THE SCEPTRE

A Jonster the Monster and the Bear Adventure

Young Adult Novel

by

B. E. Boucher

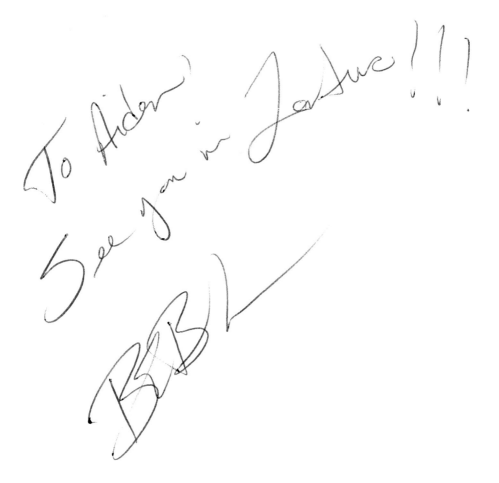

To Aiden,
See you in Joshua!!!
BB

Published by Mindstir Media, LLC
45 Lafayette Rd | Suite 181| North Hampton, NH 03862 | USA
1.800.767.0531 | www.mindstirmedia.com

Printed in the United States of America

ISBN-13: 978-1-7365224-7-9

To Geof,
the face of courage

Special thanks to Irina
for helping to guide
The Bear on his adventure.

PROLOGUE
The Secret Hideout

"Where is the soda?" Vivian sat on a blanket in the Secret Hideout and rummaged through the picnic basket for her favorite vice.

"You did not pack any?" Leonard asked.

"I guess not. Be a good husband and go get some, will ya?"

"Sure." Only a hundred feet off Airport Road, the hidden ten-foot deep wetland was less than a five-minute walk from home.

"Thanks, honey. And take Geof. You know how he loves to walk with you." She gave her son a big hug and kiss.

"Come on, Bear." Leonard smiled, grabbing his two-year-old son by the hand. "Mommy will die without her soda."

"Well, I might."

"Give us five minutes and do not eat all the potato salad."

"Leo," Vivian called out. "Never forget I love you boys."

"Love you too, Sweetie."

Leonard rushed down the hill to 546 Airport Road and snagged a six-pack of soda from the refrigerator. He pulled one can loose and gave it to his son. Geof carefully protected his treasure as they hiked back up the hill to the Secret Hideout.

"Mommy, I got soda," the Bear announced proudly. His mother did not answer.

"Vivian," Leonard hollered but heard nothing. The basket sat alone on the blanket. "Vivian, where are you?" he yelled again and again. Still no answer. Vivian was gone.

CHAPTER 1

Fourteen Years Later

Geof kicked back and looked through the haze at his mom and dad. Vivian sat on a blanket, a smile on her face as she fed Leonard a heaping spoonful of potato salad. He reached to grab a can of Coke, but she snatched it away and downed it in one gulp. Geof laughed at his father. The Beach Boys were having "Fun, Fun, Fun" on Geof's cell phone speaker as it lay by a pond surrounded by cattails. Someone touched Geof's hand. He looked up and saw his forever crush, Debbie Marshall, pulling him to his feet to dance. Being with his happy parents and dancing to the Beach Boys with Debbie was paradise. The best day ever.

Geof looked up, and the sky darkened, but there were no clouds. Leonard stood up and began dancing alone just as something rose out of the pond and silently pulled Vivian in. Geof tried to reach her, but his feet felt nailed to the ground.

He screamed for his father to help, but Leonard ignored him and kept dancing. The walls of the Secret Hideout closed in on Geof and swirled around him. Debbie released Geof's hands and floated into the spinning fog. Geof screamed, "Debbie, do you see my mom?" She laughed and threw something at him. He reached out and captured it as it slowly floated by. It was his phone.

"Mom… Mom…" he yelled into the microphone.

"Bear! Can you hear me?"

"Mom?"

"It's not your mom. It's Jon."

"Don't bother me. I'm having fun, fun, fun at a Beach Boys concert."

"Fun, fun, fun is your ringtone, dummy. You're dreaming. You were s'posed to pick me up ten minutes ago."

"Oh, crap."

"You're gonna make us late for school."

"Ohhhhhh, crap. Sorry, Jon. I'm coming. I'm coming."

Geof stumbled into his clothes and headed for the front door. He raced to Jonster the Monster's house with the top down on his 2004 Sebring convertible, the Bearmobile. Jon jumped in and glared at Geof. "What's wrong with you, man?"

"Sorry, sorry. I was up late last night. Real late. My dad…"

"Don't tell me he had another episode."

"Yeah. I heard him talking, but there was no one there. I think he was talking to my mom, or at least he thought he was. Then this morning, he wasn't there, but the car still was. I think he might have gone up to the Secret Hideout. I gotta tell you, man, it scares me. I'm scared for my dad. I don't know why he won't talk about it. I'm no little kid anymore."

"Maybe you can get it out of him tonight."

"Yeah. Maybe."

The loss of Geof's mother was a lump in his pillow, but knowing that his father was keeping him in the dark about it unnerved him. As he got older, he could see conflict in his dad and it was eating him alive.

The Bearmobile pulled into the Sheridan High School parking lot with a few minutes to spare. The school's main corridor was filled with waves of kids that looked like two silk dragons in a Chinese parade banging into each other as they wove their way in opposite directions down the hall. Geof scanned the sea of faces for Debbie Marshall but did not find her. High school was the perfect place for a people watcher like Geof. Of course, girls were his favorite target. But there were others... jocks, nerds, gamers, suck-ups, wimps, bullies, bookworms, alternative types, get-a-lifers, and teachers' pets. Geof had a habit of sticking his fellow students in a genre and giving them a nickname, a quirk Jon loved.

A slightly built and neatly dressed boy brushed Geof as he hurried past. He wore black, Clark Kent style glasses, but Geof sensed that there was no Superman hiding behind them. He had seen the boy before but knew nothing of him. Geof could see the kid was trying hard to keep his distance from the dragon so it could not eat him. With the boy's glasses and timid nature, Geof decided he just had to be called Clark.

Two boys with big red X's on their notebooks rushed up behind Clark. One of them reached out and swatted the books from his arm. The two punks snickered as Clark's books and notebook fell to the floor. Clark bent down to collect a book, but it was kicked by one of the punks and landed on Geof's left foot. Geof scooped it up to return it to the boy and found his path blocked by the bullies.

Geof gently but firmly moved them to one side with his arm and handed the book to the boy. The bullies glared at him but did nothing. Bullies like little guys, and even though he wore glasses, the six-foot-four-inch Geof was too big of a risk. Clark mumbled, "Thanks," and blurred into his locker-hugging sanctuary. Jonster the Monster and the Bear had so looked forward to this year and its possibilities that it never occurred to them that school could be a horror show for some kids.

Geoffrey, the Bear, Boucher was the quintessential best friend. He was loyal and solid. He liked loose tee shirts, cargo shorts, and those socks that don't cover the ankles.

He was bigger than Jon and just about everybody else. The girls liked Geof, but not in the James Dean way they liked Jon. He was the rock. The guy they could rely on. His dating card was not empty, but he never looked at dates as anything but casual fun. Geof decided long ago that he would forever keep the relationship door open for Debbie Marshall should she ever decide to step inside.

Geof and Jon met up and brashly entered room 43, only to be deflated when they saw that the homeroom teacher was sixty-three-year old Ms. Stiles. She stood less than five feet tall, but generations of Sheridan High School students were scared to death of her. A fun homeroom would have to be stricken from their list. Motion in the form of a waving hand caught Geof's eye. It was Debbie Marshall. Geof's heart raced as he snatched the desk across from her.

"Be silent, class," Ms. Stiles bellowed. "Homeroom lasts fifteen minutes. There will be no talking or socializing in homeroom... blah blah blah."

The bell rang, and the students fled Ms. Stiles' prison. Geof stalled until Debbie got up. "What's your first class?"

"English, room 220."

"I got algebra." Rats. No Debbie first period. Maybe later.

Jon casually waved bye as he bounced down the hall. Jon was an athletic, smart kid... slim, but not skinny, good-looking, and a handful. Early in his childhood, his weary parents nicknamed him "the Monster." His forehead was covered by a sandy shock of hair that dipped into his left eye. He thought it was cool. Apparently, the girls did too. They liked him. With his signature floppy hair, tee-shirt, and jeans, he was that good-looking bad-boy type that teenage girls thought they wanted.

Jon entered U.S. history and commandeered a desk in the back, as was his custom. To his right, there was a dazzling girl with long blonde hair and exquisite features. He had admired her for a long time but never met her. The kid on his left was also vaguely familiar. His name was Snively Asstead. Snively glanced at Jon and immediately looked away as if he had sized him up and passed judgment on his inferiority. On his desk was a loose-leaf notebook with a big red "X" on the cover. Class ended, and the blonde girl was busy fiddling with her books, so Jon offered his hand to Snively. "What's up? I'm Jon."

"Snively." The boy walked off, leaving Jon's outstretched hand dangling in the air like the punchline of a bad joke.

"Classic X-Club jerk," the blonde girl said.

"Uh, what's that?"

"I said those X-Club guys are jerks. I'm Patricia Chamness."

"I'm Jon."

"Somebody should put them in their place. They are the biggest…" As they walked together out of the classroom, Patricia's words faded to a soft symphony that enchanted Jon. Patricia Chamness was a dazzling sunrise.

"Well, see ya later." Patricia signed off.

Jon watched her glide down the hall and drawled, "Here's looking at you, kid."

Jon was a movie aficionado of all film eras and liked to integrate his favorite movie lines into the conversation whenever he could. He and Geof played a movie line game with simple rules. If one of them used a recognizable movie line in everyday life, he owned that line, and the other one could never use it without severe, but unknown, penalties. Jon was ahead, but Geof surprisingly held his own. It was good mental exercise and cheap entertainment.

CHAPTER 2

The Bear and the Bullies

The bell rang for lunch. Teacher grades were fine for parents, but the lunchroom was where kids received their crucial peer grades. A good peer grade was far more important to any high school student than an "A" in Biology. Lunch was truth serum, where every kid's place in the pecking order was either earned or assigned.

Jon met Geof at the door. "You're late as usual."

"Yeah, yeah." Geof walked past him without stopping. His eyes zeroed in on Debbie. She was sitting with a group of girls, laughing and carrying on. As Geof stared at her, the cafeteria darkened, and the entire student body stood up and started yelling at Geof. He could not recognize the words at first, but soon he realized they were screaming the word "Searcher" at him. Their faces were contorted with anger as they menacingly closed in on him. "SEARCHER! SEARCHER! SEARCHER!"

Debbie and a pretty blonde girl sat rigidly at their table, oblivious to what was going on. A snake coiled around Debbie's ankle and drew back its head to strike her leg. Geof tried to warn her, but his voice was drowned out by the crescendo of voices yelling, "SEARCHER!" Terror gripped the Bear as he knew that the love of his life was about to die right in front of him, and he could do nothing.

Jon caught up to Geof, and seeing the look on his face, punched him in the arm. "What is wrong with you, man?"

Geof shook his head back to reality, looked at Jon, and back at Debbie. Everyone was sitting and enjoying lunch. There was no snake, and nobody was yelling at him.

"You're scaring me, Bear. What's the deal?"

"Oh… uh… Nothin'." Geof looked back over his shoulder a couple of times and wondered if he were the one who was suffering from hallucinations and not his father.

The boys loaded up their trays and looked for an open seat at the picnic-style tables. Since Geof was late, there was only one opening. Two boys were sitting at that table on opposite ends. One boy was a red-headed kid with average clothes and a ruddy face. The other Geof recognized as Clark. Not much of a surprise that he was in Siberia. Jon slid in next to Clark with Geof opposite him. Geof looked back at Debbie. Everything was still normal.

The Bear tried to get Clark's attention, but he avoided eye contact. Geof reached his hand across the table and waved it under his face. "What's up? I'm Geof, and he's Jon." Clark limply put out his hand. His soggy handshake was what Geof and Jon impolitely referred to as "the squid."

"His name is Fred Lake," the other boy offered. "He doesn't talk much. Everyone just calls him Flake."

Jon jabbed Clark in the side with his elbow. "You can talk, can't you?" The sadly unresponsive boy shamed Jon for his mean comment. He repeated softly, "You do talk, don't you?"

The other boy said, "My name is Glenn Morgan, but everybody calls me Morgue. And I talk quite a bit." Wow. Morgue. Fancy meeting a kid who already had a cool nickname.

Geof turned to Fred. "So, Clark. What's up with the hall this morning."

"My name is Fred." The boy never looked up and said the words like he feared them.

"Don't sweat it, Freddy." Jon smiled. "Geof gives a nickname to just about everybody. He thinks he's Dragline in *Cool Hand Luke*." Fred looked vacantly at the Monster.

"You know… *Cool Hand Luke*. The movie where Paul Newman should have won the Oscar… ahh, never mind."

Morgue laughed, and Fred continued to look at his plate. Geof smiled wickedly at Jon. "What we got here is failure to communicate." Bingo. Geof just scored one of the best movie lines ever, and Jon foolishly gave him the perfect setup by mentioning *Cool Hand Luke*. Geof would have loved to shove Jon's face in it, but he was concerned that he had offended the defenseless Clark. "Sorry, man. No harm intended. It's the Clark Kent glasses. But Jon's right. I usually give my friends nicknames. It's my thing."

Fred looked halfway between his plate and Geof. Nobody before had ever apologized to him for anything. Not only that, but Fred had not heard his own name and the word friend in the same sentence since first grade when kids didn't know any better. He looked at Jon and Morgue, and they were both smiling. But it was a different smile than he was used to seeing. It was a nice smile, not the mean or sarcastic smirk found on the faces of X-Club types. Fred decided to take a chance. What difference would it make if two more guys picked on him?

"Uh, so what is your nickname?" he asked Geof without looking up.

"I am *the Bear.*" Geof roared, thumping his fist on his chest. "But I can't claim my own nickname. My dad gave it to me. But forget that. What's the deal with those guys this morning messing with your books?"

Fred shrugged meekly.

"That had to be the X-Club." Morgue answered for him.

"Yeah. What's up with them anyway?" Geof asked.

"Hey, you know what?" Jon asked. "I got that Snively in U.S. History."

Morgue closed his eyes and shook his head. "Snively Asstead. His dad is loaded. They moved here a couple of years ago from Boston or somewhere. Snively is like the leader of the X-Club. Everybody is afraid of them."

"They don't look very scary to me," Geof laughed.

"That's easy for you to say. They would never mess with a guy like you, but most of us are fair game. They push you around in school, and if you show any backbone, they gang up on you later on more favorable turf."

"Is that really true, Morgue? I thought modern bullies hid behind the internet."

"Oh, they're really good at that too," Morgue said. "You should see some of the crap they put online about Fred. But they really get off on making him feel like a leper at school. Sometimes I sit here so he won't feel so alone, even if I have to keep my distance."

"Bogus," Jon growled. He had seen Fred sitting alone at lunch all last year, but to his remorse, he never thought much about it.

"Why don't you tell your parents about this stuff?" asked Geof.

After what seemed like forever, Fred said quietly, "My mother is drunk all the time, and if I say anything to my stepfather, he will call me a baby and hit me."

That had to be the most words Fred had said to anybody in years. He was afraid but hoped these guys were different. Maybe there was a chance that high school could be at least bearable. His father left when he was four. He could never understand why he was left behind to deal with his boozing mother. When he was six, she married Arnold Lake. Lake was not an alcoholic but seemed to like having a wife who was. Arnold Lake forced Fred to take his last name, which Fred hated. Fred had the first name of the father who deserted him and the last name of the stepfather who abused him. At school, he was bullied. If there ever was a teenager at risk, it was Fred.

The Bear felt a hand on his left shoulder. He turned his head to see two guys standing behind him. Jon recognized one of them as Snively.

"Yo," the Bear said.

"Why are you guys sitting here?" Snively sniffed. He sounded like that rich jerk in the *Titanic* movie. He kept his mouth nearly shut, so it seemed like he was talking through his nose.

"Ran out of tables," Geof said.

"That happens. But surely you know how things are around here."

Geof grinned at Jon. "Enlighten us."

"There are certain people you shouldn't associate with."

"Yeah. I can see that. Thanks for the tip."

"I mean losers like him." Snively pointed at Fred, who riveted his eyes to the floor.

Geof's gaze bayoneted Snively. "I see no losers at this table."

Snively tried to maintain his air of superiority, but Geof was getting on top of him. He patted Geof on the shoulder like they were best buddies so everybody would see.

"Enjoy your salad," Snively faked.

Geof stuffed his mouth with salad and said, "Mmmhmm."

The two X-Clubbers retreated, feeling their reputations were intact. They remembered Geof's interference in the hall earlier, and now this. As they left the cafeteria, Snively assured his co-snobs that he would soon take care of that interfering smartass.

Lunch was over. "Later," Jon said.

Geof reached out his fist to Fred. "Later, Clark. I mean Fred."

Fred slowly stood up and stuck out his hand to bump Geof's ham-sized fist. It was the first time he had ever done that. "I... I think Clark is a good nickname."

Geof and Jon obliged each other with a high five. "Clark, it is!"

CHAPTER 3

Innocence Lost

Jonster the Monster and the Bear headed off to class, unaware of the impact they had on Fred. He had hope for the first time since he was a little kid and too young to realize how depressing his life was. It was bad at home. It was bad at school. A friend could change everything. Clark felt happy.

Geof and Jon met when they were in the first grade. They had been best friends ever since. They frequently spent the night at each other's house on the weekends. Lots of pizza from their friend Larry Carbone's pizza place. Lots of video games. Lots of girl stories.

Geof lived with his father, remembered little of his mother, and did just fine. Leonard Boucher never remarried. He was a consultant of some kind with a home office that allowed him a flexible work schedule and ample time for his son. Geof never could figure out exactly what his dad did for a living, but it did not matter. Life with Dad was good.

After sixth period, absent-minded Jon remembered he had forgotten something in his locker. "I'll meet you in the parking lot," he yelled.

Geof could not find Debbie. Bummer. Giving her a ride home would have been a nice exclamation point on the day. He hopped in the driver's seat of the Bearmobile and immediately put the top down. It was his dad's old car, and a bit beat up, but it worked for him. It once was a classy gold but now had a primer gray driver's door, gas cap cover, and front bumper cover, reminders of driving mishaps in times gone by.

Geof looked around and, to his excitement, saw Debbie in the distance. Her perfect image grew larger, and he realized she was walking toward him. Geof waved to get her attention. She came up to the car and said cheerfully, "See ya tomorrow."

"You wanna ride home?"

"Thanks, but my mom is picking me up."

"Uhhhh, well, okay. Maybe another time. Jon and I go right by your house, you know."

"Okay. Maybe another time. There's my mom. Bye."

"C' ya."

"Let's roll." Jon's cheerful voice broke Geof's trance.

Jon tossed his books on the back seat, and Geof stepped on the gas. Ten minutes later, the Sebring purred into the driveway at 546 Airport Road. The Bearmobile had a lot of miles on it but ran like a top. Geof adored it.

Geof's home was the last house on the way to the airport. Leonard told his son he lived there most of his life. Geof assumed he inherited it from his parents but really did not know the whole history. In fact, he did not know a lot about his father's past at all. Kids don't think about that. Geof watched his home change from a lone house surrounded by cow pastures to the entrance to a large subdivision. Leonard said that in his youth, he and his brother, Miles, would ride their bicycles the short distance to the airport and watch the afternoon planes land.

Times and kids were different then. And still, when Geof was very young, he loved his father's story of how he and Miles first discovered the Secret Hideout hiding in plain sight only a hundred feet from Airport Road. They would ride their bikes through weeds alongside the pasture, and it would appear. The top of the hideout was level with the pasture and nicely hidden by vegetation. There was a gently sloping path that bicycles could negotiate in and out of the hideout. Those inside could not see out, and better yet, those outside could not see in. Leonard and Miles sometimes diverted their airport rides at the last minute and wound up spending hours in their own secret place. No parents. No teachers. No school and no chores. It had to be the best place in the world. Geof heard stories about his uncle Miles but never met him.

The hideout was a sweet oasis about one hundred feet long and fifty feet wide. It had a few trees and an oval-shaped pond about twenty feet long. The pond was accessible from only one side as ten-foot-high rock walls wrapped snugly around its back. Erosion marks in the walls looked like two hands were holding the pond and presenting it to the lucky lads as a gift for their loyalty. At the other end of the pond was a group of cattails standing like security guards to prevent anyone but invited guests to enter.

Leonard's bedtime stories were wonderful tales of strange exploits he and his brother had in the hideout. Exotic landscapes, weird creatures, and grand adventures captivated the two boys.

Geof listened with the wonder only a child can experience as his father told him of the magic pond. He said they could even talk to other people below the surface of the water. The pond people would show him inviting scenes from their own world. Young Geof was captivated and begged to hear more.

"Why would you not want to be part of that wonderful world, Daddy? Why would you stay here and miss all that cool stuff?"

His dad just looked at him, smiled, and said, "I saved that for you." Geof always wondered what exactly was being saved for him. He, like his father, had gone to the Secret Hideout since he was very small. It was cool, but he never saw anything in the pond but water. It appeared he never would as a housing development was rapidly encroaching on the hideout. Perhaps because of this, Leonard's trips to the Secret Hideout increased. Could it be he was afraid he was about to lose something?

The boys bailed out of the car and were accosted by Geof's three dogs, Barney, Pop Tart, and Barsik. They instinctively knew when Geof was arriving and made a ritual of crashing through the doggie door to greet him. Wire-haired Barney was a fifty-five-pound, brown and white ball of love. Pop Tart had similar coloring, short hair, and was about half his size. Barsik was a Yorkie and the only purebred. They were all Humane Society alumni and displayed the qualities that make rescue dogs the best. The dogs made sure they received a proper amount of attention before releasing Geof and Jon. Leonard was in his home office, finishing up his work for the day.

Jonster found some leftover pizza in the fridge, curled around it like a fullback, and dodged Geof as he headed for three black, theatre-style recliners placed in front of a sixty-inch TV. Geof inventoried the fridge for some time but wound up taking only a Coke.

Leonard exited his office to greet them. The office had a heavy glass door that kept the noise out but still allowed him to spy on Geof. As he walked into the room, he said, "How was school, boys?"

"Good. Fine," they answered automatically.

Leonard sat in one of the three chairs itching to have a conversation. "Let me hear it."

Geof squirmed in his chair. "Dad, can we talk about something else?"

"Sure. Like what?"

"Mom. Every time I ask you about Mom, you change the subject."

Jon was caught off guard and felt like a peeping Tom. "I, uh, guess I'd better go." Leonard held out his arm and stopped him.

"You are like my son. And Geof will just tell you what I have to say anyway. You might as well stick around. Okay, Geof. We will talk about her."

"Really?" Geof and Jon blocked out everything but the sound of Leonard's voice. They felt they were about to be told the secret of life, and in a way, they were.

CHAPTER 4

Bedtime Story

"I'm gonna get a grape juice," Mr. B said. Jon and Geof waited nervously. Would this finally be it? Leonard grabbed the top of the juice bottle and twirled it between his index finger and thumb. "Your mother is a wonderful woman."

"Is?" Geof blurted.

Leonard shrugged. "You know, since Vivian disappeared, I... well... I never gave up hope that she would come back."

Jon put his hand on his best friend's shoulder. "Mr. B, what happened?"

"It was a beautiful July day. A beautiful, cloudless, Wyoming day. And we decided to have a little picnic up at the Secret Hideout."

"You took Mom to the Secret Hideout?"

Geof's father exhaled, and the right side of his mouth curled into a smile. "I, uh, used to tell your mother stories about the Secret Hideout, and she fell in love with it. We used to go there on, uh, dates."

"Jeez, Mr. B, what kind of date could you have in the Secret Hideout?"

"Well—you know. Anyway, she fell in love with the people in the pond stories. We would go for walks, stop by the Secret Hideout, and sit by the pond."

"Did you ever see any?" Jon asked.

"You mean people? Funny thing. I never did when I was with her. But I think she might have."

"Come on, Dad. Really?"

"Son, there are a lot of things in this world we do not understand. Who is to say there were no people in the pond? Who is to say there is not another world somewhere? Who is to say we are who we or everybody else thinks we are?"

"You aren't serious, are you, Mr. B?"

Leonard stared silently into space. "Yes, Jon. I am serious. I think it makes sense. Anyway, we went on a picnic. We would just grab a basket, fill it up with food, and go. After all, the Secret Hideout was so close. What started out as an occasional thing turned into a regularly scheduled event. Your mother insisted on it. At the end, we were going to the hideout three or four times a week. But something did not jive. I began to sense a change in your mother."

"Was she mad at you, Dad?"

"No. Not tha… no. She never got mad at me. No. It was different, more like she was distracted. I would try to get out of her what was going on, but she would just change the subject."

"That's wild, Mr. B. Then what happened?"

"Well, we were up at the Secret Hideout having a picnic by the pond. You were with us, Geof. All of a sudden, she said she forgot the drinks. She volunteered us to run to the house and get some."

Leonard got up from his chair and walked to the wall. He held his drink in both hands and spoke softly. "We went down and got the sodas. Ten minutes later, we got back, and she was gone. Just gone. The picnic basket was still there. The blanket was still there. But she was not. I figured she just took a walk and would come right back. But she never did."

"I wish I could remember, Dad, but you know I can't."

Leonard threw his arms up. "Maybe I should stop."

Geof was insistent. "No. I want to know."

"Okay, son. We searched and searched for her. We looked everywhere. But nobody had seen her. Nobody. She just vanished."

Geof knew this part, but nothing more. "What do you think really happened?"

"Geof and Jon... do you remember some of those old Indian stories I used to tell?"

Both boys nodded. Sheridan, Wyoming, was ground zero for some of the best Native American culture in the country. Years before, All-American Indian Days was held annually in Sheridan, and native peoples from across the United States would come, celebrate and tell stories of their past. An artifact from that time was one of Leonard's most prized possessions. Hanging on the wall adjacent to the large TV was a painting of a white buffalo by the Sioux artist Godfrey Broken Rope. When All-American Indian Days came to town, Broken Rope came with it. He would set up shop in front of a main street store and was quickly surrounded by eager customers. Broken Rope would take money and ask what the person wanted in the painting. In fifteen to thirty minutes, he would hand them a piece of masonry board with a beautiful painting on it. Most of Broken Rope's paintings were landscapes, so the white buffalo was a rarity and something Leonard cherished.

Leonard glanced at the painting as he stood in front of it. "Do you remember the story old Donald Deernose used to tell about the magic healing waters?"

Of course, they remembered. What kid wouldn't remember something like that? Donald Deernose was a Sheridan fixture, kind of the town character. He was perennially dressed in blue jeans, an open-collar white shirt, and a red bandana around his neck. And he never wore a coat, no matter how cold the brutal Sheridan winters were. No one knew how he made a living, but he was around town a lot and would never miss a chance to delight kids with his legends about the colorful Indian past. One of his favorite stories was about magic spring waters he said were scattered all around the world. Everyone always took that story as folklore, but Mr. Deernose swore it was true. Then two years ago, Donald Deernose disappeared from Sheridan. He always said his home was somewhere else, but he would never say where. And yet, there were times when Geof was sure his father knew where he was.

"Well, old Donald Deernose always said that there was a way to become part of the magic waters. I think that is what happened. I know it sounds nuts. But think about it. Vivian sent me home for an insignificant reason. When I came back, everything was there but her. It could be something enticed her into the pond."

"Or took her, maybe?" Geof frowned.

"Yes. Or took her."

Jon and Geof looked at each other.

"Truthfully, I do not think she went anywhere, boys. Not anywhere as we know it. I think there really is something magical about the Secret Hideout, and it might have taken her somehow, or somewhere." Leonard's last sentence seemed to hang on his tongue for an eternity. What could a son say about a statement like that? Was the old man off his cork? Did he really believe what he was saying, or was he pulling their legs?

"Are you being serious, Mr. B? Because..."

"Yes. There have been times when I am almost certain I have seen her."

"I'm sorry, Mr. B., but that all sounds pretty crackers to me."

"It is okay, Jon. It does sound crazy. Why do you think I never told you before?"

"But, Dad, if Mom really is out there somewhere, why would she not try to come back to you? Why would she leave in the first place? You said you and Mom had a great life. Why would she want to leave it?"

"I do not know, Son. Maybe she accidentally did something that... well, caused the pond to claim her somehow. I cannot get to her, and she may not be able to get back. Donald says there may be a way, but he does not say what it is. I used to beg him, but he said the time was not right and that I was not the right one. I have no idea what in the heck that means, and he will not tell me. I am just supposed to wait for the right time and the right one. I do not know if he knows anything or not. What else can I do? So I wait."

"Mr. B, you said that Donald Deernose disappeared, but you keep talking about him in the present tense."

Leonard smiled at Jon but did not respond. "Anyway, that is the story you have wanted to hear for years. Was it worth it, or do you think your old man has gone nuts?"

"My father is the sanest man I know. You know I believe in you, whatever you do, or think for that matter."

"That goes for me too, Mr. B," Jon said.

Leonard pulled Jon out of his chair and patted him on the back. "Thanks, pal. Now I think storytime is over. I am sure you boys have a lot to do." Without another word, Leonard turned and headed for his bedroom.

Geof and Jon stood speechless, staring at each other as though the sky would fall if anybody uttered a word. "Well, I guess I'll get home and annoy my own parents," Jon finally said.

"Good plan."

Geof watched Jon walk down the sidewalk. His brain did need a rest—too much input for one day. Neither of them could guess that this was the beginning of a series of events that would change their lives forever.

CHAPTER 5

The Bearmobile

Geof did not talk to his father for the rest of the night except to say goodnight. But sleep did not come gently to him. After midnight, he was awakened by his bed shaking. The bedroom swirled violently around him. Geof grabbed the sheets as he desperately tried to hold on. Lights flashed on and off as the room spun around his bed at dizzying speed. As Geof struggled to breathe, his flailing arms knocked a lamp to the floor with a crash. The door to his room opened, and his father stood in the doorway. Everything was back to normal.

"Everything okay, Bear?"

Geof relaxed his grip on the sheets, "Yeah, Dad." First the snake, and now this. His father left the room, and Geof stared blankly at the ceiling for the rest of the night.

The next morning father and son sat down to breakfast together as always. After ten minutes, Geof hugged his dad goodbye and headed for the door. He wanted to make sure he did not miss Debbie Marshall.

Jon hopped in Geof's car and clicked on his seat belt. An uncomfortable conversation was waiting to happen between the two boys. "All right, Bear, what's up with your dad anyway? I mean, that was some heavy stuff he was laying on us."

Geof wanted to tell Jon about the cafeteria snake and the creatures from last night, but he could not bring himself to say it. "Yeah, I couldn't sleep thinking about what my dad said. But as far out as it sounds, I have to believe him. My dad's not crazy."

"I know. That's what scares me. What if he's right, man?"

"I dunno. I hope my mother is out there somewhere. I really do. I don't even know why I care. I don't remember her. But I do care… now more than ever because I'm so worried about my dad."

"You wanna know what I'm thinking?"

"To be honest, what you're thinking always scares me."

"That's funny. But I think we should check out this Secret Hideout magic thing. Even if it's a load of bat guano, it would be fun to run a Jonster the Monster and the Bear style investigation on it. Come on, wouldn't it?"

"How are we supposed to find out about magic waters and people who might be living in a pond? Sounds to me like you'd need a sorcerer or something."

Jon nonchalantly stuck his hand above his head and let the wind blow through his outstretched fingers. "Or Donald Deernose."

"What are you talking about? My dad said he left a long time ago."

"Look, Bear. I understand that yesterday you were messed up with all that stuff about your mom, but that's not exactly what he said."

"I haven't gone deaf. Dad said this Deernose guy hasn't been around for a long time."

"Yeah, that's true enough. But yesterday, I got the feeling that your dad was holding out on us."

"Holding out?"

"Yup. You remember when I asked him why he always talked about Donald Deernose like he was practically having tea with him every morning? You remember?"

"Yeah, I guess I do."

"And what did he do? He blew me off like I was asking to see his underwear drawer."

"Well, maybe. But I don't think it meant anything. Besides, why would he care if I knew that old Indian storyteller was still around?"

"Maybe to protect his son."

"Protect me?"

"Maybe he is trying to protect you by stopping you… by stopping you from doing what we're about to do."

"What are we about to do?"

Jon smiled. "Find Donald Deernose, silly."

"Then what?"

"I don't know."

Sheridan High School rolled into view, and Jon said, "We'll talk about it later. I'll research this Deernose guy. Maybe we can get more about him out of your dad."

Geof shook his head. "I feel a nightmare coming on."

Geof pulled the Bearmobile smoothly into the parking lot. In seconds the electric convertible top was up, and the Sebring began its ritual of waiting for her master to return, turn the key, and give her life again.

As they exited the car, the boys noticed Clark a few feet away.

"Hey Clark," Jon yelled, running toward him. "What's up?'

"Ehhh, nothin'. Nothin' new."

Geof playfully punched Clark in the arm and said, "Walk in with us." With his new protective escort, Clark entered school feeling great for the first time.

Lunchtime. Jon, Morgue, and Clark were sitting at the outcast table munching when Geof came in. They acknowledged each other with a flip of the head, and Geof went to stand in line. A few feet in front of him, Debbie was talking to Pat, the blonde girl who made Jon's head spin. Again, he saw a snake, but this time it had legs. Snively was standing next to her.

"Let's go," Geof heard Snively say. "Quality girls like you should be sitting with the A-team, not the gaggle of losers wasting space all over the place."

Debbie eyeballed Snively. "I think I'll pass."

"Can you guess what the 'A' in A-team stands for, Debbie?" Pat giggled.

"It's pretty obvious," Debbie laughed.

Snively grabbed her arm. "Cute. But I don't think you understand, girl. You don't turn down an invitation from Snively."

Debbie flashed icy eyes at Snively. "A-Team. X-Club. They must be serving alphabet soup at your table. I stopped eating alphabet soup when I was six. Now let go of my arm."

"You don't get it. I am the leader of the X-Club, and I—"

"I said, let go of me!" Debbie punched Snively in the stomach and jerked her arm away.

Snively grabbed his stomach and sneered, "You'll change your mind."

Debbie and Pat pirouetted and walked past Geof. Snively followed but was blocked by the Bear. "Looks like the conversation's over," Geof said.

Snively recognized the four-eyed ape that yesterday had the gall to defend that Fred weenie. "You—you really need to mind your own business," Snively stammered.

"I am minding my business. I invited Debbie to have lunch with us today."

"Both of us," Pat chimed in. She waved at Jon.

"I'm sure a gentleman like you would not want a girl to break her word, would you?" Geof asked with his head cocked to one side.

"Uhhh. Well, uh… since you put it that way, of course, I wouldn't," Snively squirmed.

Geof slapped Snively on the shoulder. "Good man."

A shamed Snively walked off without another word. When he got to his exalted table, he explained to his underlings, "I decided they aren't X-Club material." But he knew that nobody bought it.

"That guy is creepy. Thanks," Debbie said as they walked to the table.

"I didn't do anything. Remind me never to tick you off," Geof grinned, holding his hand protectively over his stomach.

"I can take care of myself. By the way, this is my new friend, Patricia."

Jon ran up to them. "Hey Pat," he said.

"Hi, Jon."

Geof looked at Jon and received a cryptic smile.

When they got to the table, Morgue and Clark were inhaling their lunch. Jon pointed at their two new friends and said, "This is Morgue and Clark. Morgue and Clark, Debbie, and Patricia."

"Hey," the girls said together.

"My real name is Fred, but Geof nicknamed me Clark."

"Ohhhh yessss," Debbie laughed. "Geof had quite the reputation at Woodland Park for dishing out nicknames whether anybody wanted them or not. Everybody but me, that is. Why was that?"

"I dunno," Geof muttered. He could not admit he found no nickname for perfection. Geof smiled weakly and Jon noticed an edge to his normally easy-going friend. "Are you still hung up about your dad?" he asked.

Geof looked squarely at Jon and squinted. "Yeah."

Jon instantly knew he'd made a deep breach of bro code by bringing up something so private.

Debbie looked at Geof. "What happened with your dad?"

Geof squirmed. "Uh, well, my dad knows this old Indian named Donald Deernose—"

"Really? Mr. Deernose? The old medicine man? I know him. He used to do some work on my father's ranch. One time he helped my father find water by just walking around with a stick."

Jon and Geof looked at each other. "Funny you should say that," Jon smiled.

"What does your dad have to do with Donald Deernose?" Debbie asked.

"Apparently, he has some very interesting theories about Geof's family," Jon tiptoed. "But this probably isn't the time or place." Jon felt bad about opening a can of worms and making his friend swim in it. "I was just shooting my mouth off."

Geof let out a deep breath. "What the heck. Everybody's got somethin', right?" He took a few minutes to hurry through the story of his missing mother and how his father believed that somehow Donald Deernose had the inside track on what happened. He gave a non-Secret Hideout version to keep Debbie from thinking he'd lost it.

Debbie stared at the table. She said, "Of course I've known for years that your mother wasn't around. We all did. But I just thought your parents were divorced or something. I'm really sorry." She placed her hand softly on Geof's forearm.

She did? She knew about the no-mother situation? It felt great to know it actually meant something to her. "No worries. I didn't mean to ruin everybody's lunch."

"No way. That was one of the wildest things I have ever heard, true or not," a revved-up Patricia said, pointing at Geof's chest.

The fact that Patricia was intrigued jump-started Jon. "The Bear and I are going to go undercover to get to the bottom of this. Even though most folks around here think this Deernose character bailed on Sheridan years ago, we're still going to try to find him."

Debbie grinned. "He lives in Story."

"Whu—" Geof gulped. "How do you know that?"

"My father rents him a house there."

"Holy cow. Why don't you tell us where it is, Debbie? Geof and I have a few questions to ask him."

"I'll do better than that. Let me hitch a ride and I'll show you. That is, if it's okay."

"Okay? Well, yeah, sure. I mean, if you really want to." Geof was excited about getting Debbie in the Bearmobile for the first time, but the thought of meeting the elusive Deernose unnerved him. He wanted to learn about his mother. But he was also afraid.

"Yeah," Debbie said happily. "I think it would be fun. You can drive us out there on the weekend. It isn't even twenty miles."

"I'm free this weekend," Jon said, looking hopefully at Patricia.

"Can I come?" she asked.

"Suits me fine," Jon smiled. A Jonster the Monster setup, when executed to perfection, was a thing of beauty.

"I guess it'd be okay," Geof surrendered. Morgue and Clark looked at each other. They would like to go, but the passenger limitations of Geof's car meant that there would be four for Story. Neither of them said a word.

"This is going to be so much fun," the girls laughed and clicked their glasses.

Lunch was nearly over, and Snively walked by, followed by his band of not-so-merry men. He was annoyed to see that everybody at Jonster's table was laughing and carrying on. "I can't imagine what you dweebs could be celebrating," he snarled.

I can't either, Snively, Geof thought.

CHAPTER 6

The Song for Tomorrow

Geof did not feel good about going behind his dad's back, but when he got up on Saturday morning, his dad was again gone. There was a note apologizing for missing breakfast along with eggs and sweet potato hash browns in the oven. Geof wondered what he was up to now.

At 8:45, Geof woke up the Bearmobile. It was cool and a great day for cruising with the top down. He turned on the digital stereo, an upgrade from his dad when he was given the car for his sixteenth birthday. He directed Spotify to play "Fun, Fun, Fun" for good luck. The plan was to meet his fellow sleuths at the old Woodland Park parking lot on Coffeen Avenue. Geof was five minutes late, not bad, and the gang was already there. Jon hopped in the back seat behind Geof, assuring a boy/girl seating arrangement. "Debbie, you better sit up front so you can give directions."

"Good boy," Geof hummed under his breath.

Debbie slid her jeans onto the bucket seat, closed the door, and pointed to the left. "Just head for Story." The twenty miles separating Sheridan and Story felt like seconds. Debbie steered Geof off Route 193 and onto Fish Hatchery Road. Story is a charming town of about a thousand souls. It has a school, a couple of churches, a restaurant or two, a bunch of llamas, lots of trees, and eye-popping scenery. "Turn on Rosebud," Debbie directed.

"Rosebud?" Jon laughed.

Debbie gave Jon a tepid look, but Pat laughed with him. "*Citizen Kane*, I get it. I like to study movies. Good cultural education."

"Me too," Jon smiled.

"That's the house," Debbie shouted. She pointed at number 24. "That's it."

The four teenagers approached a farmer's porch that spanned the length of the two-story yellow house. The yard and exterior were neat but sparse. Two large trees stood in the front yard, and a sofa-sized glider rested alone on the porch. They assembled around the doorbell and stood staring at each other for a moment. Rankled by everyone's indecision, Debbie squeezed between Geof and Jon and pushed the button. There was no response. She rapped sharply on the door.

The six-paneled, oak door opened slowly, and standing before them was the fabled Donald Deernose, red bandana and all. Despite his years, he was tall, slender, and straight. His face was weathered with high cheekbones, a large nose, and dark brown eyes. Long, gray braids fell over each shoulder. Debbie stepped forward. "Hello, Mr. Deernose."

"Hello, Debbie. Come in."

The bright façade gave way to a dimly lit interior. Native American rugs covered a worn hardwood floor. The small entryway opened to a large living room on the right, a stairway in the center, and what looked like a study on the left. Mr. Deernose motioned toward the living room, and the teenagers filed in.

"Please sit," he said in a gravelly whisper.

The living room was generously furnished with an assortment of chairs and couches. Six pillows were placed on a rug in a semicircle in front of a large stone fireplace. The house was an incredible museum of Native American artifacts from an assortment of tribes. There were elaborate headdresses, lances, bows and arrows, handmade pots, blankets, and clothing adorning the walls and dangling from the ceiling. As cool as it was, it was also intimidating and eerie.

The four guests were directed to the pillows. Though it was warm outside, the fireplace was a grand stage, with yellow and orange flames flitting about like ballet dancers. Donald Deernose tossed a large pillow in the middle of the semicircle and sat down. He crossed his legs, looked down at the floor, and sat quietly.

"This guy is creepy. Why doesn't he say something?" Jon murmured to Geof.

"I dunno."

"Well, say something."

"Mr. Deernose, my name is—"

"Geof Boucher," the Indian interrupted with a slow and ominous voice. "What took so long?" He captured Geof's eyes with his own and would not release them.

"You—you were expecting us?" Geof asked nervously.

"You mostly. For long time now. For long time."

Geof squirmed as he tried to avert his eyes but could not. "What do you mean expecting me, and how do you know who I am?"

"Expecting wrong word. Hoping."

"What were you hoping, Mr. Deernose," Debbie asked.

"Salvation. I hope for salvation."

"How can we, or one of us, or, well, anybody give you salvation?" Jon asked.

"Only one way, young Jon."

A feeling of fear tingled up the back of Jon's neck. Wondering if his promotion of this adventure was a mistake, Jon asked, "How do you know my name?"

The medicine man ignored Jon's question and turned to Pat. "You have strength, but your soul torn in two pieces. You need look inside. You must decide who you are."

"I—I—Okay." Pat looked hopelessly at Jon, who was pouting at being dismissed.

Debbie interceded. "Uh, Mr. Deernose, I, that is we, have come because we are friends of Geof's."

"Yes, he must bring friends. It is good. There is no brighter light than friend. Soon you understand the strong light that shines between you and Geof and how that light protects all of you."

"Uhhh. Okay. If you say so." Debbie smiled.

"Mr. Deernose," Geof said, "we are very sorry to bother you, but I came about my father."

The Indian looked at the Bear like he had bypassed the physical Geof and addressed his spirit directly. "No. You come about your mother."

Geof felt Deernose's eyes burn his soul, and fear welled up inside him. "Well—I mean—well, yeah, I guess. Did you know my mother?"

Donald Deernose continued his visual assault. "I did. In her time of need, I give her hope."

"I don't understand."

"You not meant to understand before today."

Pat tugged on Geof's sleeve and whispered, "This guy seems shifty to me. Be careful what you say."

Donald Deernose continued, "Young Geof, do you believe there are worlds beyond the one you live in?"

"Outside of my favorite comic books, who knows? I'm just a kid. I don't think about stuff like that," Geof said, finally breaking eye contact.

The black eyes of Donald Deernose drew him back. "I think maybe you do. You come looking for answers about mother you do not remember, from man you never met, while betraying trust of father you love."

"He's good," Jon elbowed Patricia.

"He knows too much," she whispered back. "He scares me."

Donald Deernose both looked and sounded scary. "You do not believe your mother is any more part of this world. So why do you seek Donald Deernose?"

Geof regained his footing. "My father seemed to think you might know something. And it sounds like you do. How did you give my mother hope?"

The Indian softened his tone. "Your mother very ill. Your father not know this. She tell him visits to doctor were for headache. But her brain had disease. Her time like snowflake in summer. White man's doctors fail her. She come to us."

"Us?" Debbie asked.

"Vivian one-quarter Sioux. Mother of her mother give her gift of Sioux knowledge. But knowledge alone not change weather or heal sick. Knowledge only guide one to right path. Mother's knowledge guide her to us. When I hold my hands above her and feel her spirit, I know her time not long. She ask us for help, and we not deny her."

Debbie reached over and squeezed Geof's hand as a lump rose in his throat. "Sometimes, I hear my dad talking to her. Is he really talking to her?"

Donald Deernose shrugged. "I cannot say what is possible."

"Wait a minute," Jon interrupted. "Why did you keep Mr. B in the dark?"

"Yes," Pat said, "To lie to him is wrong."

Deernose ignored them and concentrated on Geof. "Your mother swore my sacred silence."

Geof looked at Jon and Pat. They were clearly wary of this guy. But he had come this far. He chose to move ahead. "My father has this cockamamie notion that she might have disappeared into this little pond near our house where they used to hang out. And to top it off, he thinks this pond might be somehow connected to ponds all over the world. I mean, my dad is a level-headed guy. But he is completely flipped out about this. And what about Debbie's question? Who is us?"

"Us—the medicine man before you, his ancestors, and the spirits. We are one, though many. You must not disrespect father. He is man of greater courage and knowledge than you imagine. Your mother leave because she have no choice."

"I don't s'pose you could let us in on what my dad does and does not know—or shouldn't know. Or whatever," Geof said.

"When you ready. Man only allowed to understand secrets of his life when his time to receive them. It is so for your father. It is so for you."

"What on earth does that mean?" Jon asked, his irritation at the constant evasiveness growing.

"The truth to one's life is key that unlocks many doors. Your spirit will guide which doors you choose open and which rooms you choose to enter." He looked squarely at Geof. "In these rooms, your destiny find you."

"Oh man—," Geof said.

"If you want to find mother, you must accept risk. Are you willing to risk all to find truth about mother?"

"Maybe."

Donald Deernose raised his voice for the first time and sent a chill down Geof's back. "Do you want to find mother or not?"

"Yes, I do."

"Then I ask you, Geoffrey, son of Leonard. Are you willing to risk all to receive truth about mother?"

"Yeah. I guess so." Still mentally cowering to the mysterious Donald Deernose, Geof gave the answer he thought he wanted.

Donald Deernose thundered at Geof. "*Man* must answer, not boy. Are you willing to risk all to receive truth you seek?"

"Yes. I am willing," Geof said with a resolve he almost believed. "But what about them?" he asked, pointing at his friends.

"Without them, you fail."

"Fail what? I don't think I should drag them into this."

Donald Deernose shrugged. "You no longer have control of that."

"It's no good. I can't ask this, whatever it is, of you guys," Geof said.

Debbie shot to her feet. "We will decide for ourselves. And I say I want in."

Jon stood by Debbie. "You're crazy if you think I'm gonna let you run off on some kick-ass adventure alone while I wind up with nothing but a thumb drive full of pictures of what I missed."

"What about you, Pat?" Debbie asked.

"I am not sure."

Debbie took Pat's hand. "I understand. But I know Mr. Deernose. Don't be afraid."

Pat looked at her new friend. There was a righteous strength flowing from her hand to Pat's manicured fingertips. She said, "Count me in."

Donald Deernose studied them carefully. "I accept your oaths. Young Geoffrey, Now, you must know you will only receive the truth you seek when you face those who would destroy you. Your father is right."

"I knew it," Geof smiled.

"And your father is wrong."

"Do you ever get to the point?" Geof snapped.

"I believe your father is right that your mother alive. But he is wrong about pond. Pond window, not door."

"Where is she?" Geof pressed.

"Remember when I say exist other worlds?"

"How could I forget? But I thought you just said she was not in the pond."

Donald Deernose stood up and left the room without a word. The four teens watched and waited. The medicine man returned carrying a piece of animal hide tightly strung between four branches. He held it close to his breast like a baby. The object appeared to be very old and very fragile. It was about twelve by eighteen inches and in the shape of a trapezoid. He grasped both sides of the object, held it with his arms outstretched, and said, "The Song for Tomorrow."

He returned to his pillow and placed the Song for Tomorrow on the floor. On it were several crude symbols drawn by someone long past. One symbol resembling a pond surrounded by cattail plants jumped out at the boys. "Whoa," Geof shouted.

"Until now, only medicine men see Song for Tomorrow. No white man."

"What makes us so special?" Debbie asked.

"In the early days, there was a spirit with the name Inktomi. Inktomi was sent on a quest to find people for the amusement of gods. In search, he discover a world deep inside our world. Inktomi promise food and luxuries to trick seven men from interior world to come to our world. But once they come to surface, they were forbidden to return. They doomed to live their lives on earth. But these seven have extraordinary knowledge and become founders of seven fireplaces of Sioux Nation." The old man spent the next half hour recounting the fascinating history of the Sioux people, or his version of it anyway.

Debbie was captivated. "That is so interesting, but why keep it from your people?"

"I do not. My people know our history. But the Song for Tomorrow..."

Debbie touched her finger to her lips. "You act afraid of it."

"After living on surface for many years, one of seven men from interior world reveal secrets of his home to my ancestor, Running Fox. Running Fox drew symbols you see before you and command that only medicine men have such knowledge until right time. We do not understand Song for Tomorrow completely. Only Searcher can bring full truth of Song out of darkness."

The word "Searcher" made the top of Geof's head tingle as he flashed back to his lunchroom hallucination. What did that word mean to him?

Jon scratched his cheek. "You still didn't answer Debbie's question. If this thing is so important or secret or whatever it is, why tell a bunch of high school kids?"

"He thinks Geof is that Searcher guy, dummy," Patricia smiled sweetly.

Donald Deernose bowed approvingly to Patricia. That was good since, until now, he looked more afraid of her than he did the Song.

"I still don't get why the big secret," Jon pressed.

"The man tell Running Fox how interior world was place of great magic. He tell of medicine man with the name Strong Bear from Lakota, who was wounded hunting buffalo. He found place of solitude on mountaintop and waited for death to relieve suffering. But he did not die. He fall asleep and wake up in strange interior world. He survive his wounds and live long time in interior world. In time, he return to his own world and find his tribe. When he enter teepee bearing his mark, he find wife still young, as was he. Strong Bear stay with wife until she die. His body stay strong, but hair became gray. At wife's death, he disappear."

"Whoa! That's radical," Jon yelped. "But why keep it from the tribe? Or anybody? Maybe there's some kind of secret squirrel thing down there that cures disease and keeps people from growing old."

"Strong Bear tell other medicine men interior world alive with strong magic, many wonders, but also terrifying creatures and much danger. Seven who come to our world all good men, and they too tell of many dangers. To people, it is just

legend. But ancient medicine men fear that interior world and our world are much like fire and water. To mix will destroy both. Strong Bear tell medicine men this was so. To protect all generations, only medicine man know of these things until time of Song for Tomorrow to be fulfilled."

"You gotta be kidding me," Jon choked. "You're telling us to go save a place where there are things nasty enough to destroy mankind? Us?"

"You aren't afraid, are you?" Pat chided.

"Right up to my eyebrows. I think being a little cautious when it comes to world-destroying, people killers is a semi-prudent thing. But I'm in if everybody else is. I have to protect my homeboy."

Debbie found herself unexpectedly jazzed by the prospect. "Come on, guys. This has got to be more fun than algebra."

Oblivious to all the activity swirling about him, Geof lifted his right hand, index finger extended, and caught the old man's eye. He said very slowly, "In the interior world... you... might not grow... any older... so that is why—"

"Your mother want to go there. She see chance to stop disease, not die. She know dangers, but hope that she survive there until cure found here. Then maybe your father find her and she come back... reunite with family."

He pointed to the Song for Tomorrow and said, "Geof, your mother enter interior world through doorway in mountains. I think mother alive."

"You really think so? That's incredible. My poor dad is always looking for her. He even thinks he talks to her."

The medicine man got up and walked over to Geof and put his hand on his shoulder. "I am sorry, young man. Eyes see what heart desire. He want to see her so he see her. But he will not find her now. He not Searcher."

Geof stood transfixed for a moment, the word Searcher pounding in his head. "I—I don't get it."

Jon was spellbound. "Me neither."

"But you helped my mother get there, didn't you? You must know how it works."

"I reveal possibility for her. Same as I do for you. Heart tell me she fulfill destiny foretold by ancestors in Song for Tomorrow. Heart tell me Searcher also come and fulfill destiny."

"How will we know who that is?"

The medicine man looked Geof in the eye. "We know."

"Now wait a minute," Geof argued. "I'm just a kid. The only thing I ever want to do is play video games."

"You do not have choice."

"Oh man. I could be home right now playing some meaningless, ultra-violent, role-playing video game. I'd be relaxing and slicing up nice, fake monsters. Instead, you're telling me I am hand-picked by some ancient wise guys to dive into an alternate universe where there might be real monsters and, and—well, real monsters are enough. You don't know it's me."

"Donald Deernose think your mother only able to enter other world because she was mother of Searcher."

"I—don't—I mean you—why did you tell my mother to go if you weren't sure?"

"I know your father. I know your mother. I believe she was mother of Searcher. I believe it then. I believe more now that you reveal yourself as Searcher. Her life short. Because of your age, time now short for Song for Tomorrow to be fulfilled. When mother enter interior world, key turn and Song for Tomorrow set in motion. Nothing we do can stop it."

"What's the big deal about the Song for Tomorrow being fulfilled anyway?" Jon protested. "Geof and his mom go to the interior world. So, what? That's a pretty insignificant item to cause some Indian Nostradamus to make a big deal out of it a thousand years ago."

The medicine man grew grim. His dark eyes now captured Jon's eyes and would not let go. "Prophecy reveal fears of my fathers. Fear will be war between interior world and your world. War destroy both. Unless—"

Jon squinted, "Unless what."

"Unless Searcher and Searcher's friends stop it."

"Oh. That sucks. Did you say friends?"

"Yes, young Jon. Searcher and friends must come with free will. Geof mother come before, and now Geof come. And you follow. I pray and fast because I believe you come. I believe Geof is Searcher, and if I help you—"

Debbie listened intently and something stirred inside her. What did Donald Deernose mean about friends and light? Why did he come to work for her father, or rent a house from him? Why did she fall into this thing with Geof? Was it all coincidence? She looked at the medicine man. He looked back and slowly nodded. She rose from her pillow, stood before Geof, and held out both hands to him as she did in his dream.

"I don't know if you are this Searcher person or not," she told him. "But I think if your mother is alive in this world or any other, you should try to find her. And if this weird prophecy is true, you have no choice. We have no choice."

"Debbie's right," Jon looked at Pat. "What about you?"

Pat looked Donald Deernose up and down. "Sounds kind of scary. But it also sounds worthwhile."

Donald Deernose released the Song for Tomorrow from the branches that had protected it for generations. He rolled it up and handed it to Jon. "Study," he commanded. "If Geof is Searcher, he sees what others not see. If he is not Searcher, we all know soon. Jon, I tell you now, do not let Geof touch Song unless in safe place."

"Uh. Sure, pal."

Geof reached out to touch the Song, but Jon swatted his hand away. He looked at Donald Deernose. "How will I be able to tell from this? It's just a bunch of pictures?"

"And not very well-drawn ones either," Jon deadpanned.

"Song for Tomorrow will reveal itself to you in ways others not see. I tell you this… Searcher will know. Then friends know."

The four teenagers left their pillows and milled around the room, looking at the treasure trove of artifacts. Geof approached the old man. "What am I to do? This thing is supposed to tell me how to save the world from all kinds of nasty creatures or whatever. And tomorrow I go back to school where I am petrified of a five-foot-tall, hundred-year-old teacher named Ms. Stiles."

"You right to fear. I hear Ms. Stiles is terrifying," Donald Dearnose said without a smile.

"Ha ha."

"I know humor help you. Use it. Geof Boucher, son of Leonard, take Song for Tomorrow with you. Song for Tomorrow reside within you now. You know what you must do. You just not know that you know."

With that, the teenagers found themselves on the front porch bidding farewell to the enigmatic man. Was he truly a pivotal figure in the history of mankind? Were they? Or was he just a fruitcake, and they were the nuts?

When they got back in the Sebring, they talked nonstop. As soon as they were out of the house, what seemed so real a few minutes before, now just did not add up.

Geof stared at the animal skin lying on Jon's lap. Without thinking, the words flew out. "Anybody wanna come over and check this thing out?" There were no objections.

The Sebring disappeared in the distance, and two bicycles arrived at the home of Donald Deernose. An old man with a red bandana opened the door.

"Mr. Deernose. I am—"

"Morgue, I believe they call you. Come in."

CHAPTER 7

The Medicine Wheel

Geof's fingers trembled as he left Story. "I'm going to El Tapatio Dos and buy some cheese enchiladas." He wanted to say something else, but this was a good stall.

"I feel like I'm in a B-movie," Jon said. "Do you believe that guy?"

"He's kind of creepy," Pat said. "I don't know."

"I believe him," Debbie said firmly.

"One way to find out," Geof said. "Let's check it out."

The Sebring pulled into the driveway at around 3:45. Enchiladas in hand, his friends piled out of the car, and Jon gingerly removed the Song for Tomorrow. It slipped from his grasp. Instinctively Geof dove to the ground with surprising speed and cupped it in his hands. The Bear regained his feet, and the Song for Tomorrow squirmed free a second time. Geof popped it from one hand to the other before finally getting it under control.

Jon rolled his eyes. "What's wrong with you, dude?"

"I dunno," Geof stammered. "It's like—it's alive."

"Right. You're just a klutz. You drop that thing again, and it'll probably blow up."

"Not funny," Geof sniffed. "I'm tellin' ya, this thing acts like it's alive."

The Song broke free again, and Jon snatched it out of midair. He raced past the normal doggie welcome wagon to the unlocked front door. He opened the door and held the Song for Tomorrow above his head while dancing and singing, "Praw-fe-sie, praw-fe-sie, praw-fe-sie." He slipped inside the door, poked his head back out and cried, "It's alive!"

Geof waved him off and motioned for the girls to go inside. He said, "Grab a drink from the fridge and let's go to the basement."

The Boucher family basement was a not large, but well-designed man cave. There was a big-screen TV and a curved fabric couch with recliners on each end. To the side was a poker table complete with chips and an unopened deck of cards. Geof went to the poker table and removed the cards and chips. He motioned for Jon to unroll the Song for Tomorrow on the green felt tabletop.

Jon carefully placed the document on the table. Before them lay several crudely drawn figures on the ancient animal skin. The four teenagers pored over the figures looking for something that might give them a clue to its meaning. There was a bear, a butterfly, a campfire with a long-haired figure sitting next to it, a two-headed snake, a fish with its mouth open, a pond with cattails, six human stick figures in various poses, and a circular symbol that looked like a bicycle wheel. At the bottom, there were more faded and indecipherable figures.

"Can anybody tell what these things are?" Pat asked, pointing at the blurry figures.

Everybody leaned forward. Three middle fingers of Geof's right hand rested on the edge of the Song for Tomorrow. The instant his fingertips touched the Song, the figures began to move. He closed his eyes and shook his head. But when he looked again, they were not only moving but levitating from the surface. Geof tried to jerk his hand away, but it felt glued to the table. The figures continued to rise and take form, writhing and crashing into each other like a drunken hologram. The bicycle wheel spun and rose above the other figures, revolving slowly at first and picking up speed as it whirled.

Geof yanked and jerked his hand as hard as he could to free himself from the invisible force. Jon, Debbie, and Pat looked at him like he was goofing off. After a few seconds of rolling eyes at Geof's childish antics, Debbie said, "All right, Geof. We get it."

Geof struggled to turn his head to look behind him. His face was contorted into a collage of terror and helplessness. He tried to say something, anything, but the words would not come out.

"All right, William Shatner, enough is enough," Jon said. With Jonster the Monster fanfare, he reached out his right hand to grab Geof's shoulder. His hand found his large friend, but he had no strength. He could barely move. He looked at

the Song for Tomorrow, and it came to life before his eyes. There was something directly in front of his face spinning crazily. He felt drawn to it and was powerless to resist. Jonster the Monster, king of the quip, could only manage a warbled, "AHHHHHHHHHHH!"

Beneath the spinning wheel, the table was alive with a two-headed snake slithering around and striking out at Jon, a bear with a dog face standing on its hind legs growling and snapping, butterflies flying all around, a small dog, and stick figure people running wild while battling something unseen.

What looked at first like a gag suddenly became very scary. "Oh my God," Pat cried. "That Deernose guy is the real deal." She grabbed Jon's arm with her left hand, but rather than rescue him, was herself drawn into the Song for Tomorrow. The three were trapped in the swirling nightmare, unable to respond to Debbie's screams.

Debbie resisted the temptation to grab Geof and slapped him instead. When she touched him, an impossible scene exploded before her eyes. The table became a stage delivering a terrifying command performance with non-refundable tickets. Debbie was also under the influence of the Song but somehow mustered the power to resist. With her free hand, she grabbed a chair and threw it into the center of the hologram. The instant the chair pierced the hologram's plane, it disappeared like a popped bubble, and the chair crashed to the floor. The hologram's hold relaxed, and three liberated and exhausted teenagers collapsed in a heap. Debbie helped Geof, Jon, and Pat to their feet. The four stared at a now benign game table partially covered by an old animal skin displaying a group of cave painting figures. Nothing was moving. Nothing was scary. Nothing was out of the ordinary at all.

"What the heck was that?" Jon yelled.

Debbie took a deep breath. "I don't know. But one thing I do know. Geof has gotta be that Searcher."

"Forget it." Geof stammered.

Patricia said, "Remember what Donald Deernose said. You have no choice."

Geof held his clenched fists next to his cheeks, looked up at the ceiling, and screamed, "Noooooooooo!"

"Oh, yeah?" Jon barked. He took a folding chair and placed it about five feet from the game table. He grabbed the distraught Geof's shirt and made him sit down. "Well, you sure are somethin', and we're all stuck with it. We're gonna stay here and figure it out right now."

"But…"

"And you, my friend, are gonna stay out of range of that *thing* while we think."

Jon and the girls approached the Song for Tomorrow. They collectively studied it for about five minutes. Jon impatiently blurted, "I can't make heads or tails out of this thing."

Debbie took Jon's arm. "Keep trying. It sounds like the world needs us…"

"At the moment, I don't care all that much about the world."

"Fine, Jon. But what about our families? Don't you care about them?"

Jon knitted his brow. "Yeah, but did you see that snake thing? A head on each end? I don't wanna get eaten by something that can't even poop me out."

Debbie glared at him. "Well, there's an intelligent concern."

"Okay, okay. What about that wheel thingamajig? And this is just a little drawing. Can you imagine what a big one would do?"

"I wonder what it is," Pat said like she already knew the answer.

"Maybe it's a flying saucer," Jon offered.

"Maybe it was a wheel from a cart of some kind," Debbie said.

Geof stood up and slowly approached the table but was blocked by Jon and Debbie. He placed his hands between them and gently pushed them apart. "Medicine Wheel," he whispered.

"What wheel?"

"It's the Medicine Wheel, Pat. My dad used to take me there."

"What is a—a—a Medicine Wheel?" Pat asked.

"You've only lived here a few years, right?"

"Yes. I came from the, uh, you know, Northeast."

"Well, the Medicine Wheel is this big stone circle up in the Big Horns that was built by some Native American people maybe seven hundred years ago or something like that."

"But what does it do?"

"It doesn't do anything, I don't think. But it was, or still is sacred to many Indian tribes. Young braves used to go there to purify themselves and become men. Native peoples still come to the Medicine Wheel from all over and pray. The Medicine Wheel is the key to what we are searching for."

"Exactly what are we searching for, Bear?" Jon asked.

"The entrance to that other world and our place in it."

"I was afraid you'd say that. What about all that other stuff? Maybe it's just some dead guy's imagination. Maybe it's just a bunch of meaningless pictures."

"They didn't seem so meaningless to me. I think those scary things are what waits for us. But forget it. I can't let any of you go any further in this. This whole thing has nothing to do with you."

"Don't presume to tell me where I can and cannot go," Debbie snapped. "This isn't just about your mother anymore. It's about every mother, father, and child. I have the right to do everything I can to protect my family... just like you do."

"But you are just kids."

"And what are you? The Ancient Mariner?"

"You guys wouldn't even know about this if it weren't for me. I can't—"

"But we do know. And we are here. And we have seen this thing. Come on. Let's try to figure this out together."

"I have a question," Jon interrupted. "What's with those six guys here running around all over the place?"

Everybody instinctively looked at Geof. "I think they could be us."

"I know you're better at math than that, old buddy. There are only four of us here."

"I know. Maybe we're supposed to meet two other people somewhere."

"You already have," came a voice from the top of the stairway.

Everyone turned sharply to see Donald Deernose and Leonard Boucher descending the stairs.

Jon gasped, "You mean it's you two?"

Donald Deernose turned and motioned to the top of the stairs. "Not us. Them." Clark and Morgue tentatively walked down the stairs.

"Where did you guys come from?"

"Sorry, Jon.—I mean we—well—we kind of—"

Morgue shoved Clark out of the way. "Spit it out, man. We got this mysterious call to go to Story and meet with some guy who said you guys might be in trouble and need our help."

"Uhhh, we needed your help?" Geof laughed.

"The Song for Tomorrow promises six warriors," the Indian explained.

"What does that have to do with anything?" Jonster asked. "Just because there are six stick figures on this thing—let me repeat that—*Stick figures*—doesn't mean jack."

"There must be six of us," Geof said quietly.

"And you know this for sure because you are..."

"The SEARCHER," Debbie interrupted.

Geof looked over at his dad with puppy dog eyes. "Help me, Dad."

"Son, it is not up to me. What I saw from the top of the stairs was no act. I have always known you were something special."

Geof looked over at Donald Deernose and saw a firm look on his face. "This is like the young braves, isn't it? They went to purify themselves at the Medicine Wheel. They went to become men."

"Yes. But wheel have more significance for you."

"I think I understand the significance, Mr. Deernose. But it is almost impossible to fathom that the six of us are key to... to anything."

It did not add up to Debbie either. "So why do we... why does Geof... have to go there?"

"To fulfill prophecies in Song for Tomorrow. Medicine men long past believed that Song for Tomorrow tell of world we are not meant to know. They see danger. It is journey Geof and friends must take."

"Son, you know I would go in your place. I want to go in your place. But..."

"I don't want to stand in your way if you really want to go, Mr. B.," said Jonster the Monster. "I'll sacrifice and give you my spot."

Everybody but the medicine man laughed. "It must be you, Jon. You are to stand beside the Searcher."

"Yeah. You can be my sidekick," Geof laughed.

"Do not be too cocky, young friend," the Indian cautioned Geof. "Searcher not royalty. Without the help of father and friends, Searcher fail."

"Yeah. Yeah. Get that? We rule."

Geof bowed to the barrage from his friends. "Okay. Okay."

"Let us go upstairs," Leonard said.

Jon looked back. "Would somebody other than Geof please bring that stupid thing?"

At the top of the stairs, Geof said, "Dad, I don't know what to do. I can't leave you like Mom did."

"This decision was made for us long ago. Besides, your mother did not leave me. She went to try to save herself, maybe all of us."

"Dad, I . . ."

"Donald told me. I have faith in you, son. Have faith in yourself."

"What are we supposed to do now?" Pat questioned. "What about our families?"

"Each must choose. You are fine young men. I am proud that you consider walking in footsteps of my ancestors."

"In case you hadn't noticed, Pat and I aren't young men."

"You have strength. You have wisdom. You have courage. These gifts are not only the ownership of men."

"We know that," Debbie said.

"Besides, Donald Deernose not think these two guys can find Colorado River in Grand Canyon without your help."

"Hardee har," Geof moaned.

"It's just that my parents…"

Leonard Boucher put his hand on his chest. "Debbie, I am happy to say that I may well be the only parent to suffer."

"How do you figure that?" Debbie asked.

"Do you remember Strong Bear? He was lost in the other world for many years, but his wife was still young when he returned. Two hours in our world might be a month in that world. Might be many years."

Leonard's knowledge of Strong Bear surprised Geof. "But wait. My mother has been gone for what? Fourteen or fifteen years? If that's true, it would mean..."

"She might have lived as much as a hundred years or much more where she is."

"Then what you are saying is that even if we are gone for a while, our parents might not even notice?"

"I do not know, Pat. Maybe. There are risks."

Geof and his father looked at one another and nodded. "I'm going, Dad. I guess I gotta go."

"I know."

The house went silent. Nobody said anything. Nothing could be said. Maybe they could ignore the whole thing away. Maybe.

"Mr. Deernose, do you know what happens now?" Debbie asked.

"We go to Medicine Wheel."

Jon looked at Pat. He said softly, "Are you sure you want to do this?

"I have always been intrigued by prophecies. It would mean a lot to me to know if this one is true or not. Plus, I bet you really would need Debbie and me to find the Colorado River in the Grand Canyon."

"Smart girl. Come on, sidekick," Jon shouted to the Bear. "At this rate, we'll all die of old age before we even get a chance to live forever."

Donald Deernose was driving an older Jeep Cherokee. Morgue put his hand on the hood. "Nice ride, Mr. D."

"I call her Mankiller," the medicine man smiled.

Morgue jerked his hand away. "Did you say Mankiller?"

"You not worry, kid. I not say, white-man killer. I name her Mankiller after Wilma Mankiller, first female chief of Cherokee. Get it?"

"If you say so."

The medicine man leaned out the window and hollered at Geof. "Follow me."

Geof waved in response. The two cars headed down Airport Road on their way to the Big Horn Mountains, the Medicine Wheel, and destiny.

CHAPTER 8

They're Gone

Mankiller and the Bearmobile cruised through Sheridan on their way to Dayton-Kane highway. As Mankiller exited the small town of Dayton and began the ascent up Dayton-Kane, Leonard Boucher glanced out the window. Visions of past adventures on the mountain helped insulate him from today's unnerving reality. Sibley Lake. Fallen City. Steamboat Rock. Like a receiving line of old friends, they welcomed Leonard with warm and happy recollections. He wondered if they were also talking to his son. Were they saying hello... or goodbye?

They stopped at the empty parking area a few feet from the Medicine Wheel ranger station. The medicine man lifted Mankiller's hatch and removed a large drum.

"What's that for?" Morgue asked.

"I think I might need it."

A forest ranger stepped out to greet them. He asked the group if they had any questions. There were none. Seriously. What would one ask?

Pat peeked past the ranger to a clump of short grass less than a hundred yards away. One little black and white head bobbed up, looked at her, and disappeared. Then another. And still another. The scene looked like a whack-a-mole game, but nobody would want to hurt these little cuties. "Ooooh. They are adorable," she squealed as she ran toward them.

"I wouldn't do that, ma'am," the ranger cautioned. "Them's badgers."

She stopped and looked at the ranger. "So?"

Jon grinned. "So, if you want to take a hundred percent of your body to the Medicine Wheel, I suggest you leave them be."

"Oh. Okay."

The trek up to the hill was not long, and within minutes, the Medicine Wheel was in sight. It lay before them majestically as it had for centuries, the eternal guardian of the mountain. A wire fence adorned with colorful prayer flags protected the Wheel.

Donald Deernose stood before the group. "This is sacred Medicine Wheel. Flags are prayers of native people. Respect them. This not just pile of rocks."

"Do you know why it was made?" Debbie asked.

"No man can be certain. Medicine Wheel points to stars. Twenty-eight spokes inside wheel may be like days of month."

Jon smirked, "Geez, Don. This is your gig. Don't you know for sure?"

"If you want more scientific explanation, Google it." Deernose smiled.

Geof pointed at Jon and laughed.

Leonard patted Geof on the back. "I feel like a bad parent letting you do this. But…"

"You always told me to do the right thing, Dad."

"Geoffrey Michael Boucher! Just because you are this alleged Searcher does not give you the right to interrupt me."

"Ooooo. Sorry, Pop. Habit."

"What I was about to say is that I feel like a bad parent, but I also know that my greatest accomplishment is you. I have always known you were destined for great things."

Geof hugged his father tightly. "I love you, Dad."

Jon looked at Debbie. A tear was rolling down her cheek. "Get me a bucket," he said, rolling his eyes.

"What?" Debbie sniffled.

"This sappy scene makes me want to barf."

Morgue and Clark laughed while Debbie gave Jon the stink eye. "I think it's beautiful."

"All right, all right. What are we supposed to do now?"

The medicine man told each of the five, not including Geof, to stand in the five stone circles that touched the outside edge of the wheel. "Most important not to disturb stones."

"What about me?" Geof asked.

"You are hub. Go to small circle of rocks in center."

Leonard counted five small rock circles surrounding the larger stone circle and one just inside it. "Hey Donald, there are six circles, not five. Does the one inside the circle line mean anything?"

"Yes. That circle is key. Gatekeeper stand there."

"Gatekeeper? You mean you?" Leonard asked.

"Not me, old friend. You. You are father of Searcher. You must guide him on most important journey."

"Of course, I will. What am I supposed to do?"

Donald Deernose leaned close to Leonard and said in a whisper, "You know what to do." Leonard nodded. "When Geof takes place in middle circle, he reaches out hands to you. You must reach back to him. You must keep strong bond with him. He know when to let go, and you must let him go."

Jon turned toward the group, and solemnly lifted his right hand toward the sky. The others reached up and clasped hands. They looked at each other for a few moments, each waiting for someone to say something inspiring. Jon pulled back, thrust his index finger to the sky, and yelled, "To infinity and beyond!"

Five arms went limp.

"*Toy Story*?" Debbie gagged. "That's it? *Toy Story*?"

"Well… it's the right sentiment," Jon said defiantly. "And now I own it." He did an about-face and marched triumphantly toward one of the five stone circles.

When the five outer circles were filled, the Bear looked back at his father and Donald Deernose. Careful not to disturb anything, he stepped into the middle of the wheel. He turned toward his father and nodded. Leonard tiptoed into the key and glanced at Donald Deernose, but he seemed to be looking right through him. The eyes of father and son met. Geof reached out both hands to his father. Leonard reached out to his son. At that moment, Geof felt a power flowing from his father that he had never experienced before.

Jon, Debbie, Pat, Clark, and Morgue looked across the wheel at each other and waited. Nothing happened. After what seemed to be the climax of anticlimaxes, a chorus of nervous laughter broke out. It was all nonsense, after all. Donald Deernose was just an old kook and the Song for Tomorrow was simply a piece of art by some ancient Native American Picasso.

Jon looked at Geof with a big grin on his face, totally appreciative of the bag job that was just played on them. He leaned forward to get a better look. Geof was not looking back. His eyes were welded to his father, who was equally oblivious to everything around him.

Jon tried to step out of his stone circle but was pushed back. He turned to go the other way but wasn't going anywhere. Jon could see his friends pushing against the same unseen captor. His attitude quickly changed from the good-natured victim of an elaborate practical joke to the edge of terrified.

Jon balanced himself against the force field and looked at his feet. The ground moved beneath them. The world outside swirled around him faster and faster. The spinning landscape should have been blurry, but it was not. In that movement, there were endless scenes of people, animals, and strange creatures. And every one focused on him. Some looked friendly and talked to him while others screamed unintelligible threats. Some were animals, and some were human. But there were other creatures he could only classify as monsters snarling and clawing at him, one after another.

Debbie screamed as she found herself the lead in the same terrifying play. She ducked, dodged, and did her best to evade the monsters that were intent on destroying her. She was not alone. Morgue and Clark were equally terrified. Only Pat was unmoved. Rather than trying to evade the boiling creatures, she looked upon them with interest and curiosity.

Geof stood in the hub of the Medicine Wheel, eyes fixed on his father. Leonard's eyes held steady on Geof, but they showed no emotion. Donald Deernose began to mumble Native American chants and beat his drum as he watched the scene unfold. Geof and his father stood rigid. As the swirl reached redline RPMs, it began to grow upward and inward until it came together in a cone shape directly above Geof's head. Donald Deernose chanted louder and louder and beat his drum harder and harder until he had no vision beyond the whirlwind. His new friends were now invisible. In an instant, the drum was ripped from his grasp and hurled into the tempest. With that, it all ended. Donald Deernose was standing a few feet from the Medicine Wheel, his friend Leonard standing unfazed in the keyhole near him.

Donald scanned the Medicine Wheel. They were gone. They really were gone.

CHAPTER 9

Uriah

Geof stood in the center of the Medicine Wheel, his mind without a concept of time. Debbie was lying on the ground.

"Are you okay?" he quivered.

"Geof. What... oh wow. What a dream I just had."

"No dream, I'm afraid."

"That was wild," Jon said, skipping toward them. "But nothing's different."

"Nothing's different? You see my dad anywhere?"

"Or Mr. Deernose? Where is he?" Debbie asked.

"Look," Clark said with uncharacteristic self-assurance. "Things look the same, but they're not. Look at the sky. It's green."

Everybody looked up. It looked green, all right. But something else. The sun was red.

"So, where are we then?" Debbie asked. Everyone instinctively looked at Clark. He lived in an alternative universe most of the time, so if anybody had an answer, it would be him.

Clark instinctively looked toward the ground. "I'm a nerd, not a psychic. We could be anywhere…"

Or any time, Geof thought.

"Hey, look," Morgue called out excitedly. "It's not all that different." He ran to the top of a gently sloping hill. Everyone ran after him. In front of them a small cocker spaniel. He looked like pictures of Leonard Boucher's beloved cocker spaniels from his childhood. He was blond with large tan freckles on his face and a white patch that started on his nose and rode up between his eyes to the top of his head. His tail was long, and it was wagging. "Oooh, how cute," Debbie cooed as she ran to pet him. She squatted in front of him and turned back toward the group. "Do you think he's lost?"

The dog stared at her.

"Nice doggie," she said, reaching out to pet him. When her hand was an inch from the dog's forehead, he opened his mouth to the size of Debbie herself and let out a roar that sent Debbie reeling.

Geof threw himself protectively between Debbie and what was not your father's dog. The dog stood his ground, closed his mouth, and stared at the mortified teenagers. He cocked his head to one side and started to open his mouth again. The kids imploded into a group hug. The dog did not roar but spoke. "Did not mean to startle you, but you cannot be too careful these days."

"That's all folks. I'm outta here," Jon said. He grabbed Pat's hand and yanked her in the opposite direction of the dog, or whatever it was.

"Don't be silly," the dog laughed. "You have nowhere to go."

Jon stopped abruptly, causing Pat to crash into him. Geof gathered himself and stepped forward. They were on somebody else's turf now, but the Bear was a dog guy. This little guy could not be all that different.

As the rest of the group huddled behind him, Geof said, "Nice doggie."

"Doggie, you say. Did you say doggie?" the cocker sniffed. He continued without waiting for Geof to answer. "I see it is true. I must have missed it. Just went down the hill for a moment to lift a leg, so to speak."

"Uhhhhh, missed what?" Geof asked. The situation was not as difficult as he thought it would be. Geof talked to dogs all his life. They just never talked back before.

"Why, your arrival, of course. I did not see your arrival. Most extraordinary. That is what I am here for."

Clark leaned over to Morgue and said, "Does he have an English accent? Sounds like an English accent."

"Sounds more Irish to me," Morgue breathed back. "But he's a spaniel. Shouldn't he have a Spanish accent?"

Debbie looked sideways at Morgue and Clark. "Are you guys on drugs? Your reaction to a talking dog is to try to identify its accent?"

"Just curious," Clark whimpered.

"Wait a minute," Jon jumped in. "What *are* you here for?"

"To greet visitors, of course. I am Uriah the guardian. I identify those who have entered our world with evil intent. They must be classified and dealt with."

"What does dealt with mean?"

"If you pose a danger, you will be destroyed. If, in the rare case you do not, I am to guide you."

Geof shoved his palm at Uriah's face. "Can you excuse us just for a minute?"

"As you wish."

Geof gathered everyone around him. "You know, there is an Indian legend that says that when a person dies, he is met at heaven's gate by all the animals he met in his lifetime. How he treated those animals determines if he gets into heaven or not."

"You think this is heaven? I don't think this is heaven," Jon said.

"I don't know. Either way, I strongly suggest we tread lightly here."

"That's a cool legend, Geof, but I don't think it has anything to do with this," Debbie said. "First of all, we've never met this guy Uriah before. And secondly, we're not dead."

"Maybe we are. Maybe this is being dead."

Jon punched Geof in the shoulder. "Feel that? You're not dead."

Geof rubbed his shoulder. "I'm just saying."

"Why don't we just see what Uriah has to say?" Clark said, still too timid to look his friends in the eye.

"Yes. Let's," Debbie nodded. She broke away from the others and went back to Uriah. "Uriah, I assure you we have no evil intent. We're just trying to help Geof find his mother."

She pointed at her friends. "Look at them. There is no way they could be a danger to you."

Five voices supported her with a chorus of varying verses. "We are no danger. No danger at all. Us a danger? Ridiculous."

Geof straightened himself and said firmly, "Debbie is right. We mean no harm to anyone."

Jon added, "And we definitely could use some guidance."

"That much is obvious," the dog answered without a blink. "I will consider what you have said."

"You said you're the gaurdian. Guardian of what?" Geof asked.

"I am the guardian of Sergel-tuteron, of course."

"Sergel-what?"

"This is the land of Sergel-tuteron, and I am the guardian. I must decide why you are here and if you are to be destroyed."

"We unanimously vote against destroyed."

"Why are you here? There have been no friendly visitors since, oh, since a long time. Most do not intend to come here. It just happens."

"Wellll, we are here because, uh, well, there was this Indian who, uhhhh..."

"My patience grows thin."

Debbie rushed to Geof's side. "Show him the Song for Tomorrow."

Jon reluctantly handed Debbie the Song. She cautiously knelt in front of Uriah and unrolled it. He studied it for what seemed like an eternity, his eyes growing bigger with each passing second. When he looked up from the symbols before him, Uriah had a new look about him. He sat up on his haunches, stuck out his right forepaw in Geof's direction, and said, "Welcome."

Geof stood, looking at him. "Come on, Geof, shake," Jon laughed.

Geof looked sideways at Jon and reached out to grasp Uriah's paw. "Happy to be here, uh, I guess."

"Now roll over," Jon cracked.

"You've got to be the funniest sidekick on the planet," Geof growled.

"Boys, I hate to break up this little male bonding ritual," Debbie said, "but I just wonder if you could focus on the fact that we are in the Twilight Zone without our families or the slightest idea of where we are or what is going to happen to us. And to top it all off, we're having a conversation with a talking dog!" Her voice got louder with each syllable until she was shouting red-faced into the shocked faces of Jon and Geof.

"Talking dog?" Uriah looked annoyed.

"You see Mr., Mr..."

"Uriah."

"Right. Mr. Uriah. Where we come from, dogs don't talk," Clark tried to explain.

"Dogs? I have not heard this term before. Is it an insult? I am Uriah, a member of the Cain division."

"Uriah, the word dog refers to those like you and is anything but an insult. Where we come from, dogs are called man's best friend. They are highly revered and respected,"

Geof explained. "Personally, I would be honored to be called a dog."

"You have been. Just not to your face," Jon smiled.

"I do not understand this kind of speech. You are friends, and yet you ridicule each other."

"It's a guy thing," Debbie apologized. "It doesn't have to make any sense." She instinctively reached out her hand to stroke Uriah, and this time he let her.

"Tell me of this thing, this story you call the Song for Tomorrow," Uriah said.

"It was given to us by an Indian medicine man. We have come here because we are supposed to do something to stop some big disaster from happening. And I hope to find my mother."

"Your mother?'

"Yes. I have reason to believe that she might be here in.... Ser... wherever this is.

"Sergel-tuteron. And which of you is supposed to be the Searcher?"

Geof looked back and got the fish eye from everyone. "You, you know of this, this Searcher person?"

"Everyone in Sergel-tuteron knows of him." Uriah looked down and away for a moment, his face saddened. "We know of him."

"You do not look pleased."

"The Song for Tomorrow is known throughout my land, not yours. This is certain. And yet you have come bearing the Song for Tomorrow, which means you must be—well, it must mean that the time of the Song for Tomorrow is upon us."

"Is that so bad?" Geof asked.

"It is said to be a time of great promise. But it will also bring upheaval. Great upheaval," Uriah repeated with a sigh.

"We didn't mean to—I mean, we didn't think we would bring anything bad. I am definitely not an upheaval kind of guy."

"That does not matter. It is said that the Song for Tomorrow cannot be changed. If you are those foretold, these events are already in motion. Now, I ask again. Which one is the Searcher?"

Geof sheepishly raised his hand. "I guess it's me."

Uriah dropped his head and muttered, "May our queen protect us. I had hoped for a heroic warrior."

"Now wait a minute," Jon gruffed. "Geof may seem a little, you know, uh, tranquilized at times, but..."

Geof looked at Jon and raised his right eyebrow.

"But beneath all that sleepwalking beats the heart of a lion... or gorilla or something."

"The Song for Tomorrow tells of great battles and great sacrifices. It tells of one who can defeat the undefeatable. The Searcher must have more than heart."

Jon countered, "I would bet most of the great men, or dogs, of your history did not know they would be heroes until events forced it on them. And on top of that, we don't even know what's going on around here, what the big deal is, or what we're supposed to do."

Debbie shrugged. "Doesn't this prophecy thing tell what is going to happen anyway? I mean, what are you worried about? If Geof is to be the big guy, it's already set, right?"

"No, my naïve one. The events are prophesied, not the outcome. The Song for Tomorrow tells of the possibilities of our world, things that will determine our future, but not what that future will be. It tells of a great warrior and his friends. It does not say the warrior will be successful."

Geof swallowed hard. "That sucks."

"I beg your pardon?" Uriah asked.

"Nothing."

"I will take you five to the queen. She will know what to do with you."

Morgue raised his index finger. "Excuse me, Mr. Uriah, there are six of us."

"One of you is not coming."

"What? Are you going to eat one of us or something?" Clark shuddered.

Uriah shook his head. "Are such fools to be our deliverance? Have I waited all these epochs for this? Fewer than three who have come into the land of Sergel-tuteron have I allowed admittance."

"I am kind of afraid to ask what happened to the rest of them."

Uriah uttered a low grrrrrrrr.

"Oh God," Clark gasped. "You mean one of us is going to be, you know, grrrrrrrrrrrrrr?"

Uriah scratched himself with his hind leg. "I am going to take you to the queen myself. That means the wheel would be left with no guardian, and that is not possible. One of you must stay to take my place."

"Well, I s'pose that's me," Clark said dejectedly. "I'm obviously the weak link."

"It is not you. Your feet must take a different path." Uriah turned to Morgue and sat down in front of him. "You will stay."

"What the? What did I do?" Morgue yelped. "I—I don't know anything about being a—one of those—this guardian thing."

"I assure you that you will find it enjoyable. Take my paw."

Morgue tenuously reached out and took Uriah's extended foot. His eyes glazed over. When Uriah took his paw away, Morgue turned and walked back up the hill without a word to his friends.

"Morgue, are you all right?" Geof called out.

Morgue did not answer and walked to the Medicine Wheel. He turned, looked down the hill at his friends, slowly raised his right hand, and evaporated before their eyes.

"What have you done to him? Where is he?" Jon yelled.

"He is now the guardian. You must worry about yourselves. He has his job. You have yours. And I have mine. Come. We go to see the queen."

Jon took a deep breath. "Only minutes ago, we were standing on top of a mountain talking to Geof's dad. And now we're about to be led by a talking dog to see some queen in a land nobody ever heard of, for... for why?"

Geof looked at his friends. "There must be a reason. Let's get ahold of ourselves and do this thing."

Debbie put her hands on her hips, "That might be easy for you because you're supposed to be this Searcher guy. But what are we?"

"Yeah, good point," Jon said. "Maybe we're just a bunch of red shirts in *Star Trek*, you know? Somebody to get killed off so Captain Kirk can save the day, get the girl, and—"

"You watch too much TV. I think this whole Searcher thing is pretty silly. But Deernose says that I am nothing without you." The friends realized that Geof was right. One by one, beginning with Clark, they took his hand. Geof looked each in the eye, lingering longer on Debbie. He straightened himself up and said in a firm voice, "I dub thee one and all, the Protectors."

"Lame," Jon smirked.

"Better than to infinity and beyond," Pat winked.

Jon scrunched his nose. "It sounds... I don't know... subservient."

"Perfect," Geof grinned. He looked at Jon's unamused face and shrugged, "Okay, fine, you big baby. You can all be Searchers."

CHAPTER 10

Take a Hike

They followed Uriah as he effortlessly bounded down the hill. "Is Morgue going to be all right? And how far are we going?" Pat asked.

Uriah looked at her like it was dissection day in biology, and she was the frog. There was something about her that clearly unnerved him. Finally, he said, "Oh, yes. He is in good hands. You must concentrate on yourselves going forward. The lumen will set three times before we reach the queen."

Debbie looked at Pat. "I think he means the sun will go down," Pat said. "Three days."

"Ah yes... days. I have heard that simple word before. As you wish. We will call it days," Uriah said.

Pat ran to Uriah's side. "I never was much on camping. What do we do for shelter, or for something to eat?"

"Your needs will be seen to," he said without emotion.

The descent from the Medicine Wheel was easy and uneventful. About halfway down, Jon found a long stick half-buried in the rocks and dirt. It was an impressive piece of wood, about two inches in diameter and six feet long. He picked it up. "Hey, look at this," he shouted.

"Nice stick," Geof sniffed.

"Yeah, but look." Jon wiped the dirt off with his shirttail.

Geof looked more closely and saw that the stick had an ornate carving on each end with deep grooves cut in random patterns running from one end to the other. Unintelligible markings were etched throughout.

"Radical!" Geof jumped in the air. "This must have belonged to some kind of caveman or something. What is this, Uriah?"

"I do not know," a wide-eyed Uriah said.

"Don't buy it," Geof whispered to Jon. "It's obvious he finds something very interesting about that stick."

"Well, it's mine now," Jon crowed.

"Let me see," Geof said, grabbing it. He studied the carvings carefully.

"What do you think those carvings mean?" Jon asked.

"It's obvious," Geof said.

"Really? Gimme that," Jon said, reaching for the stick.

Geof pulled it away. "Not so fast. I'll show you." Geof drew Jon's face close to the stick and pointed his finger to the middle of the etchings.

"You see here?"

Jon squinted and shoved his nose to within inches of the stick. He shook his head. "I can't read it."

Geof smiled. "It says, and I'm paraphrasing here… it says a big stick for a little sidekick."

Jon snatched the stick away from the Bear. "Oh, you are just too funny, aren't you?"

Pat laughed with Geof. But she could not shake the uneasy way Uriah looked at her.

The slope of the mountain was gradual, and to kids who resided in the shadow of the Big Horn Mountains, it was just a hill. Jon held his head high and walked slowly and proudly with his cool walking stick.

"Why is he walking like that, Bear?" Clark asked.

"He thinks he's Moses."

The terrain morphed into gently rolling hills, which, in turn, became farmland as far as the eye could see. In the distance was a range of beautiful but forbidding mountains. As they crossed the bucolic countryside, they became aware of people working in the fields. People like them. There were no tractors or mechanized equipment to do the work. The heavy lifting was done by horses and beasts resembling oxen. But something was different. These horses and oxen were plowing the fields and moving the boulders by themselves. There were no humans anywhere near them.

Debbie jabbed Pat with her elbow. "If I ever get out of this place alive, I'm bringing some of those critters home with me."

"Good plan."

Before long, they were on a neatly kept dirt road that wound around fields of corn, wheat, and an assortment of crops that even Debbie did not recognize. Immaculate houses and barns were dotting the landscape. The countryside looked like an Amish calendar. The farmers, two and four-legged, stopped to watch the small band with a mixture of interest, reverence, and fear.

Pat leaned over to Debbie. "I think they are staring at me."

"They're staring at all of us," Debbie laughed. "What an ego!"

As usual, Geof trailed far behind. Jon yelled over his shoulder, "Come on, Bear. Step on it, or whatever we're searching for will be gone before we even get there."

"Heh, heh," Geof grinned.

Debbie wondered what was up with Geof. Was he afraid? Was he just antisocial? She knew that was not true. Curiosity got the best of her, and she stopped to wait for Geof to catch up to her. Geof was delighted to see his beloved slow down to join him, but he seemed unusually reserved.

"Are you all right?" Debbie asked.

"No worries. Are you?"

"Oh yes, of course."

Debbie watched Geof's face as they moved ahead. He was walking with great purpose, his head turning slightly from left to right every couple of steps, his eyes accompanying the movement of his head.

Hey! He's protecting us, she thought. He's hanging back here to see if anything might come springing out of one of these fields to attack us. Very Sir Galahad. "Do you mind if I hang with you for a while?" Debbie asked, looking up at him.

"Sure." This was good. This was really, really, really good. He had fantasized about being a hero to Debbie his whole life. And now he will probably get killed tomorrow and not be able to enjoy it. But this moment and this time was his to cherish.

Outside of Pat's paranoia, there was nothing in the faces of the locals that gave any reason for apprehension among the Searchers. In fact, they all, including animals, seemed to regard the entire group with an expression bordering on reverence. Pat sidled up next to Uriah and diplomatically tried to find out why she felt so weird. "Why are all these people looking at us like that? We don't look any different from them."

"Maybe you do."

Pat raised her eyebrows. "Okay, what does that mean? And while we're at it, how come you speak English."

"I am not speaking English. I am speaking Uni. And so are you."

"What are you talking about? I am speaking English. It is all I know."

"Yes, I have heard this word English before. But now you are speaking Uni. Everyone in Sergel-tuteron speaks and writes Uni."

"You lost me," Pat said.

"Everyone is looking at us because they are familiar with the Song for Tomorrow. And, you see, I am quite well known around here," he bragged. "The people know me and what I do, and you are with me. And, well, look at you. Why would I be with someone like you unless...."

"Oh, really! What's wrong with us?" Jon growled.

"I hope less than there seems to be."

"Cute. What you are saying that they think we are?"

"The Searchers."

"Anybody bring a Sharpie so I can sign autographs?" the Monster asked. "And Uriah, this Uni thing blows my mind."

Uriah stared at Jon, then resumed his walk. "If you are in Sergel-tuteron, you speak Uni. That is the way it is." Further explanations would have to wait.

The sun, or lumen, was going down, and a wave of nervousness swept through the party. "It's getting dark," Clark moaned.

"We soon rest," Uriah said.

"Where?" Pat asked.

"Ehhhhh. Over there," an exasperated Uriah answered.

"Too bad he's not a pointer," Jon whispered to Debbie. They both laughed.

"We are about there," Uriah said.

A simple farmhouse came into view. It was white with light blue trim and a thatched roof atop the second story. This might not be so bad. There were lights in two rooms on the first floor and in one room on the second floor. Uriah led them down a small stone path a few feet to the side of the house. "We are here," Uriah declared. He stood in front of a forty-inch high wooden door. A small light was positioned directly above the door in the center, illuminating a carved wooden sign that read, "Walk with honor."

"Are we supposed to go in there?" Debbie asked.

"Oh yes, dear," came an uncharacteristically gentle reply. Uriah reached out with his right paw and opened the door. Clark, his scientific curiosity overcoming his angst, was the first to crouch down and enter. He was surprised that inside he could immediately stand erect. He turned and motioned for the others to come in. The interior was bright and surprisingly spacious, with a ceiling high enough to easily accommodate Geof. Uriah trotted in with his tail curled above his back. He was happy to be there. Geof struggled to squeeze himself through the door but made it with minimal damage.

Uriah said proudly, "Welcome to my home."

If silence is golden, the next few moments were Fort Knox. Even Jon was speechless. He saw a room brightly lit by clusters of multi-faceted crystals. They looked like lamps, sort of. There were no shades, yet the light emanating from them was not glaring and did not hurt the eyes. Clark was hovering over one of the lights and doing his best to figure out what made it tick. There was no cord. There was no switch. And the house was lit like daylight, creating such a juicy puzzle for Clark that he did not see the black cocker spaniel enter the room.

"Searchers… my mate, Felinah," Uriah beamed.

To everyone's relief, Jon resisted another "shake" joke. "Glad to meet you," he said safely.

"Welcome to our home," she curtsied.

Debbie walked up to Felinah and squatted down to make eye contact. "We are very appreciative of your opening your home to us, Mrs… uh, do I call you Felinah?"

"Yes, yes. Please do." Her words were welcoming, but there was an unmistakable hesitance to them.

Geof leaned close to Jon's ear. "I don't think Mrs. Uriah is very glad to see us, pal."

"Mmmmm," Jon nodded.

"We really don't want to be a bother," Geof said. "If you don't have room for us—"

"Nonsense," Uriah interjected. "This is where you belong."

"Your wife, uh, mate doesn't seem all that pleased," Jon mouthed.

"Oh, dear. Where are my manners?" Felinah turned and walked into the kitchen. She looked back at Pat with a look that, If she were a dog, would be described as "the cat eye."

Uriah answered in a low voice, "It is not that. But my mate knows what your presence here means."

"Just what does it mean?" Debbie asked.

Uriah walked around in circles a couple of times before seating himself. "We are fortunate that we lived a quiet and good life for many epochs. But a storm has been coming for some time. It is inevitable. If you truly are the Searchers, that means the storm is near. Very near."

"We're bringing a storm?"

"Oh no, Geof. You must not think that. It has been foretold, and there is nothing anybody can do about it. In a way, it is good you are here."

"Why?"

"Because if you were not, it would mean the Song for Tomorrow was wrong, and I fear there would be no hope for us."

CHAPTER 11

In the Dog House

"Let me show you where you will sleep." Geof, Jon, and Clark followed Uriah down a hall. He looked up at Geof. "You said the word wife when talking about Felinah. What is 'wife'?"

"I think it is like your word 'mate'. A wife is the most beloved person in your life."

"Interesting," Uriah said. "I like that word wife."

Uriah led them to a large room with five beds. The beds were about the size of a full bed but oval in shape, having neither headboard nor footboard. They looked to be comfortable enough, even though the mattresses were more like thick pads. Multicolored, three-dimensional objects hung on the walls.

Jon leaned close to Geof's ear. "What do you think all that crap on the walls is?"

Geof shrugged. "If I had to guess, I would say it's art. Might be a good idea not to comment on it, hint hint."

Felinah collected Debbie and Pat and escorted them to a room similar to the boys' room. Crystals were prominent in most of the wall hangings. There was a small, plain dresser and hooks for hanging clothes. Crystals were everywhere and cast a dim light, nicely suited for a bedroom. Debbie and Pat nodded their approval. "Thank you. Very nice," Debbie said.

Uriah led the boys back down the hall and poked his head into the girl's room. "Come with me," he said. "We will have food, and then you rest."

When the group reassembled in the main living area, Uriah pointed toward another room. Inside was a large, irregular shaped dining room table about two inches thick, surrounded by six people chairs and four higher and wider cushioned chairs. The chairs were made of solid wood and had a mirror-like surface. They were indescribably beautiful. Clark's nerdy sense tingled as he examined his chair closely. He saw no varnish or staining agent that could have given birth to this impressive object. Maybe it came that way right out of the forest. The equally beautiful table was lavishly set with seven place settings and a center lazy Susan serving area containing an impressive array of every imaginable type of fruit and vegetable. A large, brightly colored ceramic bowl was at each place setting.

"Sit!" Uriah commanded.

The Searchers dutifully took their places at the table, and with a nod from Felinah, filled their bowls. "Now is the time for questions," Uriah said.

Geof jumped at the chance. "Tell us why we're really here."

Uriah took a deep breath. "Sergel-tuteron is comprised of Four Karrolls."

"Karrolls are what? Like our countries?" Pat asked.

"It is so. Agron, Erud, Mu-jin, and Gelog are the Karrolls. Although each Karroll has its own language, the Eruds developed Uni so that all people might communicate. The Karrolls' cultures were similar, and the people lived in peace. In Agron, we were farmers. The Eruds were practitioners of science, and Mu-jin were blessed with the thickest forests."

"And the Gelogs?

"Their land contained most of the stone quarries and minerals. It is from Gelog we get our crystals. The Eruds and the Gelogs have a close bond, and they have never had a problem. As long as everyone worked together, each Karroll prospered."

"That sounds almost like a perfect society," Pat sighed.

"Yes. I suppose it was," he said wistfully. "It had been that way for many epochs until the Great Sorrow."

Jon drew a shallow breath. "The Great Sorrow? That doesn't sound good."

Uriah looked away.

Debbie reached over and stroked Uriah's head. "What was it?"

"There was a horrible plague. The Agron, Gelog, and Mu-jin peoples were decimated. Nearly half of all divisions in our Karrolls were lost."

"And the Eruds?" Pat asked, her blue eyes boring a hole in Uriah. "You did not say anything about the Eruds?"

Uriah squinted back at her. "The Eruds feared they would be infected by contact with the other Karrolls. They barricaded themselves inside the Secret City to keep the sickness out."

"Hmmm. Smart," Debbie said, nodding her head.

"Yes. Smart," Uriah smiled sadly. He leaned down and took a bite of food from his bowl.

Clark leaned in. "What they did caused resentment, didn't it?"

"Yes," Uriah said while still chewing. "The Agrons and the Gelogs did not fault the Eruds for protecting their people. They felt that if a cure could be found for the plague, healthy Eruds were the best chance to find it. But the Mu-jinians hated them for it. The evil Mu-jin Prince Bu-usah told everyone the Eruds had a cure for the disease and kept it a secret. He spread the rumor throughout Mu-jin that the Eruds started the plague to conquer the other Karrolls."

"Did they start it?" Pat asked.

"No," Felinah said, smacking the table sharply with her paw. "The Eruds were saved from the plague because they protected themselves in the Secret City, not because they had a cure for it. They are brilliant and have made our lives easier in every way with their science. But the plague was beyond their knowledge. There had never been such pestilence in Sergel-tuteron before or since."

Geof looked Uriah in the eye. "I get the feeling there is something you don't want to tell us. That disease came from our world, didn't it?"

Uriah could not force himself to look at Geof. He excused himself from the table and left the room. His head was low and his tail down.

"What's going on?" Jon asked.

"He will be back," Felinah said. "This is most difficult for him—for all of us."

When he was able to compose himself, Uriah re-entered the room and resumed his place at the table. He took a trembling breath. "You are right, Searcher. We had not seen the like of it before. Queen Alma's books tell it is very common in your world. Your people get sick from this disease, but most do not die. You have to understand that in Sergel-tuteron, we never had what you call a disease before. This was something new for us, and we were not prepared for it."

"The flu," Clark said. "Somebody from our side gave them the flu, and they had no natural defense against it."

"Oh my God," Debbie lamented. "It's our fault."

"No, child. It is our fault. We did not protect our world," Felinah said. "How could we possibly know of the existence of something so terrible?"

Debbie was crushed with guilt. "So now you welcome us to save Sergel-tuteron when we might bring even more disease to you. Oh my God."

For the first time, there was defeat in Uriah's voice. "We are without choices. Like you, we must risk all."

Debbie looked at her companions and back at Uriah. "Tell us the rest. We will do everything we can to help you. Everything!"

"Prince Bu-usah was angry with the Eruds and forced weak Mu-jin King Mar-lev to attack the Secret City. He knew much stronger Mu-jin could overrun the Eruds with ease. The Eruds are not a fighting people. They are scholars."

"Jocks versus nerds Sergel-tuteron style," Clark moaned.

"Hey, man. You know what my dad always says? The jocks may get the girls, but the geek shall inherit the earth."

"Thanks, Geof. I'll try to remember that."

"The Eruds were in a state of desperation," Uriah continued. "They turned to the wisest person in their land, Sergel Tuteron. He was an inventor and scientist from parts unknown, and he offered a way to withstand the overwhelming Mu-jin forces."

"How?" Clark blurted.

"The Secret City had no military, so he made the Mu-jin navy work for him."

"I can't think of any military strategy in the history of the world where anything like that was done. Did it work?"

"Come on, Clark," Jon snapped. "Why do you think they named the country Sergel-tuteron? Besides, what would you know about it?"

"Actually, the study of military campaigns and battles is a hobby of mine. Every week a group of us, uh—"

"Nerds?" Jon helped.

"Okay fine, nerds." It was time to wear that title with honor. "We recreate some of the great historical military battles, dissect them, and try to see what alternative strategies might have resulted in a different outcome. It's great fun and very educational."

"Get a life, get a life," Jon sang under his breath.

Debbie smacked Jon behind the head.

"Here is how it happened," Uriah continued. "Mu-jin laid siege to the Secret City knowing that even a plague weakened Mu-jin army could defeat the Eruds. But Erud had a natural defense. The Secret City is built into the side of a cliff, and the only way to approach it is from the Great Sea through a narrow opening between two cliffs called the Gates. But, the Gates alone could not keep the superior numbers of Mu-jin out forever. Sergel Tuteron devised a plan to confuse the Mu-jin ranks. They wound up killing large numbers of their own army, and the siege of the Secret City failed."

"How did he do it?" Clark salivated.

Uriah shook his head, causing his large furry ears to flop wildly. "At the harbor of the Secret City were twelve giant crystals, each about the height of two Geofs." Everybody looked at Geof, causing him to squirm in his chair. "The Eruds developed power in the crystals even the Gelogs did not understand," Uriah explained. "The mysteries of the Secret City are closely guarded. Sergel Tuteron knew the Mu-jin ships would attack in darkness. Legend says that Sergel Tuteron harnessed the power of the lumen to flow through the crystals and shine blinding light into the ships of the Mu-jinians. The light was there for a blink of an eye, and then it was not, then it was, again and again."

"Strobe light. Fascinating," Clark smiled.

"Thank you, Mr. Spock," Jon half-eyed.

Uriah went on. "How Sergel Tuteron harnessed the power of the lumen at night is not known. But the blinded Mu-jin navy could not tell who was friend or enemy. They turned their weapons on anything that moved. With the Eruds safe in the high walls of the Secret City, the Mu-jin navy destroyed itself."

"Radical!" Clark jumped up and down.

His four friends gave him a naughty boy stare.

"What?" Clark asked sheepishly.

"Well, uh," Geof shrugged. "Oh—nothin'."

Debbie stayed focused on Uriah. "So, the battle was won."

"Fearful of what other magic weapons the Eruds might have, Mu-jin retreated. King Mar-lev of Mu-jin was killed in the process and was replaced by his son, the evil Bu-usah. King Bu-usah withdrew his shattered forces, vowing to gain revenge for the death of his father. But some say he just wanted the throne, and it was Bu-usah himself who took advantage of the confusion to kill his father. As time passed, his greed and his obsession with the Eruds caused him to destroy the forests and resources of Mu-jin to build palaces, ships, and weapons."

"That is a fantastic story," Pat said.

"It is just the beginning. While the Karrolls of Sergel-tuteron struggled to recover from the plague, King Bu-usah spent the wealth of Mu-jin on himself while his people starved. It is said that even his own family does not know the extent of his evil."

"His family does not know? That is hard to believe," Pat said.

"King Bu-usah is a treacherous man, loyal only to himself."

Debbie tried to complete the puzzle. "So, I assume everybody was so impressed by Sergel Tuteron that they decided to name everything after him."

"Yes, but not in Mu-jin. Unlike the other Karrolls, they do not recognize Sergel Tuteron's honor. It is good for all that they have maintained the peace, at least until now. I think it is all a ruse. I think they have been building weapons and plotting a strategy to attack all this time."

"I am afraid to ask why you think that?" Pat said.

"Many captured spies have eagerly told of Bu-usah's plans. They are all terrified of Bu-usah and do not want to go back to Mu-jin."

"He is a bad man," Felinah interrupted. "An evil man."

"I get it. He is setting you up for a do-over of the Great Sorrow war," Jon said.

Uriah looked perplexed.

"He wants another shot at the Eruds," Geof clarified.

"Yyyyyes. King Bu-usah wants to break the peace. The Eruds do not say much, and Agron and Gelog have no armies. I am sure Bu-usah has many spies in all the Karrolls now." Uriah cast a protective glance toward Felinah. Felinah again looked suspiciously at Pat.

Jon looked over at Pat, who was deep in thought. "What's up?"

Pat looked into the eyes of a staring Felinah, who quickly looked away. "Why is Felinah staring at me like that?" she demanded. And looking back at Uriah, she complained, "And, why do you?"

"Remember, I said the Mu-jin have spies everywhere?"

"Yeah, so what?" Pat asked.

"I don't mean to be cruel, dear," Felinah answered. "But you look like a—a Mu-jinian."

"You think I am a spy?" Pat sputtered.

"Well—"

"Forget that," Jon interrupted. You mean to tell me the Mu-jin—uh—ians all look like Pat?"

"Identical," Uriah answered warily.

"Whoa! And they're the bad guys?" Jon smiled from ear to ear. "Look, if anybody needs someone to go undercover in Mu-jin, I volunteer,"

"You, Jon, also could pass in Mu-jin with little notice," Uriah said, looking away.

"You bonehead," Geof glared. "Can't you see they think your girlfriend's a spy?" Pat and Jon both blushed. "I assure you, Uriah and Felinah, Pat is no Mu-jin spy. Her idea of sneaky would be to hide a dress the day before it goes on sale."

"Thanks for the vote of uh… confidence, Geof."

"I'm just sayin'."

"After King Bu-usah retreated to Mu-jin, he closed it off to everyone. The only knowledge we have of Mu-jin is what their spies and our own spies tell us."

"What do they tell you?" Pat pressed.

"That Mu-jin is dead. Bu-usah has destroyed their forests and farmland. Mu-jin was once the most beautiful of Karrolls, and now the land is barren. Where there were fields of crops, there is now dirt. People are starving because Bu-usah destroyed their means to create food.

"Do the spies give much information about Bu-usah's battle plan?" Pat asked.

"No. What they say is that there are rumors of the monstrous Unborns. Just rumors."

Pat sat up and zeroed in on Uriah. "Did you say Unborns? Who are they?"

Uriah jumped from his chair and said, "Nobody. Come. Time for rest." The conversation was over.

CHAPTER 12

Gone Fishin'

In bed, Geof again was tortured by nightmares. "Searcher, Searcher, Searcher," cried hundreds of strange beings as they charged at him and dissipated just before attacking him. Geof woke up in a cold sweat more than once this night. In the morning, Uriah emerged from the house. "You need to ready yourselves. We have a long way to go. Felinah has provisions for you."

Each extended thanks to Felinah for her hospitality. In return, they received a sack the size of a basketball containing food and other essentials. Pat lingered a bit, unsure of how Felinah would receive her. "Goodbye, Felinah, and thank you for everything," she said in a friendly tone. Felinah acknowledged her gratitude and handed her a sack.

Pat faced Felinah and said, "I do not know if you believe this, but I really am not a Mu-jin spy. I never even heard of Mu-jin till yesterday."

Felinah nodded slowly. "I am sorry, dear. But…"

"But what?"

"I fear for you. Many will think as I, and you may encounter problems."

Pat smiled. "I think we already have problems."

"I understand. But for your safety, remember what I tell you now. Listen to Uriah. Make your friends listen to him. He is wise and sees what others do not." Felinah stepped back. Her long black ears glistened in the sunlight as it broadcast through the door and amplified the look of deep concern in her eyes. Pat again thanked Felinah and went outside.

A businesslike Uriah was standing ten feet in front of the Searchers. "It is time to go," he said. "It is very important that you do as I say at all times. Being too adventurous will be dangerous."

"Wait a minute," Jon interrupted. "I thought Agron was safe."

"Most of the creatures that live here are peaceful, but there are threats. Spies are everywhere, and we don't want to call attention to you." Uriah turned and walked down the road.

Jon grabbed his trusty walking stick and shoved it in Geof's face. "In that case, I better not forget this bad boy," he laughed.

"Good idea. You never know when we might need a little firewood."

The trek began without incident. Geof hurried to the front to accompany Uriah. Uriah shot him a glance that was not especially welcoming. The spunky cocker spaniel clearly relished his role as leader and was not all that interested in

sharing it with Geof, at least not until it would be to his advantage. Geof could see he was an unwelcome guest. He would live with it as he saw this as an opportunity to learn things everybody was dying to know.

"Uriah," he began timidly. Uriah raised his nose and looked sideways at him. "I wonder if I could ask you some questions."

"I am very busy now."

"No, you're not. You're just walking in the middle of nowhere, and I think we have a right to know a few things."

"What do you want to know?"

"Well, for one thing, what sort of dangers are we facing?"

"You are in an unfamiliar land, so everything is dangerous for you. There are Mu-jin spies. There may even be small bands of Mu-jin soldiers. Bu-usah wants to do everything he can to disrupt the peace outside of Mu-jin. There have been assassinations, farms destroyed, and rumors of Mu-jinian sightings near the Secret City."

"At least, those are things we can prepare for. I was more interested in things like, you know, monsters."

"There are divisions unfriendly to us, but it is unlikely we will encounter them for some time."

"For some time? What does that mean?"

"It means if we encounter them, you will know it."

"Thanks. That's very helpful."

Uriah gave Geof a long look and adjusted his attitude. "As you are the possible Searcher, it is much more important that I know everything about you."

"Okay. You should hope I am more generous with my answers than you are."

Uriah grunted. "The Searchers are the most important visitors ever to come to Sergel-tuteron. It is for that reason that I take the greatest care to investigate you."

"I guess that's fair."

"In our legends, the Searchers are the most glorious warriors. They are brave, strong, intelligent, and steadfast leaders. I have a hard time finding those qualities in you. I am sorry. I do not mean to insult."

"I agree with you. We may appear to be lacking in some of those qualities. But we aren't losers. And for that matter, I doubt that we even are these so-called Searchers."

"We will find out soon enough. I think if I knew more about you, I would feel better."

"Not a lot to know."

"The female, Debbie. Is she to be your mate, or... uh... wife?"

"What? My what?" Geof's not-so-classified adoration of Debbie was obvious even to a talking dog in an upside-down world. "I have no way of knowing that."

"You mean it is not decided?"

"How can it be? We're just a couple of high school kids."

"In Sergel-tuteron, such things are often decided in youth. More time to prepare, you know. I am no fool. I know you want her to be your wife."

Geof shuffled along, conflicted by reality, and what he was willing to reveal to the secretive Uriah. "You are scary smart,

Uriah… Okay. Here is the truth. I have loved Debbie since day one in first grade. The only reason I looked forward to going to school was that I knew Debbie would be there. If she was home sick, school sucked for the day. There. I said it."

"That is interesting," Uriah mused. "Quite interesting. And Jon and Pat? Are they like you and Debbie?"

"Nah. They just met not long ago. Jon usually goes from one girl to another when he gets bored. But I will say this. Pat is digging into his hide like nobody I've ever seen."

Uriah stared at Geof like he was the suspect in a lie detector test. "Even more interesting."

Uriah's familiar "I know something you don't know" attitude was really beginning to bug Geof. "Look man. What do a couple of high school crush stories have to do with anything? What possible significance can it have to you and this crazy place?"

"Nothing really. There is a legend…. but it does not matter."

"Legend? What legend?" Geof demanded. "What are you trying to pigeonhole me into now?"

"It is nothing," Uriah dismissed. "What about Clark."

"Forget Clark," Geof snorted. "I want to know what legend."

"What about Clark?"

Geof clenched his teeth. "Let me just say that you are the first dog I ever met that disproved the adage that happiness is a warm puppy."

Uriah did not understand or care about Geof's observation. "It is important that I know about Clark."

"Fine. FINE. I don't know Clark that well. All I know is that he is super smart, and his life basically sucks. We are his only friends, and his parents treat him like dirt."

Uriah looked up at the sky, his face the picture of contemplation. "He who is despised shall wield the sword of wisdom to destroy his enemies," he said under his breath.

Regretting he chose to engage Uriah in this useless dialog, Geof said, "Did you just say something? On second thought, forget it. I think I'm done here."

Uriah ran around Geof's words like they were a pothole. "I want to know more about Pat. Tell me more about Pat."

"She really bugs you, doesn't she?" Geof laughed. "I don't know much about her. Maybe you better ask Jon. She's more his territory."

"I will ask Jon. Tell me about your father."

"All right, but after this, I'm done." Geof was openly annoyed about Uriah turning the tables on him. He wanted to pick Uriah's brain. Instead, he found his own brain under relentless examination. He would play the game a bit longer to see where it went. "My dad is the greatest. He does everything for me. He completely supports me in everything. He even gave his blessing for me to come here, which had to be hard."

"What does he say about your mother? Does he speak of her?"

"Sometimes I think he speaks TO her. But I don't know. I'm like any kid. I know about him since I was little. But now that you mention it, I don't know much about his life before me. Never thought about it."

"Thank you," Uriah said. "Most illuminating." With that, Uriah picked up the pace and left Geof wondering what had just happened.

Seeing Geof by himself, Jon scurried up to him to get the scoop. "Did you get anything out of him?"

"You know how you have to pick up your dog's poop back home?"

"Yeah."

"Same thing here."

"Tough audience, is he? Maybe I should give it a shot."

"Knock yourself out, pal. But before you know it, the score will be Uriah ten, Jon, zero."

"You know what, Bear. I doubt it matters. I'm going to go back and tell Pat how much she likes me."

"Go for it, Monster. Best idea I've heard all day."

For two days they traveled, camping at night. Rolling hills and charming farms dotted the landscape. The scene was so peaceful it was impossible to think that there could be danger anywhere. On the third day, the loose dirt and sand became speckled with rocks. Small rocks grew in size and abundance, but the change was gradual and not observed by anyone but the curious Clark. The smoothness of the rocks suggested they had been polished by water long ago, but there was no water anywhere. He tapped Geof on the shoulder. "Look at these rocks."

"Yeah. What about 'em?"

"They're smooth."

"Wow. You don't miss a trick."

"But WHY are they smooth? There is no water."

Geof looked down at Clark. "How should I know? How did we get here? Why is the sky green? Why are we obediently following a talking dog? Surely there are things a little bit more curious to you the last twenty-four hours than smooth rocks."

Clark looked down. "I guess so."

Clark's deflation made Geof feel like a bully, but he was given no time to dwell on it. Uriah stopped suddenly. "We have come to our first challenge," Uriah said without emotion. "We must cross the Canyon of the Pecash. You must stay close to me as we enter the canyon."

Geof and Jon looked at each other blankly. "Uh, no disrespect Uriah, but I see no canyon anywhere," Jon said.

"It is right in front of you."

Jon looked at Geof again and shook his head. "I'm... I'm sorry. But there is nothing in front of us but farmland." Jon stared at Uriah, waiting for a response, but Uriah just shook his head.

Finally, Debbie said, "Uriah, there does not look like there is anything in front of us except for that little gully."

"Gully? What is a gully?"

"That!" Debbie exclaimed, pointing at what looked like a rocky irrigation ditch a few feet in front of them.

"Yes. That is the Canyon of the Pecash. Now follow me and step only where I step." Uriah turned and muttered, "What canyon indeed!"

Jon threw up his hands in frustration and looked at Geof in a silent bid for backup but got none.

Uriah moved toward the ditch expecting everyone to follow him, but no one did. "Come," he said impatiently.

"Where?" Debbie asked softly.

"Into the canyon."

Pat remembered what Felinah told her about trusting Uriah. She flipped her sunny hair over her right shoulder, and confidently said, "I think we should stop wasting time and follow Uriah."

Satisfied, Uriah turned and trotted forward. Pat marched confidently behind him. Uriah looked back at Pat one more time and said, "Remember, walk only where I walk."

She nodded.

Uriah stepped over the edge onto a rocky trail and vanished from sight. Pat dutifully took a leap of faith and followed his path. The instant she stepped onto the trail, the landscape changed. Before her eyes, the far side of the canyon moved away at blazing speed. The two rims of the canyon separated in a blur and what had been the bottom of a three-foot deep ditch became a drop of a thousand feet. The trail was no more than three feet wide and felt like a catwalk without a handrail. Pat white-knuckled every sharp rock that jutted out far enough to grab. She pressed her face against the canyon wall and inched forward, one step at a time.

Uriah looked back at her with exasperation. "At this speed, we will never get anywhere," he barked at her.

"I'm... I'm sorry. This is very scary. I don't like heights."

Uriah sighed. Pat closed her eyes and tried to move more quickly when she felt Geof's hand crushing her right wrist. It felt firm and reassuring. "Just think of it as being at the top of the escalator at Bloomingdales," he said.

Pat faked a grin. Geof had a black belt in hiking, but this had to be the scariest trail he had ever seen. Debbie followed closely behind Geof, holding tight to his extra-long shirttail. Clark followed Debbie and was as intrigued as he was terrified. His eyes drank in the scene with child-like wonderment, and Jon, walking behind him, could almost see the questions shooting out of his nerd brain like Roman candles. Jon leaned close to Clark's ear, "If you say something like 'fascinating', I'm gonna shove you right off this ledge."

Clark glanced back and said, "Huh?"

"Just pay attention, will ya?"

The treacherous trail seemed to have no end, but the pace quickened as the unsteady explorers grew accustomed to it. Time went by, but there was no reference point. It could have been minutes. It could have been hours.

The trail looked like it was ending, and Uriah stopped. "You must be very careful to do only as I say from this point forward. There is danger ahead."

"Danger ahead? What do you call this?" Jon grilled.

"Walk only where I walk. Touch nothing and keep your hands close to your bodies." Uriah ordered. "Follow me."

What looked like the end of the trail was, in fact, the beginning of a long turn. At the end of the turn, the trail was engulfed by a red mist, which Uriah entered without hesitation.

"Man, did you ever see a red mist in any movie that was good news?" Jon yelled to Geof.

Geof did not look back but shook his head. Pat was next to vanish. The temperature inside dropped by several degrees. It was cool, but not cold. Hazy but not opaque. And humid. Very humid. Like ten Floridas.

As they moved forward, Debbie felt something bump against her, and she let out a shriek. Geof whirled instinctively to protect her and punched the air to ward off her assailant.

"Noooooo!" Uriah cried out.

His warning was too late. Geof's hand was instantly caught in something, and he was whisked off the ledge like a leaf in a hurricane. Debbie let go of his shirt just in time to save herself.

"What was that?" Jon yelled. "Where is Geof?" He had not gotten the words out of his mouth before objects in the mist appeared from nowhere and looked at him like he was an appetizer.

"What are those?… Wait a minute. Those are fish!" Debbie cried. "But it's crazy. There's no water, and there are big, ugly fish."

Uriah charged toward Jon. "Keep your hands in. Keep your hands in." Uriah ordered. "I told you to keep your hands in."

"It's my fault," Debbie said tearfully. "Geof was trying to protect me."

"Where is Geof?" Jon cried.

"He has been taken by the Pecash."

"Taken where?"

"Taken. Our mission is in grave jeopardy."

A large Pecash swooped by, his huge tail churning the red mist into a cauldron of confusion. In its mouth was the unmistakable outline of a large boy.

"A little help." Geof's voice stabbed through the fog.

"What do we do? What do we do?" Jon shouted at Uriah.

"Follow me."

The group followed Uriah around the corner and into a small cave opening in the side of the wall. The fish approached the cave but stopped short of going in.

"We will be safe here," Uriah said. "For now."

"What about Geof?" Debbie sobbed.

"I... I don't know what to do," Uriah said, hanging his head. "The canyon is immense. We might never find him, and if we did..."

"We have to do something," Jon yelled back.

"If you go out there now, they will take you too. We must wait."

"Wait? We have to help Geof now!" Jon screamed.

Clark rummaged feverishly through Felinah's goodie bag. He pulled out some food wrapped in a shiny, tin foil type wrapping and dumped the food. "Give me all this stuff you have," Clark said in a commanding voice that surprised even him.

"Why?" Pat asked.

Debbie's eyes scanned Clark and saw something new and strong in him. "Just do what he says."

Clark collected all of the shiny foil and moved to the mouth of the cave. He grabbed the piece of rope Felinah provided to tie his care package together and flicked it to Jon. "Tie this thing around the end of your stick. Maybe he can grab it,"

"Okay." Jon was not used to taking orders from Clark. This felt different.

"They wait for us. If you go outside, you will also be taken," Uriah warned.

"Who cares," Clark dismissed. "Geof is the only person in the world who ever stood up for me. I'm going to try to lure them back here. Jon, if you see Geof, try to grab him and pull him into the cave. Those fish things look afraid to come in here."

Jon nodded. "I know. I can't help but wonder why."

Clark moved to the outer edge of the cave and waved the wrapping furiously. Nothing happened. He moved several feet away from the entrance and continued to wave. Uriah screamed at him to come back, but Clark ignored him. Within seconds the first Pecash appeared. Then another, and another. The first fish nearly caught Clark's hand, but he jerked it back just in time, and it swam harmlessly by.

"Geof!" he cried out. Silence.

"Geof!" Five voices called out in unison.

"Here." It was faint. But it was Geof.

They yelled louder, and Clark waved his lures more vigorously. Fish after fish passed by, each taking a shot at Clark. Jon stabbed at the monsters with his walking stick to keep them at bay.

"Look!" Jon yelled.

Geof's fish reappeared, its mouth still firmly clamped on Geof's right wrist. Even though he had Geof, the greedy predator was also interested in Clark. "Get him closer. Get him closer," Jon hollered. Clark stepped further out and waved crazily, inviting another host of curious Pecash. Geof's fish stayed out of reach.

The Pecash operated as a group. They attacked together and swam away together. Geof was visible in the distance and alive, but now he and his captor were attracting some interest from the other Pecash. Pat walked to the edge of the trail and said in a low voice, "They are going to try to steal Geof from that fish. He will be torn to bits."

The group stood paralyzed by helplessness. As the gang of Pecash moved in to pilfer Geof, his captor darted toward the questionable safety of the cave to evade them. The fact that there was no honor among Pecash worked in Geof's favor. The Pecash would turn on one of their own if it meant a good meal. The hunter was now the prey as long as Geof was in its mouth. Trapped between his hungry cousins and whatever was in the cave, the big fish chose the cave and moved within reach of Jon's walking stick.

"Now's our chance," Jon yelled. Clark waved frantically, hoping it would loosen his grip on Geof long enough for Jon to grab him. The Pecash stopped momentarily and fixed its six-eyed gaze on Clark. It was only for an instant, but long enough for Jon to reach out with his walking stick and give Geof a lifeline. Geof grasped the stick and slipped his wrist through the loop. A bizarre tug of war ensued. Clark, Debbie, and Pat grabbed hold of Jon. But it was not a fair fight. The fish was huge, and he had the home-court advantage. The jerking back and forth tightened the strap around Geof's wrist, and he was stretched out like a rubber band.

"Ahhhhhh!" he cried as he felt his bones being pulled apart.

The battle was violent, and the teenagers lost ground as they ran out of gas. Jon looked down at his feet and saw them inching ever closer to the edge of the trail. Through his pain and fear, Geof could see that his friends were about to be pulled off the ledge.

"Let go," Geof yelled. "Let go. You'll all be killed."

Jon's insides were shredded. His choice was to hopelessly hang onto his lifelong friend and probably kill everyone else or... there was no other choice.

"You have to let go, Jon," Geof cried out again. At that instant, Jon saw a flash in the corner of his eye as Uriah blew past him.

"Hang on to him, Jon," Uriah yelped as he streaked to his side.

Jon dug his feet in behind a rock and pulled with every ounce of strength left in his depleted body. The noise caused the fish to turn and face them head-on, placing Geof within inches of the trail. Jon squinted to block out the grotesque fish's gargoyle face inches away.

"Hang on, JonnnnnnnnnArggggggggggggh!" The word "Jon" morphed into an ear-splitting roar accompanied by Uriah's mouth gaping to the size of a dump truck. Uriah's signature attack move startled the Pecash. The shock and awe

were enough to force the big fish to loosen its grip on Geof for an instant, causing him and his friends to fall backward into the tentative safety of the cave. The fish stopped and stared at them but did not advance.

"What in the heck are those things?" Geof yelled out in frustration.

"They are called Pecash," Uriah woofed.

Geof pounded his fists on the ground. "Somebody please tell me what fish are doing swimming around in a fog? They are supposed to be in water. Do you see any friggin' water?"

"It is said there once was," Uriah answered as calmly as he could.

Geof collapsed against the wall. His face and arms were cut and bruised from banging against the canyon wall. Otherwise, he looked surprisingly unscathed. As good as he was on the outside, Geof was demolished on the inside. "Thank you, everyone," he panted. "Thank you, Jon."

"Thank Clark," Jon answered humbly as Pat and Debbie nodded. Jon explained the ingenuity and courage Clark displayed. "You can also thank my walking stick you were so happy to make fun of."

"Come here, Super Clark," Geof said, ignoring the walking stick comment.

Also wasted from the ordeal, Clark crawled closer to Geof and received a coveted fist bump. "Thanks, Buddy," Geof huffed. Clark smiled.

"Whatever made you think those things in the food bags would be of any interest to those monsters?" Pat asked.

"They're fish, aren't they? I'm no fisherman, but I read they are attracted to shiny things. This stuff is shiny. Looks like fish are fish everywhere."

The brilliant simplicity evoked a round of tension-reducing laughter and applause from everyone, especially Geof. Debbie hugged an overwhelmed Clark and moved closer to the Bear. She took his arm and looked it over. There were bruises from the mouth of the fish and scrapes from the walking stick noose, but little else. "I was so scared you'd be killed. It's like a miracle. You hardly have a scratch." Debbie continued to hold Geof's arm and rub it to ease the pain. "You saved my life and almost lost yours," she said through teary eyes. She reached up and tenderly kissed Geof's battered cheek. "All this has to hurt so much."

Geof smiled and leaned against the gray and black cave wall. "No worries," he smiled, looking into her eyes. "I never felt better in my life."

CHAPTER 13

Welcome to Lantuc

The exhausted explorers kicked back and waited for their strength to return. Debbie sat next to Geof on one side of the cave while Jon, Pat, and Clark rested on the other. Uriah lay flat on the floor, his head between his feet.

"Jon, look at Uriah," Pat squealed.

"Yeah, he's cute. But who knows what's lurking inside that head?"

"Felinah told me to trust Uriah. I think we should."

"What are you guys babbling about?" Geof boomed from the opposite wall.

"We were just wondering what the scoop is with this cave."

Geof pointed at Uriah. "Ask wonder dog over there. He seems to have all the answers."

Uriah lifted his left ear an inch or two off the ground. "Nothing but insults," he growled. "Nothing but insults. You have not asked me any questions."

"I got one," Pat said. "Does this cave go anywhere?"

Uriah lifted his head. "I really don't know. I was never in here before."

"But you seemed to know all about it. You led us right here. How did you know it was here?"

"I saw it from the ledge."

"Um," Pat scrunched up her face, "soooo you don't know anything about this cave."

"No. Not really." His tone was firm but unconvincing.

"I don't mean to put ice cream in a microwave," Jon said, "but does anyone besides me appreciate that we are stuck in a cave surrounded by gigantic man-eating, no-water-required fish... and they are afraid of something in here with us?"

"I was trying not to think about that," Geof frowned. "But now that you mention it, Uriah, what do you say we get out of here?"

"I do not think that is a good idea right now."

"Why not?"

"Pecash are an interesting division, yes, definitely interesting," Uriah explained. "They will not come in. They will wait for us to come out."

Debbie looked at Uriah and shook her head. "Doesn't sound to me like they're that stupid."

"They are quite stupid. They will starve to death waiting for us."

"If we do not starve to death first." Pat whimpered.

"Well, since we're gonna be here a while, I guess I'll look around," Jon said, hopping to his feet. The adrenalin-pumping rescue of Geof jump-started his personality. Jonster the Monster was back online.

"Come on, Dude," he motioned to Geof as he headed toward the darkness.

Geof was quite happy with his current position next to Debbie. But he knew Jon was right. They could not just sit and wait to be Pecash snacks. Geof dragged himself to his feet. "Hang on. I'm coming. I don't know why, but I am."

Geof stretched his legs and lumbered after Jon. He looked over his shoulder at his uneasy friends. "Maybe you'd better wait here. No point in all of us getting killed."

"You should not do this," Uriah said.

Jon and Geof ignored Uriah and were quickly engulfed by the darkness. Before they had gone far, the others could hear Jon's voice floating to the front of the cave. "Hey, you still got that keychain?"

"Keychain. Yes!" The Bearmobile keychain was a birthday gift from Jon. It was in the shape of a Sebring convertible, and the headlights were small LED lights. Geof put his right hand in his pocket, pushed the button on the keychain, and saw a light shine through his cargo pocket. "Thanks to you, yes."

He punched a gold-colored button, and the cave was softly illuminated twenty feet in front of them. "Boy, these things are amazing," Geof beamed. Applause came from the front of the cave as the light filtered outward.

"I guess we didn't get very far in yet," Jon smiled.

"Well, let's take it easy. Neither one of us is Indiana Jones, and if there's any way to avoid whatever freaks out those fish, I'm in favor of it."

"Maybe there isn't anything. Maybe they just don't like caves."

"Yeah. That's probably it."

The boys made their way a few hundred feet without incident, guided by Geof's trusty keychain light. The cave smelled musty, and condensation dripped on their faces. Geof ran his hand along the jagged wall and found a three-by-four-foot indentation that was promising but went nowhere. They moved forward another hundred feet, and the circular glow of the keychain beacon molded itself to the shape of the cave until its diameter equaled that of the tunnel itself. As they advanced, the diameter of the light ahead decreased in size. With each step, the circle of light got smaller until they realized the light was shining on a wall. The cave was a dead end.

Jon and Geof felt relieved but disappointed. No nasty Pecash-type creatures were waiting to put them on the menu. But there was no way out either.

Jon scratched his head. "I don't get it. Those stupid fish seem so scared to come in here, and there's nothing here."

"Maybe they're as stupid as they look." The jaw-tightening anticipation of something beyond scary at the end of the tunnel failed to materialize. Geof laughed the relief laugh movie audiences make when a scary sound in a horror movie turns out to be the cat knocking over a garbage can. "You know what? I don't think I've fully recovered from being bait," Geof said, hunkering down on a large rock.

"Oh, let's get back, Bear. They'll be worried about us."

"Aw, come on, man. I'm comfortable. This doesn't feel like a rock at all."

"What does it feel like?"

"Like it's moving. YEOWWWW!!!"

Geof jumped up and landed next to Jon. He swept the Bearmobile light back and forth across the rock like a spotlight chasing an escaped convict. The rock exploded into a ten-foot, pulsating, blackish green blob with multiple eyes and mouths. Each mouth had several rows of jagged, slobber-dripping teeth. Jon and Geof were face to face with the grossest looking creature conceivable.

"AHHHHHHHHHHHHHHHH!" they yelled at each other. They had about a fifteen-foot head start when the creature bolted after them. On their heels was a chorus of grunts and splushing, which got louder and louder with each panicked stride.

Jon yelled, "Everybody, get out of the cave and hide NOW!" In mid-sentence, he felt a vice grip on his shoulder and was yanked into the wall cutout Geof had found only moments before. Geof squashed Jon against the wall, and the beast whooshed by them without slowing. It was the weirdest creature. Almost perfectly round with dripping mouths, flaring nostrils, and multicolored eyes everywhere, some of which stared blankly at the trembling teens as it sailed by. The Pecash were no dummies for being afraid of this thing.

Jonster the Monster and the Bear charged after the creature. It was not possible to tell what propelled it. It just rolled and bounced off the ground and walls. The boys saw the monster shoot through the mouth of the cave like a giant spitball and quadruple in size as soon as it left the confines of the cave. As the beast blasted into the fog, the Pecash scattered in every direction. It caught one Pecash in its giant teeth and spun to grab a second with another mouth.

Thinking their friends had been gobbled up as the monster rolled by, Jon and Geof dashed to the cave opening where Geof crashed into Debbie, Pat, Clark, and Uriah, as they re-entered the cave. They heard Jon's warning and curled around the outer edge of the cave seconds before the monster blew past them. Their re-entry into the cave was perfectly timed to be flattened by their friends. The cave provided questionable shelter again, but their situation was now even worse. The Pecash were outside, and that thing was out there too, enjoying a meal of two writhing Pecash at the same time.

Inside the tenuous safety of the cave, everyone froze. They tried to think of something to say or do other than scream and run. Jon snapped at Uriah. "No offense, but you can keep Agron as far as I'm concerned."

"I warned you there were dangers."

Geof shook his head. "You call these dangers? We've had two, count 'em, two encounters with rather nasty monsters in the space of a few minutes. And did I mention they both want to eat us?"

"I hoped the Searcher would be stronger," Uriah grumbled.

"Well, excuuuuse me," Geof shot back. "We're here, aren't we? And I don't give a flying f—"

"Look," Debbie shouted excitedly while directing a slender index finger toward the back of the cave. It was not bright, but Debbie found a dim light emanating from deep in the cave. "Maybe there's another way out of here."

"Been there, done that," Jon said.

"I think it would be wise to... how does Jon say it? Check it out?" Uriah said.

"You don't have to ask me twice," Geof said, whipping his trusty LED light about until it intersected with the light in the cave.

"I get it. You couldn't see the light in the back of the cave because that thing blocked it." Debbie said.

Clark was less thrilled. "I just hope that light isn't coming from that great big, round, ugly man-eating thing's family sitting around watching a great big, round, man-eating TV."

"Don't worry," Jon smirked. "They don't have TV." He laughed as he leaped forward and snatched the keychain from Geof's hand.

"Hey!" Geof yelled.

"Last one in's a dropped call," Jon laughed. Geof watched the Monster's hair bounce up and down as he ran.

Pat shook her head. "They don't call him Jonster the Monster for nothing, do they?"

"Nope."

Jon disappeared for a few seconds. But everyone knew he was still with them as the glow from the LED light was visibly dancing about in the distance. The light stopped moving. Geof sprinted forward and saw the outline of his friend staring into a giant cavern. It was illuminated from below by lights, many lights.

"Wow, man. What's that?" Geof asked breathlessly. "Jon? Hey, I'm talking to you, boy."

Jon turned slowly to face Geof and tilted his head to the right. Four large creatures stepped out of the shadows. They looked like grizzly bears with Saint Bernard's faces. The "dogs" were eight feet tall and had metal armament circling their torsos. There was a large sword dangling in a scabbard across the chest armor of each of them.

"Stop," Geof grunted, stretching out both hands to block the advance of his friends. Uriah ran up next to him. Geof looked down and said, "I don't s'pose that wide mouth thing you do would do any good right now."

Uriah moved between Geof and the grizzlies. He raised his right paw. "I am Ur—"

"We know who you are," the leader of the grizzly dogs growled. His fur was long and brown, his face was all business, and he was powerful. Even his muscles had muscles. "You will come with us."

"Delighted," Uriah smiled. "Simply delighted."

"Looks like you got us in the soup again," Jon chided Geof.

"Me? ME? I believe the term 'last one in is a dropped call' came from a certain ne'er-do-well runt with floppy hair."

"Are you guys at it again?" Debbie snapped.

"Be silent," the lead grizzly dog barked. "The queen will know what to do with you."

A trail wound its way down into the cavern and morphed into a road of smooth cobblestones. The light shone brighter, and evidence of a great civilization was everywhere. As they descended, the cavern broadened and structures began to appear along the road. There were buildings but no visible inhabitants.

With each step, the scene grew more astonishing. The cobblestone road widened and looked like it was coming to an end at the edge of a precipice. The grizzly dogs separated and motioned for the group to step forward. Their eyes beheld a fantastic site. Several hundred feet below was a grand city. It was brightly lit with a beautiful stone castle at the far end. Creatures were milling about below, but in the distance, it was impossible to determine what they were.

"You will follow," the head grizzly dog snarled.

"Happy to," Jon smiled.

They were led onto a round platform. It was ten feet in diameter with no visible means of support and no railings on the outside.

"Holy smoke," Clark chirped. "This is an elevator. I am dying to see how they make this thing work."

Pat looked at him glumly. "You just might get your wish."

CHAPTER 14

Queen Andi

The round platform dropped a few inches and clicked firmly into an unseen framework. Geof situated himself at dead center, followed quickly by four nervous friends. The floor slowly rotated and descended. The spinning platform picked up speed with each revolution, and everyone locked arms. Everyone that is, except for Uriah, who sat unconcernedly on the floor, licking his paw.

Debbie hated merry-go-rounds. But to her delight, as the elevator rotated faster and faster, she felt nothing. "Are my eyes playing tricks on me or what? This thing is spinning like crazy, and I don't feel a thing."

Clark held his glasses against his nose with his middle finger, but there was no need. "Logic would dictate that we should be splattered all over those walls from inertia," he observed. "But we're standing here like there is no outside force working on us at all. It so violates Newton's first law of motion. It's as though there is a suspension—"

"Look, Stephen Hawking," Jon interrupted. "I'm just glad we're not cave paintings, and I don't really give a damn why."

"Amen," Geof agreed.

Debbie snapped her fingers. "Hey, geniuses. Drop the science class and check this out." The soft focus of the city sharpened into images of buildings, roads, and the city's inhabitants engaged in their daily routines.

The elevator stopped on a wooden platform standing four feet off the ground. Connected to the platform was a stairway, but the grizzly dogs made no effort to disembark their guests. The elevator sat in a public square surrounded by stone buildings. People, dogs, horses, and other animals milled about in a businesslike fashion with one eye on the newcomers. Geof looked at his friends and saw a panorama of human disorientation. He stood sound and confident to give them courage, even though he was scared to death. He shot a question at the head grizzly dog. "Do you plan to take us somewhere?"

His question was met with silence.

"I demand to know your intentions," he said, amping up his tone.

A grizzly dog walked up to Geof and towered over him. "You will be taken to the queen. For now, you wait."

The wait was not long. Six humans on horseback approached the elevator, which was a hopeful sight. They had five beautiful specimens of horse in tow, two black and three white. Debbie looked them over closely. She owned horses her whole life but had not seen the like of these before. They were horses, to be sure, but their legs were twice the size of Sheridan horses. Debbie got the attention of one of the grizzly dogs. "Excuse me. Where we come from, we call these creatures horses. By what name do you call them?"

"Horses. We brought them to help the weaker species move about Lantuc."

"That would certainly be us," Jon smiled.

"Lantuc?" Pat inhaled. "I thought that was a legend."

Uriah looked suspiciously at her. "How is it that you have heard of Lantuc?"

"Did you say Lantuc? I thought he said Atlantis."

Uriah shivered, "Everyone has heard of Lantuc. But it is a—a—legend. A great and advanced civilization that disappeared long before recorded history. I—I never believed it was real."

"Everything about it sounds like Atlantis, but this looks pretty real," Geof said. "Let's hope it's as advanced and great as the legend."

The humans maneuvered the horses close to the platform and motioned for the teenagers to climb aboard. Debbie hopped on with the skill of a rodeo rider and sang out with a thick western twang, "Let's go y'all."

Geof climbed boldly onto a black horse directly behind Debbie's white. Jon approached a white horse and looked back at Pat. She and Clark were staring at each other like two naked mannequins in a store window.

"Come on, guys. I don't think it's a good idea to piss off sasquatch here," Jon urged.

The grizzly's menacing face helped Pat and Clark snap out of their catatonic states.

"The closest I ever got to a horse was to stand next to a mounted cop in New York City," Pat admitted.

"Come on," Jon implored through gritted teeth. "It's bad form to keep a queen waiting."

Jon held out his hand and gently helped Pat onto the back of the smallest big horse. Geof looked at a trembling Clark. "Let's go, man. It's time to put on the red cape for a while."

Clark sucked it up and crawled onto the last horse. He grabbed the horse around its neck and wrapped the reins around his hands so tightly he nearly cut off his circulation.

"Fake it and sit up," Geof ordered. "You don't look like much of a hero in that position."

"Hero, schmero," Clark mumbled.

The head human directed his horse to the road before them. He was a handsome, powerfully built man and exuded an air of authority. He was dressed in a white sleeveless pullover shirt with a V-neck and no buttons. His thigh-length tan trousers clung tightly to his muscular legs. He wore no insignia, but it was obvious he was a man of importance.

The road was bordered by large stone block buildings that might be found in Zurich, Chicago, or any other metropolitan city. After a few minutes, the road made a forty-five-degree turn. As they rounded the corner, an incredible sight awaited. It was a boulevard, as wide as a six-lane highway. The street, teeming with activity, had no street signs or visible markings of any kind. And yet all the horses, wagons, and pedestrian traffic moved with a precision never seen in places like New York City with their stoplights, speed limits, and crosswalks.

The road beneath them was not like any in Sheridan. It consisted of twelve-inch square bricks, but they were not gray or brown. They were gold with a small crisscross pattern cut in the top and beveled edges that butted against each other with a jeweler's precision.

Clark did not follow Geof's "man up" instructions and was still leaning forward with his arms wrapped firmly around the powerful neck of his mount. His position, while comic, provided him with a sharp view of the road. As he bounced around, he noticed how beautiful and atypical the road was. Despite being scared out of his wits, he quickly came to an inescapable conclusion. This road was not just gold in color— it was gold! Clark mustered the courage to push himself erect and sputtered to Debbie, "This street is made of gold."

"You mean gold gold?"

"Yeah... yeah... yes. I'm certain of it."

"Just a minute," she said as she trotted to the front of the pack. She pulled next to the leader and waved her hand to get his attention. "Excuse me, sir, can I ask you a question?"

"Yes," he replied without turning his head.

"What is this road made out of?"

"It is called gold."

Debbie looked over at Geof, who tilted his head. "May I ask why this substance is used to make the streets?"

"It is easy to work with, plentiful, and integrates well with our energy sources."

"Did… did you say plentiful?" she asked incredulously.

"Why, yes. Look up."

Everybody obeyed. The walls surrounding them were bright and luminescent from countless crystals and balls of gold suspended like stars. Strangely, they could not be seen from above. But from below, they looked like a thousand mini suns sharing their brilliance with the city. The gold balls appeared to interact with the road in some way and convert what should have been a dark cavern into a huge hemisphere of daylight. The dimensions of the cave seen at ground level were expanded a thousand times. Viewing the spectacle before them, the awestruck Searchers engaged in a collective silent "WOW" but said nothing more.

Debbie asked," May I ask your name, sir?"

"Edgal," he replied without looking her way.

"Are you a military person or something," she asked, knowing she might be pushing her luck.

"I am Supreme General of Lantuc. I have been sent to welcome you."

"That… that's nice," she said, struggling to find something intelligent to say. Her words failing, she turned her attention to Pat. Leaning close, she said, "He's hot!"

"Totally," Pat purred as her eyes zeroed in on Edgal's muscular upper arm.

Geof and Jon looked at each other and seethed. Geof started to say something but decided that keeping his mouth shut was the wisest course at the moment. This was not the time to express any jealousy, as before them stood a castle that would rival the finest palaces in Europe. It was made of stone blocks the size of school buses. A wide staircase of at least thirty steps rose in the center to a two-piece wooden door twenty feet high. Running the length of the palace were five stories of thirty arches, each of which Clark estimated to be nine feet across. Geof was immediately reminded of the Piazza San Marco in Venice, which he had been fortunate to visit with his father two years before. The castle was longer than the Piazza, taller, and no pigeons. The overwhelming size of the castle was pure evidence of the majesty of the country they found themselves in.

This was the seat of power for Lantuc. On either side of a stairway stood a double line of men dressed like Edgal. They were as rigid as statues and held in their right hands a shaft that looked like a spear with a crystal on the end. It was a weapon of some kind, but its function was not discernible. Citizens milled around at the bottom of the stairway unchallenged by the guards who seemed more style than substance.

Edgal dismounted and motioned for his companions to follow him. Debbie threw her right leg over the horse's head and hopped to the ground.

"Show off," Geof smirked as he slid off his horse.

He was followed by Jon, who chivalrously held out his hand to help Pat. Everyone looked impatiently at Clark, who continued to hold onto the horse's neck while inching very carefully to the ground. After an agonizing wait, the horse turned its head to Clark and knelt as if he read Clark's fear.

"*Ahhhhhhhhhh!*" Clark shrieked as he fell awkwardly over the horse's head onto his face.

"What is wrong with him?" Edgal asked Debbie.

"His mother dropped him on his head when he was little."

"Oh."

Clark could swear he heard the horses laughing as they walked away. And why not? He had to admit, this time, he really did look funny. Geof grabbed Clark's hand and yanked him to his feet in one motion. "Dude. Not in front of the Lantucians."

"Right." Clark hauled himself to his feet with marginal dignity.

Edgal led the newcomers up the stairs past the motionless honor guard of Edgal clones. The huge doors opened before them with no visible assistance from outside. As they entered, they noticed that there was no visible assistance from inside, either. So, who opened it? And more importantly, who would be closing it? The group followed Geof nervously as they crossed a large foyer to another set of large doors with a guard on either side. The doors were not as large as the outside doors but were still impressive. There was a beautiful carving of a coat of arms on each door. The background of the carvings bore a strong resemblance to the palace, with the profiles of a dog and a cat facing each other. It was weird but beautiful. Above the door were some illegible markings.

"What does that say?" Pat asked.

"Great Hall," Edgal answered.

"Very original," Jon said. The guards opened the doors revealing the appropriately named great hall. The floors were constructed of large squares of highly polished wood inlaid with gold. The hall was devoid of furniture, except for a row of sparsely occupied benches along each wall. The walls were alive with stained-glass windows and twenty-foot high tapestries the entire length of the hall. Gold and marble were everywhere.

Edgal led the Searchers into the great hall, where they immediately fixated on the queen's throne straight ahead. "Your Royal Highness, the kingdom has guests," Edgal announced.

"You may proceed." The throne came into focus, and a small dog lifted her head from a lavender pillow. She was covered by a beautiful purple robe with gold trim, and though she could not have weighed more than forty pounds, her countenance overflowed with authority.

"Queen Andi," Edgal announced.

"Whom do we have before us?" Queen Andi sniffed.

For a moment, the teenagers looked at each other like they were trying to avoid being called on in chemistry class. Debbie looked at Geof and motioned for him to step forward. He obeyed.

"Uhhh, my name is Geoffrey Boucher, uh… Your Highness."

"Why are you in Lantuc?"

Uriah jumped in front of Geof. "I am Uriah of Agron," he said. "We have traveled far to see you. This one is a stranger and does not understand our ways."

Andi leaned over to a table containing two cats lounging on a purple pillow. One was a gray, tabby type, and the other was a calico. While the gray cat looked like a Sheridan cat, there was something distinctly different about the calico. It was the eyes. Andi conferred with the cats for a few moments and then looked squarely at Geof. "We will wait for your answer."

Geof looked at Jon for backup and was urged on with a nod. "You see, I am not from Lantuc, or even from Sergeltuteron. My friends and I were sort of summoned to save your world from some kind of war or something."

Queen Andi looked at the cats, threw back her head, and laughed. "You do not look like you could save yourself from a sore paw, let alone save our world."

Again, Uriah interceded. "I admit they don't look like much, but they defeated the Pecash and that monster guarding the entrance to your kingdom."

Andi looked at Edgal. "They defeated the Rodart?" she asked.

"It would so appear, Your Majesty. They are here."

"Your Majesty, if I may," Uriah said cautiously. "Regard the windows surrounding your magnificence."

Andi looked at the stained-glass windows, and her eyes engaged each finely drafted panel. Her gaze was followed by her guests who, upon seeing the windows, gave an audible, collective gasp.

"Those—those windows have almost the same pictures to that animal hide thing Donald Deernose gave us," Pat gulped.

Andi whisked back the cape to reveal herself. She was jet black except for a white diamond on her chest. She had the face of a black Labrador, though her snout was not so long, and she was smaller than most Labs. Her legs were short and her body long. Her broad tail curled over her purple robe. She carried herself with such elegance that the only word to describe her was regal.

The queen studied the windows carefully. She raised her eyebrows, looked at Edgal, and zeroed in on the nervous teens. "General Edgal, make sure our guests are comfortable. We will be having them for dinner."

"Oh dear," Jon moaned. "I remember that line from *Silence of the Lambs,* and I don't think it worked out too well for that jerk psychiatrist."

"Mmmmmm," Geof grunted.

CHAPTER 15

King Bu-usah

Mu-jin King Bu-usah's face was intense. He impatiently tapped his yellow fingernails on the gilded arm of his gaudy throne. The throne room's opulence rivaled the Great Hall of Queen Andi, but it was not as cavernous. Despite its splendor, this great hall was dim, though not from lack of light. It was a dimness that comes from a depletion of heart and soul. The hall reflected images in a clouded mirror, unable to reflect the beauty and dignity of a world that once was. Guards standing shoulder to shoulder lined both sides of the hall all the way to the king.

King Bu-usah looked down at his subjects from his elevated throne. In Mu-jin, two things were evident. King Bu-usah was the absolute master of his domain, and his people were beautiful. The guards were all handsome, muscular, and tall. Their hair ranged from Jonster the Monster light brown in a few instances to sunlight blond in the majority. The women of Mu-jin were beautiful in face and body. They wore white tunics that revealed athletic midriffs, and their short skirts were slit on both sides to their thighs.

The men wore kilts that, unlike colorful Irish kilts, were the product of unimaginative designers. They were white and plain except for the figure of a snake with a head on each end. One head was triangular with an open mouth, fangs prominently protruding. The other head was round with a forked tongue that looked to be searching for something as the kilt swished back and forth.

The king's subjects walked an emotional tightrope. An appearance of calm was imperative to keep the king's legendary temper in check. Those who mistakenly offended the king paid for it by death or a one-way ticket to what the king called his University. Many painful lessons were learned in the University, but students never graduated.

"Where is he?" Bu-usah roared, rising to his full height of six feet. "Vandu-un... Bring him before me at once."

"Your Majesty," Vandu-un said reverently while bowing slightly toward the king.

Vandu-un was Bu-usah's right-hand man, or more accurately, his right-hand henchman. Vandu-un was not like the other citizens of Mu-jin. He stood only five feet six. His head was too large for his body and his face unattractive. His hair was Mu-jin blond but messy. His arms were short, and he displayed a paunchy stomach uncharacteristic for Mu-jin. He was not one of them. And yet, he stood above them all at the right hand of the king. The people of Mu-jin laughed at him behind his back, but only in the most trusted quarters as discretion was scarce in Mu-jin.

Vandu-un circled the throne and descended the stairs. His gait was peculiar but not mocked by any member of the populace who was fond of his own head. He briskly tottered his way to the large doors at the end of the room, grabbed the nearest guard by his collar, and thrust him toward the door.

"He should have been here long ago," Vandu-un said in a thick voice. "Bring him before the king at once."

"I obey." The large door swung open, and to the guard's relief, his exit was brief. He only took two or three steps outside when he found himself face to face with the object of the king's obsession. A man out of breath and wrinkled, straightened himself and panted, "I am here to see the king."

Vandu-un brusquely shoved the guard out of the way and said, "You have kept the king waiting. Your news better be good."

The look on the man's face betrayed the fact that he had no good news. Vandu-un frowned and pirouetted, and the man dutifully followed him to the throne and its king.

They stopped six feet from the bottom step. Bu-usah tapped his fingers on the tip of his pointy nose as he sized up the man standing before him. The king rose, a maneuver that rendered the entire room motionless. He stepped forward, strode down the stairs, and stood face to face with the man before him.

"You were sent to bring me the head of Sergel Tuteron. Where is it?"

"I… I do not have it, Your Majesty."

"Am I not talking to Halb-ean, Protector of Our Homeland and Commander of the First Legion?" The king's voice rose with each description.

"Yes, Majesty," Halb-ean said firmly.

"And did I not give you the honor of performing this simple task for me?"

"Y… yes King Bu-usah, and I do have information in this regard for you."

"Information? Information? I did not send you for information, but for the head of Sergel Tuteron. Why do you not have it?"

"Because he is long dead," Halb-ean said.

The king stepped back a pace and looked Halb-ean square in the eyes. "How do you know this?"

"My spies in Erud tell me that Sergel Tuteron no longer lives."

"What does that mean?" He grabbed Halb-ean by the shirt with both hands and pulled him to within inches of his face. "Take me to his grave."

"I… I do not know where it is. Nobody knows."

The king whirled and shouted at the top of his lungs, "Then why do you think he is dead?"

"It is common knowledge. He left Erud. He went off to die."

"Die? From what?"

"It is said he fell ill with the pestilence. That he still lives is just a lie concocted to occupy your majesty's time.… Of course, I am certain your majesty did not fall for such a crude trick."

"I have not heard this. No one in Mu-jin has heard this." Bu-usah turned his back to the man, spread his arms out before him, and bellowed in the direction of the soldiers, "This is a joke, is it not?"

An imperfect silence hung over the hall like a dark cloud too frightened to release its rain. "Is it not?" Bu-usah wailed in an even louder voice.

One soldier chuckled weakly, a sound that drew the attention of the king. Members of the palace guard froze. Was this man a fool or very smart? Did he just fall into one of Bu-usah's traps that guaranteed a one-way ticket to the University? King Bu-usah enjoyed watching his subjects squirm as they struggled to figure out what he wanted from them. Was he looking for laughter in his reference to a joke? Was he looking for outrage? The wise strategy was to stay neutral until someone else had the courage or stupidity to roll the dice to curry favor. King Bu-usah walked past a line of rigid faces and stopped in front of the soldier. He had a tentative but broad smile on his face. Bu-usah looked the soldier squarely in the eye and said quietly, "Is it a joke?"

The soldier straightened his shoulders and said confidently, "Yes, Your Majesty. And it would appear that you and I are the only ones who find it funny."

Bu-usah stood passively for a moment, then put his hands on the shoulders of the young man. Vandu-un placed himself in a position that would allow him to react to whatever way the winds of Bu-usah's uneven temperament blew.

Throwing back his head, Bu-usah laughed and broke the tension. The soldier in his grasp laughed more loudly, and soon the entire complement of soldiers and spectators was laughing with them. The merriment went on for several seconds until Bu-usah suddenly stopped laughing. The temperature of the room again went cold as the sound of laughter evaporated.

"And why do you think it is a joke?" He squinted at the now trembling soldier before him.

"Because there is no way Sergel Tuteron is dead. And it is a joke that anyone could hope to betray your wisdom with such a lie."

King Bu-usah nodded his head slowly. "How sad it is that only one in my elite guard should recognize such an obvious thing."

With that, he took the young man by the arm and guided him toward the throne. When he reached the steps, he turned to Vandu-un and nodded. Vandu-un walked up to Halb-ean, pulled a knife from his sash, and thrust it into Halb-ean's stomach. Halb-ean let out a scream and crumpled to the ground.

"Somebody kill this maniac before the Unborns destroy us all." he cried with his dying breath.

Halb-ean's desperate message fell on deaf ears. Not a soul had the courage to challenge the king.

Unconcerned, Bu-usah again addressed the man before him. "What is your name?" Bu-usah asked quietly.

"It is Desde, Your Highness."

"I shall give you a new name." The king swept his white-robed arm out with a flourish. "You shall henceforth be known as Des-dean."

The young man bowed his head. "I am honored, Your Majesty."

Bu-usah turned the young man to face the crowd. "I give you Des-dean, Protector of Our Homeland. Commander of the First Legion."

The young man's gamble paid off. A second ago, he was nobody. Now he was powerful beyond his wildest dreams, and a room full of soldiers looked back in regret that it was not they who laughed. Now knowing which side of the bread had the butter, the soldiers cheered wildly and called out Des-dean's name. "Des-dean, Des-dean," they cheered so convincingly that the king could not hear the hollowness in their voices.

"I give you a new life. What will you do for me?" the king asked.

"I will bring you the living or dead body of Sergel Tuteron."

"Vandu-un!"

Vandu-un stepped smartly forward. "Take our new commander and make sure that he lacks for nothing in his quest to bring us the head of Sergel Tuteron." Vandu-un bowed and led the newly minted commander to his tenuous future.

The Kingdom of Bu-usah was a dichotomy of beautiful people and not-so-beautiful landscape. At one time, Mu-jin was the most dazzling land in all of Sergel-tuteron. Her people worked the lush land, tended the forests, and enjoyed the good life. But all that changed with the emergence of King Bu-usah. The massive forests that once spread far and wide in Mu-jin were destroyed with cruel efficiency. Endless fuel was needed for the royal foundries that operated day and night to build ships and Bu-usah's multiple palaces. Exquisite inlaid wood floors and walls in the king's many palaces accepted only the finest wood. Precious log after log was burned as garbage when it did not meet Bu-usah's standards.

Bu-usah lulled his people into a stupor by providing for all their needs. In a short time, they became dependent on him, totally unaware that they had surrendered that most precious of things, their freedom, to a man who had a vision for their future that would have terrified them. Before Bu-usah, Mu-jinians were subjects of King Mar-lev. He was a just king who understood that his power came from his people's goodwill, not their subjugation. While living under this mantel of benign governance, the people of Mu-jin loved and trusted their king without pause and would do anything for him. This blind allegiance was transferred to the evil Bu-usah and became their undoing. To him, they were a means to an end. He was the ruler of the most beautiful people in his world, and it was only fitting that all other creatures should become his chattel. He coveted the intellect of the Eruds and resented their position as the rock stars of science. Bu-usah vowed they would soon kneel before him and beg to give him their wisdom.

CHAPTER 16

Constantine

Edgal led the wide-eyed Searchers to a room behind Andi's throne. It was well appointed with a large Persian-style rug and a broad selection of furniture designed for human and dog. Against the far wall was a Victorian couch with scrolled arms and no back. It was finely upholstered with elegant, purple fabric, darkened by countless tiny black hairs.

"Wait here," Edgal directed. "If you need anything, pull this." He gestured to a braided rope, about two inches in diameter and gold in color. Edgal exited and left the five teenagers to stare at each other.

"Check it out," Jon said, walking over to the rope. "This is just like those things they always had in the old movies... you know... people used to pull them to call their butler. In the movies, they never make a sound, but servants just show up. I always wanted to try it. Feeling the power, you know," he said as he grasped the rope in his right hand.

"If you pull that thing, I am going to rip off your arm and beat you to death with it," Geof growled. "We need to figure out what to do."

"Well, I wasn't reeeeally gonna pull it, you know. But now that you mention it, I do know what I need to do now."

"You do?"

"Yes. Pee. I have to pee."

"Say what? We may be about to—"

"Do you know why I love movies so much?" Jon quizzed before Geof could finish his sentence.

"Because you don't have a life?"

"Clever. But no. It's because nobody ever has to pee in the movies. I mean, wouldn't that be great?"

Geof was uncomfortable with a conversation that, in his mind, should be reserved for boy-only company. "I never thought much about it."

"Well, you should. Remember that scene in Harry Potter where that troll thing traps the girl—"

"Hermione," Debbie and Pat chirped in unison.

"Yeah, Hermione. Anyway, she gets trapped in the bathroom by this troll because she is in there crying. You get that? Crying in the head. Not peeing like she should be. People cry in movies all the time, but they don't pee! And then she hides by crawling all around the toilets like no girl on earth would ever do because they are yucky. But she does it because she knows they aren't the least bit yucky. And do you know why?"

"Huh-uh."

"Because toilets are never used in movies because nobody ever has to pee. That's why."

Debbie and Pat giggled uncontrollably. Geof grunted. "Oh, what the heck." He walked past Jon and yanked the cord.

Immediately the door opened, and before them stood two large English bulldog types, the perfect servants.

"May we be of assistance?" one of them asked.

"Uh, yeah. Well, I mean, uh, do you have a bathroom? Restroom? WC?" Jon asked timidly.

The two bulldogs looked at each other questioningly. "Ah," one finally said. "You need the priv."

"The priv, yeah. Sure. The priv. If you wouldn't mind."

"Males follow me, females follow her," the larger bulldog said. As they led the way, the small bulldog laughed loudly to the large one, "The humans never can hold it."

The group was led down a long hall to two sets of doors. Above one was a large circle for girls and above the other, two circles. After the call of nature was satisfied, they returned to Andi's luxurious study to chill. Queen Andi smartly walked in, and her guests instinctively jumped to their feet. She crossed the room, nodded slightly, and hopped up on the backless purple couch.

"Are you the ones?" she asked, dismissing any small talk.

"The... ones?" Geof asked.

"The ones. You know very well of what we are speaking."

Geof did not know what to say. His better judgment said it might be best to play it cagey. He had no idea if this latest version of lingual lapdog was friend or foe. "That is what everybody keeps telling us. But to tell you the truth, we don't know. You all keep saying that I am this Searcher guy, but I don't feel like it."

Andi's gaze fixed on Geof for an eternity. Her eyes consumed every line and angle of his face. He could feel her spirit tearing through his physical and psychological barriers one by one until his soul was laid open. His nerves tingled from the knowledge that his mind ceased to be his own.

"We understand that our world is foreign to you," she said, releasing him. "But we see that hidden in you is much courage, much fear, and much passion. Such are the qualities of a great leader."

"Excuse me, Queen. I am Debbie, and I have a question."

"You may speak."

"Uriah gives us the impression that Lantuc is just a legend to everyone. We don't know if he brought us here on purpose or by accident." She looked at Uriah who strategically looked the other way. "So how come you seem to know so much about what is beyond your walls? And how do you know about us what we don't even know?"

"If you study our colorful windows, you will see that we are perfectly educated about you or who you claim to be."

"Those windows are pretty scary."

"Lantuc occupies a unique position," Andi continued. "It is our duty to be aware of anything that might endanger us."

"She means they spy on everybody," Jon smirked.

"That makes sense," Clark said. "If you fear your country is in danger, smart leaders prepare, and spying's been fair game since before there were any countries."

Andi acknowledged Clark and continued. "Those with less strength must utilize more intelligence. With what we have learned, we believe we may be of service to you, and by doing so, help ourselves."

"You will help us?" Geof asked, hopefully.

"We do what we must for our survival. If that means helping you, then yes, we will help you."

"Seems kind of self-serving," Pat said.

"Is not everything?" Andi shrugged. "Deception has kept Lantuc secure for many epochs. We have done much to convince all those except the Eruds that our existence is merely a legend. But now we feel that Lantuc may soon be discovered, and with King Bu-usah ready to destroy everything, we feel we are in grave danger."

"I feel like we are bringing trouble to everyone," Debbie said.

Uriah shook his head. "No, child. Trouble is already here."

Sensing they were about to be dismissed, Geof blurted. "I am trying to find my mother. Do you know anything about her?"

"That is a strange question," Andi said. "Why would you ask that of us?"

"Well, to be honest, trying to find my mother is the reason we came here in the first place, more or less."

"Interesting. Most interesting. We do not know of your mother, but if we can assist you, we will try."

"Okay, thanks. I was just checking."

"Do not look so sad, young Geof. If your mother is here, she is safe, and you have a good chance to find her."

"Thank you."

"But for now, we have other issues. We will provide you with someone to help you, to guide you, to teach you. If you are who we hope you are, you will soon be teaching him. And if your presence here is in error, we will deal with you in another way."

"Yeah, we know. Grrrrrrrr," Geof snorted. "When do we meet this person?"

The door swung open on cue, and the familiar face of the large grizzly dog announced, "Your Majesty, Lord Constantine." A man about six feet tall stooped to enter Andi's private chamber. Once inside, he stood erect and bowed his head. "Your Majesty," he said. Upon acknowledgment by the queen, Constantine directed himself toward the royal guests. A strange look overcame his face, but he said nothing as he continued to study them like ants.

"Constantine, escort our guests to your section, interview them, and if they are of substance, counsel them."

Constantine nodded. "Follow me," he said without looking at them.

Lord Constantine turned and bowed, followed by Uriah and the others. He was wearing a flawless, full-length white robe with a gold sash. His sleeves extended to the midpoint between his elbow and wrist. There was no collar, and a bold but unfamiliar design bordered the V-shaped opening in front of his neck. He was completely bald and sported a neatly trimmed, black goatee. His face was slightly round but was taut and without wrinkles. His dark eyes hinted of oriental ancestry. There was something about Constantine, but whatever it was, Geof could not put his finger on it. Was it sinister? Was it divine? What he did know was this guy was different, but strangely familiar.

Lord Constantine led the way down a series of spectacular marble hallways adorned with now-familiar artwork. In every hall were full-size bas relief carvings of men and women from assorted professions. The journey ended at a large, carved, wooden door that was secured by four locks. Constantine raised his right hand, and three carvings emerged from the wall, produced a key, and unlocked the three bottom locks. When finished, they returned to the wall and again became one with it.

"Yikes," Clark gasped. "Whatever's behind this guy's door is more securely guarded than the queen's private chambers. I wonder why."

Constantine removed a key from a large pocket in his robe and unlocked the final lock. The door swung open, and he entered. The spacious domain of Constantine was as intriguing as the man himself. The walls were irregular with endless nooks and crannies that contained an impressive variety of scientific instruments, paintings, sculptures, books, and models. At the far end of the room stood a large fireplace. To the left of the fireplace was one long, continuous wall. It was close to twenty feet high and was packed with row after row of books. There were thousands of volumes accessible by a ladder on wheels. Could these books contain the collective wisdom of Lantuc? Clark was blown away and dying to dive into this ocean of prose and intellect.

Geof felt lost. It was too much. How could he possibly gain any insight that would help him find his mother, save a world, or just figure out how to operate on the most basic level in Sergel-tuteron? Debbie leaned over a large wingback chair and petted two cats. They looked suspiciously like Maximillian and Crystal, the very cats seen less than an hour earlier by Andi's side in the throne room. They were as receptive to her attention as cats allow. Even though Debbie was petting them, it was Pat who held their interest.

Geof walked up to Debbie, smiled at the cats, and pulled her to one side. "What's going on here? These are the same cats that were sitting next to Andi when we first met her."

"Yeah, so?" Debbie answered.

"And..."

"And what?"

"And how did they get here?"

"Walked?"

"Oh, come on," Geof said. "Did you see all the rigmarole this Constantine guy had to go through just to get his own door open?"

"Well, maybe they have the run of the place. Or maybe there's a top-secret, cats only, tunnel somewhere."

"I don't know. I think it's fishy," Geof said.

Geof and Debbie's aside was interrupted by Lord Constantine, who directed them to a businesslike corner where a round table eight feet in diameter awaited them. There were eight chairs, and with Uriah curled up on one of them, a solitary chair was left empty. Geof looked at the chair and thought of Morgue. He felt bad that in all the excitement, little thought had been given to Morgue by anybody. Uriah promised Morgue would be in great shape. But how much could they trust this enigmatic little dog?

Lord Constantine told his guests to wait and left the room, his white robe billowing behind him. He returned less than a minute later with a ceramic urn cradled gently in his hands. The alabaster urn was a foot tall and without handles. He set it in the middle of the table and retrieved a crystal from his pocket. It was dodecahedron, two inches in diameter. He placed the crystal in the center of the urn where it floated in midair. "Watch," Constantine ordered.

The Bear and his friends waited in subdued anticipation. A cylinder of light beamed upward through the top of the crystal and saturated the ceiling twenty feet above their heads. Shapes and movement took form within the boundaries of the light and dazzled the wide-eyed teenagers below.

"Here we go again," Jon moaned.

The shapes in the cylinder came and went rapidly, but some were recognizable. There was a frighteningly familiar scene of several young people under attack by the Pecash. The throne room of Andi with people milling about was also familiar. And there was Pat standing before a man in a white robe, but the man was not Lord Constantine. The play before them was hypnotic. Some scenes were of things that had already happened, and they became darker and more sinister as the images in the cylinder continued to develop. Seeing Pat as a hologram was a shock, particularly to Jon. The showstopper was a vision of Geof, a chain attached to a collar around his neck, being led by a woman in white.

Geof leaped to his feet, crashing his chair to the floor. "What is that? What is that?"

"Concentrate," Constantine commanded.

Debbie grabbed Geof's arm with one hand and picked his chair up with the other. The scene of him in chains mercifully vanished and was replaced by another. There were thousands of flying snakes flailing about in a chaotic ballet. A large bear stood on its hind legs and let out a fierce growl, but there was no sound. Geof appeared again, unchained and battling a monstrous snake, a sword in his hands.

The images disappeared and Constantine sat quietly for a moment, waiting for acceptable blood pressure levels to return to his guests. When they crawled back to their seats, he said, "Do you now still question who you are? Do you now still question that you are the Searchers?"

The kids looked at one another. All the words in every known language could not be combined to explain the meaning of a twisted nightmare that surpassed reality long ago. Constantine waited for someone to speak, his hands folded in front of his waist like an altar boy. Clark gawked at the table. Deep inside, he felt that if he did not grasp a rudimentary understanding of things, he would violate his position as nerd emeritus.

"What does this all mean?" Clark asked. "Are these scenes that will take place... or maybe... or I mean, might take place? Or are they just possibilities spawned by people's imaginations?

Or dreams… And how does this crystal have images of Geof and Pat as actors in events that haven't even happened?" His voice was trembling almost as much as his body.

"We do not know," Constantine said, shaking his head. "It was hoped you could help us understand it."

"I… I don't know," Geof shook his head. His gaze locked on the intractable face of Constantine. He could not get over how black his eyes were. His pupils were indistinguishable from his irises. What a thing to notice at a time like this. Who was this Constantine anyway? Was he even human, or as human as anyone could be in this society? Did he somehow conjure up those images as a means of controlling Geof and his friends for his own purpose? Was this a clever piece of Lantuc movie-making designed to manipulate them? After all, deception was their mantra.

His thoughts were disconnected by Jon's voice. "This is obviously a glimpse of what we have been told will happen to us. But I can't believe there is no choice, and we will be swept helplessly along this river just because that Song thing says so."

"It has been accurate so far, as best as we can tell anyway. That is all we know… until now."

The large room, impressively filled with books and all their collected knowledge, was at this moment the picture of confusion. Here was this guy Constantine with all these literary works and tapestries, his cool robe, and minions that pop out of walls to unlock his door. And he doesn't seem to be any more in the know than a bunch of teenagers who were cruising the halls of Sheridan High School just a few days before. And despite whatever confidence they might fake on the outside, if this world had to rely on them for salvation, it was in deep trouble.

Geof shrugged. "Okay. We have all this weird stuff floating around, but we still don't have a clue what to do or why or how we are to do it."

Uriah, who had been silent for some time, now spoke softly. He lowered his head and his long blond ears nearly touched the floor. "I do not know how you are supposed to do it, Geof. But I believe you are here to save our world."

The door swung open, and Queen Andi entered the room.

CHAPTER 17

Jok-imo, Son of Halb-ean

Queen Andi crossed the floor and pulled Constantine a few paces away from their guests. Constantine leaned down and listened as Andi peered around his robe once or twice at the visitors. Queen Andi and Lord Constantine's talk was brief and concluded by Constantine motioning toward the door with his arm. The door swung open a second time and revealed a man with his eyes covered by a gold band secured by a clasp at the back of his head. He was guarded by two large grizzly dogs.

"My Lord, I present Jok-imo from the Karroll of Mu-jin," one of the grizzlies declared.

Jon whispered to Geof, "Mu-jin? I think the plot is thickening."

"Agreed."

"Step forward," Constantine commanded. It seemed out of the ordinary that Constantine would give such a command in favor of Andi. But instead of presenting herself as the powerful monarch she was, she walked slowly to the nearest corner and flopped on the floor, her eyes looking sleepily up at the newcomer. A grizzly dog reached behind Jok-imo's back and physically straightened him up. "You are in the presence of Lord Constantine. Tell your story and be quick about it," the grizzly commanded.

Jok-imo had long blond hair that fell unkempt to the top of his shoulders. He wore a soiled white Mu-jin uniform and sported the impressive features of most Mu-jin men. He was very nervous, his face exhibiting the conflict of what he knew he had to do but was afraid to do. He bowed his head slightly and spoke in a soft tone.

"I am Jok-imo, son of Halb-ean of Mu-jin. I must speak to Queen Alma. Am I in the Secret City?"

Geof and Jon looked at each other. "Queen Alma? Who the heck is that?"

"What business do you have with the queen?" Constantine asked in an official voice.

"I have come to…" Jok-imo stopped when he realized he had no idea who he was talking to.

Constantine waited. This man's mission was clearly urgent. He was willing to put his life in jeopardy by attempting to enter the Secret City. Constantine hoped that Jok-imo was carrying information that might help prevent what looked like an inevitable war with Mu-jin. The situation called for caution. He also could be a spy who managed to breach the veils that protected Lantuc and the Secret City.

"Please sit," Constantine said reassuringly, taking Jok-imo's arm and leading him to a tufted chair. Jok-imo sat uneasily on the edge while Constantine sat comfortably across from him. The visitor could sense the presence of others but had no way of telling how many or who they were.

Jok-imo sat for a few moments, and with his limited senses, tried to size up this man of influence who had become his host. He traveled far. He knew that much. But for the past two days, he journeyed in the dark. He could still be in Mu-jin, and this could be one of Bu-usah's tricks. The man from Mu-jin decided that his options were few, and his future would be determined here and now. He would trust this man of mystery, this Constantine, and face the consequences.

"I… I need to see Queen Alma," he said tentatively.

"That is not possible. Queen Alma is not available. But do not despair, young man. I will personally convey your message to Queen Alma," Constantine said.

Jok-imo realized it was pointless to play a game of cat and mouse since he was clearly the mouse. "King Bu-usah plans another attack on the Secret City," he coughed.

"This is no secret to anyone in Sergel-tuteron," Constantine said, folding his arms across his chest. "I am afraid you came a long way for nothing. But I am curious. How did you get here?"

"I do not know. My father, Halb-ean, was murdered by Bu-usah. I have been hiding ever since. I was traveling near the Great Sea when I met two men who offered to share their food. Any offer of food in Mu-jin is welcome. I fell asleep, and the next thing I knew, I was bound and blindfolded. Then these big cains brought me here."

"One moment," Constantine said. He got up and walked over to the grizzly dogs for a private chat. "How did this come about?"

"We received a message that this man would be coming. In fact, he nearly stumbled onto the hidden entrance. Our guards fed him and caused him to sleep. They brought him to me."

"Excellent work," Constantine nodded and returned to Jok-imo.

He continued as though there had been no gap in the conversation, "Bu-usah's intent to attack the Secret City is no secret."

"Possibly. But he also has sent assassins to kill Sergel Tuteron."

"Why kill Sergel Tuteron?" Constantine probed.

"Because he feels that Sergel Tuteron is the only thing that stands in the way of him conquering the Secret City."

Constantine scoffed. "For one thing, Bu-usah holds Sergel Tuteron in far too high regard. He is just one man. And secondly, I am afraid he will be waiting a long time for that victory. The Sergel Tuteron Bu-usah fears no longer exists."

"Is this a certainty?"

"Yes."

"If Sergel Tuteron is dead, my father died for nothing."

"Why do you say that?"

"My father, Halb-ean, was one of King Bu-usah's highest military leaders. He was ordered to go out and find, kidnap, or kill Sergel Tuteron. But when he returned to Mu-jin, he reported that Sergel Tuteron was dead."

Constantine shifted uncomfortably in his chair. "And how did he come by this revelation?"

"I am not sure that he did."

"Explain."

His answer would result in a swift death for Jok-imo if he were talking to a Bu-usah surrogate. But he had come too far to turn back now. "My father grew disillusioned with King Bu-usah. He saw how he destroyed the beauty of our country and soul of our people. King Bu-usah thinks only of revenge and power. He sees the way to achieve both is to kill or imprison Sergel Tuteron. By this one act, he believes he will capture the complete fear and respect of my people."

"Interesting combination," Debbie uttered. "What happened?"

Jok-imo flinched at the sound of an unfamiliar female voice. "Halb-ean is, or was, one of a group of citizens in Muj-in who see King Bu-usah for what he is, a cruel and sadistic madman. So Halb-ean lied about Sergel Tuteron. My father was the only one with the courage to stand up to Bu-usah and put an end to the disease that is rotting my Karroll."

"Go on," Constantine urged.

"Halb-ean's courage ended his life, and he knew it would end mine. Like any father, he could risk his own life but not his son's. He secretly entered Bu-usah City to warn me. That was the night before he was to go to the King's Court, and the last time I would see my father. His final gift to me was to order me to leave Mu-jin. I did, that very night."

"And?" Jon asked anxiously.

"That same night, my father left the city under cover of darkness and returned in the light of the lumen to hide the fact that he had seen me. He went to the castle and presented himself before the court of Bu-usah. I heard he made his declaration to the king and was murdered in full view of everyone by Vandu-un."

Constantine placed his hand on Jok-imo's wrist. "I am sorry for your father. He sounds like a very brave man."

"Reality dwells in a far distant place from Bu-usah's mind. He has bewitched our people."

Debbie wiped a tear from her eye and looked at Geof. If Jok-imo's story were true, it was the final proof that this was no dream. It was the bedrock form of reality where friends might die, and worlds might end. Geof reached out and squeezed her hand. He intended to channel to her whatever strength he could muster, but when she squeezed back, it was he who felt the power.

"I must see Queen Alma," Jok-imo continued in earnest. "I must know if Sergel Tuteron is alive and if he can help me. And can someone tell me where I am?"

"You are in a safe place, and no living soul knows the fate of Sergel Tuteron," Constantine roadblocked. "It is of no importance in dealing with the defense of the Secret City and its treasures. What is important is knowing Bu-usah's plan and his ability to carry it out. If you want to help

Alma and the Secret City, make this information known to me NOW."

Jok-imo lowered his head. "I do not know his plan, but I have seen Bu-usah's entire fleet nearly complete as we speak. Soon it will be ready to attack."

Constantine feared that time may be shorter than he had hoped, but he tried not to give away his concern. "Is that it?" he asked evenly. "Do you have any allies in Mu-jin?"

"There are those who, like me, oppose the king, but everyone is afraid."

"It is good that there is opposition in Mu-jin. That means Bu-usah's intelligence is not perfect," Constantine said.

"There are things successfully secreted from Bu-usah, but they are few and done at the risk of death."

"What about this underground resistance?" Clark asked.

"We have no leader. Our people are either too paralyzed with fear or brainwashed to do anything against King Bu-usah because he has the—"

"Maybe it's because they have no alternative," Geof interrupted. "You could find him. I mean, you could look for someone—" Geof glanced over at Jok-imo and realized he was lost. "Let me put it this way, you seem to have the proper pedigree to be a leader, and you see this Bu-usah guy for what he is. Go back, put together an army, and kick his butt."

"Y... you mean ME go against Bu-usah?" Jok-imo asked incredulously. "I... I couldn't. I don't have... I couldn't. As long as he has the... well, he is invincible."

"He has the *what*?" Constantine forced. "Say the word."

"I want to tell, but it is so terrible. If I could only find Sergel Tuteron or Queen Alma—"

"He and Queen Alma cannot help you," Constantine bellowed. "But I can. Say the word."

"Sceptre. He has the Sceptre."

Constantine's face was scrutinized by everyone, but he tried to remain in control. "Describe it," Constantine said solemnly.

"Constantine knows something," Jon breathed to a nodding Geof.

"It… it is the length of a man's arm. On each end is an ornate carving. A cat-eye is in the middle, and there are markings all over it. I am told that it has infinite power. And there is no one in Mu-jin with the courage to take it from the king."

"Do you think this Sceptre gives Bu-usah infinite power?" Constantine asked.

"I do not know. But if it did, I think he would have used it by now. I think the Sceptre may belong to Sergel Tuteron, which is why I search for him."

"But if Sergel Tuteron alone can make this Sceptre max out, and he's not around, then it's worthless. So, what's the big deal?" Geof asked.

Constantine asked the grizzly dogs to escort Jok-imo from the room. When Jok-imo was safely out of earshot, Constantine told Geof, "The Sceptre is mentioned in the Song. We feared Bu-usah had it, and it must be taken from him at all costs."

"But if Bu-usah can't activate it—"

"He may be able to and just not know it... yet," Constantine sighed.

"Why don't you send someone in to snatch it from him?" Jon asked as if it were an easy thing. "You must have someone here who could do that."

"I fear there is no one here or anywhere in Sergel-tuteron."

"I have a bad feeling you're going to say until now," Geof mumbled.

Constantine nodded. "Until now."

CHAPTER 18

A Good Start

With Jok-imo safely out of the room, Constantine focused his attention on Geof and his friends. He surveyed each of them carefully and pointed at Geof. "I think I now know your purpose in coming here."

"Not on your life," Geof rebelled. "You think I'm somehow going to go to that Mu-jin place and start some kind of revolution against a real live king? I'm just a kid, and for that matter, pretty much of a goof-off if you know what I mean. Besides, I don't look anything like those guys if they all look like pretty boy Jok-imo."

At that point, Andi arose from the floor and walked towards Geof. Constantine respectfully moved out of the way. Andi, the rug dog, was Queen Andi once again.

"They call you the Bear?" she asked.

"Yeah, but that's just a nickname because I was a big kid."

"Perhaps it has more meaning than you think. The Song for Tomorrow is not completely clear to us, but it leads us in certain directions. I believe that Jok-imo is an explorer. And I believe you are the object of his journey, though he does not know it. If the armies of Bu-usah can be weakened from within, we might be able to save the Secret City and Lantuc."

"And what am I supposed to do? Go marching in there, shove a sword out in front of me and yell charge?"

"Not necessarily," Constantine said. "It may not be possible to raise an army in Mu-jin against Bu-usah. But if you can capture the Sceptre, that may be all we will need. We don't really know what you are supposed to do. But the Song says you will know and do it."

"The Song. The Song. I am getting tired of hearing about the Song. Besides, I repeat, I don't even look like those Mu-jinians."

Constantine said, "There are some in Mu-jin that do not look like Jok-imo, though they are not considered the favored people."

"Great. So, I'd not only stick out, but I'd be a second-class citizen."

"Your friends Jon and Pat do look enough like Mu-jinians to provide credibility. And if we can persuade the timid Jok-imo to guide you, I believe you can fulfill your destiny."

Geof put his hand on his forehead and shook his head. "This is too bizarre. What about Debbie and Clark?" he asked.

"I'm going with you," Debbie said firmly.

"No way," Geof shot back. "Three of us getting killed is enough."

"More than enough," Jon agreed.

"I don't think that's funny," Debbie pouted.

"Who's joking?"

"Debbie, I need you to stay with me," Andi said firmly. "It is of vital importance that you stay with me."

"And you, young man," Constantine said to Clark. "It seems you have great knowledge of military and war matters. Perhaps that knowledge could be helpful to us."

Jon elbowed Geof. "Talk about irony. They're asking a laughingstock high school nerd to prepare an army to defend an entire country against invasion. What was the author of that Song for Tomorrow thinking?"

"Sure," Clark answered Constantine, knowing there was nothing else he could say.

"What do you three say?" Constantine asked Geof, Pat, and Jon.

"Bro, if we don't do this, it would be like going to Paris and not seeing the Eiffel Tower."

"I've seen the Eiffel Tower. It's overrated," Geof said. "And what about Pat? We can't risk her life."

"You're right, man. No girls."

"Wait a minute," Pat protested. "Nobody makes decisions for me."

"But Pat—"

"No, Jon. Everywhere we have gone, people have looked at me like I was one of *them*. They even accused me of being a spy, remember? I am the best cover you have."

Jon closed his eyes and shook his head. "I don't know."

"I am going, Jon. Besides, would you deny me the chance to change a world?"

"Jon, listen to me," Uriah said gently. "I think that destiny has already decided for both you and Pat."

"That's bull," Jon argued. "I don't believe that's possible."

"Think about it," Uriah continued. "The Song for Tomorrow has been around since before anyone can remember. Our earliest writings tell of it. It is not only in our world but yours. And it brought you here. All of you. And why?"

"No clue."

"To fulfill your destiny."

"Destiny schmestiny. Maybe it's someone else's destiny."

"I think we will find out soon enough," Uriah said. "I will be going with you. I, too, will risk my life, and I will risk it to protect you and your friends. My whole family's lives are at risk. Our whole world is at risk."

Jon sighed and knelt to look into Uriah's probing eyes. Uriah placed his paw on Jon's bent knee and spoke softly. "We all have the life we want and the life we have. Seldom are the life we have and the life we want the same thing. So, we make the best of what we have. And in doing this, maybe what we have will turn out to be what we wanted all along."

Geof put his arm around Jon, "You don't get it, do ya, pal? There's something goatee face here hasn't told us, isn't there?" he said turning his eyes accusingly toward Constantine.

Constantine looked to the side. "We can't go back if we don't go forward. We are prisoners to this destiny, whether it's ours or not."

Debbie, Pat, Clark, and Jon stared at Geof. "Wh–what does he mean 'can't'?" Debbie asked. She marched to within inches of Constantine's face. "What do you mean 'can't'?"

Constantine stepped back and yielded to Andi. "What he means dear, is that from the time you entered Lantuc, you placed your feet into shoes you cannot remove. It is impossible for you to go back to your world until you have fulfilled your destiny in ours."

"You mean we are prisoners?" Debbie glared.

"We are all prisoners of our destiny," Uriah said from behind Andi. "You might find that your destiny as foretold in the Song for Tomorrow is the road that will lead you from the life you have to the life you want."

"Great. Just great. Whudda we do now?" Geof asked.

Constantine addressed the nearest grizzly dog. "Return the Mu-jinian to us."

Jok-imo found himself once again in the presence of Constantine. "It has been decided that you will accompany a small band of heroes to the heart of Mu-jin and liberate your people," Constantine said without emotion. "Will you go?"

"For my father and for the Secret City… yes I will go."

Satisfied, Constantine said, "We shall have a banquet tonight to honor our heroes and prepare for their journey. You must get to know each other. Stay here and be comfortable. I fear your comfort will be elusive in times to come." Constantine led Jok-imo to the door and exited, followed by the grizzly dogs. Andi stayed behind and mingled.

Geof and Jon found themselves in a corner alone, a rare moment to share feelings unencumbered by the interference of strange creatures and wild stories. "Man, I've got to be dreaming," Jon said, wiping his floppy hair off his forehead.

"Newsflash buddy. This ain't no dream."

"Come on, bro. You don't really think we're gonna go trucking into this Mu-jin joint, gather up an army of wannabe soldiers and kick the shit out of the Sergel-tuteron version of Adolph Hitler, do you? Need I remind you we are both scared to death of Miss Stiles."

"I think we should just go with the flow and see what happens. It's not like we have a lot of choices. Besides, we may not be going there to raise an army at all."

Jon shook his head. "I just don't get the deal with queeny over there," he said, identifying Andi as she entertained the girls.

"Girl talk," Geof smiled. "Probably sharing recipes for doggie sugar cookies."

"You sexist pig," Jon smirked. "But really, man, who the heck is she, and how does she fit into all this? One minute she's queen of the hop, and the next, she's lying around like she doesn't want anybody to know who she is."

"Probably doesn't have too many Facebook friends, that's for sure."

"Good one, Bear, but for once, I need to be serious."

"I'm afraid if I am serious, I'll have to face reality. So, the best thing for me is to live in the pleasant world of denial."

"You don't really think we can pull this off, do you?"

"I don't know. This Song for Tomorrow nonsense says we can. Besides, our pre-frontal cortexes won't be fully developed until we are in our mid-twenties, so we have an excuse for doing reckless and stupid things without considering the consequences."

"My big friend, you are reading way too many science magazines and not nearly enough comic books."

"All I know is I'm here, and as far as Andi's concerned, it's obvious she doesn't want anybody to know she's the queen."

"But why? She didn't hide it from us. In fact, being in awe of her was crammed down our throats."

"I know," Geof said. "Let's ask her."

Geof and Jon smoothly inserted themselves into the Andi, Debbie, and Pat triangle.

"Well, Queen Andi, why the floor act when Jok-imo the Dreamo was in the room?"

"It is necessary, you see," she responded like they should already know the answer. "The more things seem real, the less chance they are unreal."

Geof and Jon grunted.

Andi continued. "It is vital to keep strangers off balance until you come to know them as friends. Jok-imo did not know for sure that he was out of Mu-jin, and seeing someone like me in authority would instantly give us away. Do you understand? He must not know where he is. Never!"

"Well, that makes sense, I guess," Geof said. Jon nodded half-heartedly.

"What about us?" Jon pushed.

"Since your arrival, it was clear who you were. It is said in the Song that the heroes from the outside would be the most unlikely group. They would seem so helpless that to think of them as the saviors of the Secret City would bring people to their knees with laughter."

"That describes *some* of us," Geof smirked.

"I think Andi's just referring to the boys," Debbie smiled sweetly.

"Well, I have a real question," Clark interjected. Why do they call it the Song for Tomorrow? I don't hear anybody singing around here."

Andi gave him a cryptic look. "Perhaps you can tell us." Her probe was met with a communal shrug. One more mystery.

"You need time together. Your individual futures depend on your collective resolve. I advise you to use the remaining moments before the banquet to strengthen that resolve for the journey ahead. We will come for you in two—uh—hours."

With that admonition, Queen Andi left the room, leaving a contemplative group of teenagers to ponder their fate. Without conversation, they mingled and paced, each grappling with his or her own demons and fears.

"What do you s'pose this banquet thing is all about?" Geof asked, breaking the ice.

"Well, it's a banquet, so I think it will be fun," Debbie smiled.

"Yeah, just pretend you are in a Dickens book," Patricia smiled.

Jon stared at her blankly. "A Dickens book?"

"Well, my, uh, parents insisted I read as many of the classics as I could. I just love Charles Dickens, don't you? I bet they had grand banquets in Dickens' time."

"Uhh, yeah. Well, Dickens—heck yeah."

"My favorite is *A Tale of Two Cities*. We are supposed to read it this year in English, but I already have. You can borrow my copy if you want and save you some money."

"I'm covered. I have the CheatNotes," Jon answered.

"What?" cried a shocked Pat. "Why waste time with that garbage when I have the book?"

"You don't mean you actually read the entire book, do you?" Jon asked, unmindful of the hole he was digging with his tongue.

Pat bristled. "What kind of fool would miss the chance to read a great book like *A Tale of Two Cities* in favor of those, those CheatNotes?" she fumed.

"That kind," a laughing Geof said, pointing at Jon.

"Okay, fine," Jon retreated. "I, uh—well, I actually use the CheatNotes to enhance my understanding of a book," he added slyly, glancing over at Geof. Geof's eyes remained fixated on the ceiling convincing Jon that he had better refine his technique or fall further into Pat's no-man's-land. "Of course, I would love to borrow your book."

"Hmmmm," Pat nodded unconvinced.

The whole room burst into laughter. It felt good to laugh, so good that even Jon joined in. "That's okay," Pat forgave him. "I guess we all have our strengths and weaknesses. It is good to know all of yours are not so obvious."

Bullet dodged, Jon segued into something less threatening. "Uhhh, does anybody have anything they want to talk about while we're together and alone? I mean, who knows when that might happen again with all this 'you go here', and 'you go there' stuff."

Debbie answered immediately. "I just want everyone to know that I am proud of you all. We will all come through this stronger than we were before. I already am."

"Hear hear," Geof said, raising an imaginary glass in a toast.

"I agree with you a hundred percent," Jon said. "If anybody or anything dares to come at me, I'm gonna kick its ass." The door swung open, and a grizzly dog stood in the doorway. "Except him," Jon muttered.

The grizzly dog beckoned all to follow him. Banquet time was at hand.

CHAPTER 19

Food for Thought

The grizzly dog led his charges down a long and beautiful hallway of ornate columns with scrolls of gold decorating top and bottom. The columns impressively framed a wall of endless bas reliefs. The grizzly dog announced that they had reached the banquet hall and would be escorted to their seats. Two large, carved wood doors awaited them, massive in size and intricacy, but in light of everything else in Lantuc, not memorable. The opening doors presented a breathtaking ballroom that would humble nearly anything in the "real" world. There was a huge collection of gold decorations of all sizes on the walls, even gold doorknobs, and gold silverware. Illumination was provided by the familiar crystals that sent light bouncing in all directions off thousands of crystal and gold surfaces attached to the ceiling. Twenty feet above the tables was a dazzling light show that could best be described as a wedding of the wildest rock concert laser show and the Northern Lights. Yet below, the room was bathed in even sunlight with no distractions from the performance above. Clark added this to his ever-growing list of "how do they do that" questions.

Several large tables were laid end to end, forming a square, each one fitted with twenty chairs and layers of gold-trimmed tablecloths draped to the floor. The array of tables looked tiny centered in the middle of the spectacular room, but this gathering was VIPs only. The chairs, except for three, looked like they were designed for human anatomy. There was one quite ornate chair in the middle of one table. Its seat was several inches higher than the others and was presumably to be occupied by the queen. To the right of that chair was a wider chair, about the same height, that looked more like a bench with a back. And finally, there was another ornate high chair directly next to Andi for Uriah.

"That figures," Jon said. "That suck up Uriah managed to weasel himself a spot right next to the queen."

Geof nodded. "I'm not surprised."

The tables were buried beneath plate after plate of sumptuous, nostril-pleasing cuisine. Nothing looked familiar, but the aromas were seductive. Jon said, "I have no idea what this stuff is, but I am so starved I could eat anything."

"Yeah, it's unnatural to get this hungry. Where are all the convenience stores anyway?" Geof said without a hint of humor.

Jon cocked his head. "I was wondering that too."

All chairs were quickly filled with a precision suggesting the existence of name cards, but there were none. When everyone was settled, Queen Andi entered the room and was seated with appropriate fanfare. Constantine followed her and then, surprisingly, the two cats. Maximilian and Crystal nonchalantly hopped on the bench between Andi and Constantine and assumed classic lazy cat positions. Clark was situated on the row of tables to their right between Edgal and an unknown Erud.

An exceptionally beautiful woman with long dark hair and darker eyes eased into a chair next to Jon. When seating was complete, Andi addressed the room. "Tonight is a night long-awaited. It is a night both we and our ancestors have hoped for, and at the same time, dreaded. We have lived under the threat of war and annihilation for far too long, and it is clear that we can no longer trust the peace we have enjoyed. Never in our history has our way of life been so threatened. But in this increasingly precarious time, we have been comforted by the Song for Tomorrow. We find security in its promise that a Searcher from a foreign land will come into our home and restore peace to Sergel-tuteron."

An elegant black man sitting next to Geof turned to him and said in a deep, muffled voice, "The queen talks about you."

Geof squirmed uncomfortably in his chair. A strained "Nice," was the only response he could muster.

Andi continued her remarks, making eye contact with Geof, "You are in the presence of Lantuc's elite. Our best leaders, artists, engineers, architects, and scientists have gathered to meet and learn from you and teach you."

Geof locked eyes with Andi for a moment but quickly looked away. In any dimension, it is impossible to win a staredown with a dog.

"We have much to talk about, but now dine and enjoy the best of Lantuc." With that, Andi pushed her purple robe to one side and began to eat.

Jon reached out and snagged what looked like a drumstick, but it was greenish and clearly a plant. He bit into it and smiled broadly once his taste buds captured it. With a half-full mouth, he called down the row to Geof, "Dude, these are really good." He leaned back in his chair and looked at the stunning woman to his left, who smiled and nodded at him approvingly.

"Do you mind telling me what all this stuff is?" he asked, finally accomplishing a swallow.

"Yes, of course," she said in a melodious voice that validated her beauty. "What you have in your hand is targa. These are royalons," she said, pointing to a heaping plate of round pasta-looking things. "And these, these are very special," she said with pride. "These are ansparg." The woman stabbed a circular fork into what looked like the vegetable version of a starfish. "These are a delicacy we have not had in Lantuc for some time."

"Why is that?" Pat asked.

The woman lowered her voice. "They were only grown in Mu-jin. Until tonight I did not even know they existed anymore."

Pat looked surprised. "You mean they do not grow them there now?"

Sadness overwhelmed the woman's face. "They can no longer grow much of anything. That is why legions of divisions have been consumed by starving Mu-jin citizens."

"Consumed.... what does that mean? What does that mean?"

The woman lowered her eyes in shame. "It means Prince Uriah and Queen Andi would have a very short life in Mu-jin."

Jon looked at Uriah, who was happily chomping away. "Oh my God."

"If they are starving and the Eruds are so smart, why do the Eruds not help them?" Pat cross-examined. "Why don't those Agrons give them food if they have so much?"

"What can we do? Bu-usah would never allow it. He needs us to be his villains."

"Time out," Jon gestured like a basketball referee. He motioned to Geof to join him, which he did. "Seems like I heard that before," he said to the attractive lady. "Did you say Mu-jin was across a—a great sea."

"Yes, the Great Sea."

"Not just a little sea now, but a great sea," Jon moaned. "Why can't it just be a little pond or something like that?"

Geof approached Jon and leaned over him. "Wait a minute, wait a minute. If there is this great sea, how did Jok-imo get here? This isn't adding up."

"I dunno," Jon shrugged. But I think it's time we ask baldy over there a few questions." He stood up and motioned to Constantine.

Constantine bowed to Andi and walked around the table. Jon and Geof stepped a few feet away from the others and greeted him.

"We need a little geography lesson," Geof said. "What's the deal with this Great Sea business?"

"The Great Sea separates Mu-jin from the other Karrolls."

"Yeh. That minor detail was left out when you were talking to Jok-imo. I mean, what was all that stuff about him escaping Bu-usah City and not knowing if he was still in Mu-jin or not. How could he not know if he was still in Mu-jin if he had to cross a great sea? If it's so great, doesn't it have waves or anything that might tip someone off he was on *water*?" Geof's exaggerated and loud pronunciation of the word "water" unnerved Constantine.

Constantine fidgeted and moved the boys further from the table. He drew them close and in a quiet voice said, "When King Bu-usah came to power, it was clear to the elders in the Secret City that the Great Sorrow would not be the last war. Bu-usah's strategy was to use the peace to gain time to become stronger and attack again. Knowing this, the Eruds sent a courageous band of volunteers to live in the land of Mu-jin as subjects to the king. Halb-ean was one of those volunteers."

"Whoa, you mean this Halb-ean guy was a spy and Jok-imo is actually a Secret City-an or a Lantucian or, you know... one of you guys?"

"Yes, but he does not know it. He was a baby when Halb-ean took him to Mu-jin. His father is an even greater hero than Jok-imo realizes. He lived his life in Mu-jin and helped to keep us informed about the treachery of Bu-usah. Much of what we know is from Halb-ean. We have done our best to prepare for Bu-usah, but we do not have the warriors or the military minds to confront him successfully. The sad part about it is that Halb-ean almost made it to where he could have possibly had some influence. But it is rumored he may have been suspected by Bu-usah's daughters Trixi-lyn or Irishka-ru."

"You mean that nut job has two daughters?" Jon asked.

"Yes," Constantine answered. "But little is known of them except that they are said to be the most beautiful in all of Mu-jin."

Geof and Jon looked at each other and nodded approvingly. "Oh man, this is like mondo complicated," Geof said, scratching his head. "So why wasn't Jok-imo in on it?"

Constantine shrugged. "He was too young to understand and may have put them both in danger should he talk too freely, or even worse, become loyal to Bu-usah. He will be told when the time is right. We have to be sure. Remember what we told you before. Deception is our biggest weapon."

"That still doesn't answer the part about the sea," Jon pushed.

Constantine took a deep breath. "What I tell you now is putting the lives of everyone in Lantuc in your hands. None have this knowledge except for the queen, Spoto, her most trusted confidants, and a handful of our spies in Mu-jin. If anyone in Mu-jin found out, our civilization would be in the gravest danger."

"Spoto? Who is Spoto?"

Constantine pointed to the large grizzly dog. "He is Spoto."

"That figures," Jon said. "So, what's the big secret?"

"Before she was queen, Andi discovered a cavern, much like the one you are in now. It was near the edge of the Great Sea. Guided by Maximillian and Crystal, she explored the cave and found that it went under the sea. They followed the cave and three lumens later, found themselves in a remote region of Mu-jin. The cave goes all the way from one Karroll to another under the Great Sea. With the help of Stevloyd, Jok-imo was blindfolded and taken through this cave from Mu-jin to here. He was on land all the time and had no way of knowing if he ever left Mu-jin or not. He still does not know for sure where he is, and we will keep it that way until he proves himself."

"Stevloyd? Who is Stevloyd?" Geof asked.

"The man sitting next to you," Constantine said, pointing at the black man with his hand resting on Geof's empty chair. "He is honored in Lantuc and is most valuable when traveling through the caves."

"Whaddaya think?" Jon looked at Geof.

Geof shrugged. "You can't make this stuff up."

"The cave is the only way then?" Jon asked. "Don't you have any flying dragons or anything?"

"What is a dragon?"

"Nothing. I just expected one to pop up sooner or later. I mean, what good is a place like this with no dragon?"

"We have the giant condors, but Bu-usah has imprisoned them."

"Are condors great big birds? We have condors in our world, and they are pretty big but not big enough to carry a human."

"Yes, they could carry you."

"Random," Jon shook his head. "That sounds more fun than trudging through another cave for days."

"It's weird that animals here are so accepted, and in Mu-jin, they are so mistreated," Geof said.

"Animals?" Constantine quizzed.

"You know. Everybody not like us we call animals."

Constantine explained, "In Sergel-tuteron, all citizens have value. But in Mu-jin, some are treated cruelly, and they will be treated cruelly here if Bu-usah crosses the Great Sea."

It became clear why Queen Andi became Andi the rug dog in the presence of Jok-imo. If he saw Andi the queen, the jig would be up, and he would know where he was and who he was talking to.

Feeling that Geof and Jon had heard enough, Constantine invited them to return to the table. "Relax tonight. There is much to do to prepare you for your journey."

Geof grabbed his arm. "Look. I want to know more about this Sceptre business."

"Tomorrow," Constantine said tersely.

Constantine returned to his place without further comment. Debbie and Pat intercepted the boys and peppered them with questions. "What did he say? Did you learn anything? Do we know what to do next?"

Geof and Jon gave an abbreviated version of their conversation that left everybody confused. As the evening progressed, the Searchers, as they now resigned themselves to being called, became acquainted with a dazzling variety of Lantuc talent and intellect. They got the CheatNotes history of Lantuc... the basics of their energy system, and how their government worked. It was interesting, but most importantly, they gained tips on how to survive in Mu-jin.

As the evening came to a close, Geof glanced in the direction of Clark. He was huddled with Edgal and another man in deepest conversation, oblivious to anyone else around him. Geof could not for the life of himself figure out what Clark could possibly be saying that would command so much attention, or maybe he was just listening. Either way, Geof learned one thing this night. It was time for the Searchers to surrender to the Song for Tomorrow. He looked at Jon, Debbie, Pat, and Clark and he knew. He just knew.

CHAPTER 20

Breakfast: The Most Important Meal of the Day

The Searchers were provided with sleeping quarters commensurate with castle living. Everyone slept comfortably on a night when their minds should have been enslaved by visions of uncertain days ahead. Such sleepless nights were yet to come.

A knock at the door signaled that the grizzly dogs had arrived to take their guests to breakfast. Waiting for the Searchers were Uriah, Queen Andi, Constantine, Edgal, Stevloyd, and the two ever-present cats. Debbie and Pat were seated at the round table directly across from Edgal, giving them a good view.

"You must pay close attention to what you learn from us," Andi said. "Geof, Jon, and Patricia will accompany Stevloyd to receive instructions for their journey. Clark will accompany Edgal, and Debbie will remain with me."

Stevloyd smiled at Geof and said in a deep, resonant voice, "Hello again."

"S'up Stevloyd?"

"I will be your guide to Mu-jin. The cave has its dangers, and no one knows them better than I. Once we are in Mu-jin, you will be under the supervision of Jok-imo."

"Hey, yeah. Jok-imo. Where is that guy anyway?" Jon asked Constantine.

"He will not be joining us until it is time to depart. And at that time, he will return the same way he came."

"You... you mean you must blindfold him again?" Pat asked.

"It must be, for the safety of all. He is not allowed to see anything outside these walls."

Geof cocked his head. "Uhhh... hold on now. Are you saying that the guy who is to be our protector and guide in Neverland is so untrustworthy that he still has to be blindfolded in the magic tunnel?"

"It is a necessary precaution."

"So, once we get on the other side and the blindfold comes off, he could turn on us and we would become Mu-jin slaves, right?"

"We think it unlikely. But he will not be given his vision until the entrance to the tunnel is far away and once again hidden. He will not know where he has been."

"So, you guys will be safe back here while we're thrown to the wolves...or snake."

"But you see Geof, Lantuc will be preserved, and that is the most important thing." Constantine snapped his head like he had just made an unarguable point.

"I don't mean to contradict you, pal, but we think us being preserved is pretty important too."

"Do not get me wrong, Jon. We will take every precaution to protect you. You know how important you are to the survival of our very society. And we have done much to prepare Jok-imo."

Jon shook his head.

"He's right, Jon," Clark stepped in. "Minimizing casualties is the prime goal of any operation."

"Well, thank you General Patton."

Andi walked around the table and stood next to Jon. She looked at him intently before speaking. "Jon, if you fail… if the Song is somehow wrong, it will be the end of all of us. We have friends in Mu-jin who are willing to die to protect you if Jok-imo is not true to you."

"And how will we recognize these so-called friends?" Geof asked.

"My brother will know them," Andi said.

"Your brother? Now there's a brother?"

Andi stepped back. "Introduce yourself, my brother."

Uriah hopped off his chair and strutted to Andi's side. "Greetings. I am Uriah de Lancer, Prince of Lantuc and First Defender of the Secret City."

"Why you little sneak," Jon snapped. "All this stuff about Lantuc being a legend was all BS."

"Oh no. Lantuc is a legend to everyone outside Lantuc. Just not to me."

"And all this homey little wifey and daughter business was a dirty lie..." Debbie's prosecution was interrupted by Uriah.

"Oh no. They are my mate, or wife, and daughter. And I am the, or rather a guardian of the mountain. We use—"

"Deception," Geof cut in. "Your biggest weapon. And we fell for it like a . . . like a . . ."

"Bunch of high school kids?" Pat assisted.

"Thanks," Geof nodded.

"Do not underestimate yourselves," Andi reassured. "You are here for a purpose. I know you look weak, have no judgment, and possess limited skills, but you—"

"Okay, okay. We get the message," Geof said, waving his hands in front of his chest.

"You know what? She's right," Jon said. "Forget all that Song for Tomorrow jazz. In a few days, we'll be singing 'How Do You Like Me Now?'"

"You better believe it," Geof said. "I want to know about this Sceptre. That's what this is all about, isn't it?"

"You are correct, my friend," Uriah wagged.

"So?"

"During the time of the Great Sorrow, Sergel Tuteron vanquished the Mu-jin army and sent King Bu-usah home a bitter and vengeful man. He was determined to destroy the Secret City and Sergel Tuteron."

Clark brightened. "You said before that nobody knew how the giant crystals were activated. You guys think that Sceptre had something to do with it, don't you?"

Uriah handed off the question to Constantine. "Maybe. And the fact that Bu-usah may gain permission to use it is a most unsettling thing."

Pat stroked her long, blonde hair. "I do not understand. Permission?"

"There is a legend about the Sceptre. The legend says that permission to unleash the Sceptre's powers may only be given to its accepted custodian."

"And I just bet that Sergel Tuteron was such a custodian," Geof said confidently.

"And maybe he used it to activate the crystals that turned the Mu-jinians' brains to mush." Clark nearly hyperventilated as the pieces of a puzzle fell into place.

"It would seem so."

Geof was skeptical. "I don't get it. If the Secret City is so secret, and even you can't seem to tell if Sergel Tuteron is alive or dead, how did the maniac king from across this gigantic, foreboding sea wind up with the Sceptre?"

"It is one of the most shameful events in our history. Sergel Tuteron took pity on one named Vandun. He was unattractive and an outcast in his youth. The one person who never mistreated him was Sergel Tuteron."

"I can see where this is going," Geof said. "No good deed goes unpunished."

"As Sergel Tuteron gained prominence in the Secret City, Vandun earned his friendship and confidence. Sadly, over time Vandun became jealous of him. Vandun watched Sergel

Tuteron receive accolades and prestige for his work. He felt that he should share in the glory and recognition but did not. Even though Sergel Tuteron always treated him well, he became resentful. To bolster Vandun's spirit, Sergel Tuteron entrusted him with a secret mission to deliver something of great importance to Agron or parts nearby. Nobody knows what it was or why it was important."

"Let me fast forward this thing," Jon took over. "Vandun stole the Sceptre, grabbed his bailout bag, and zipped over to Mu-jin, where he cut a deal with Bu-usah. I bet right now he lives some kind of cushy life in Mu-jin where he gets the props he never got in the Secret City. Am I close?"

"You understand," Constantine said. "He is now a powerful man in the court of Mu-jin, perhaps the most powerful man. Bu-usah gave him the honored name of Vandu-un."

"I have questions," Debbie said. "If Bu-usah has the Sceptre, why doesn't he just use it to destroy the Secret City? And two, does this Vandu-un creep know about the cave they are going to be walking around in?"

"Ahhhh. You must remember that I said the Sceptre's powers are only accessible to its custodian. We do not believe that either Bu-usah or Vandu-un have the moral authority to be its custodian. And no, Vandun has no knowledge of the cave or Lantuc."

"Well, that part's good."

Jon nodded. "I think that's why Bu-usah wants Sergel Tuteron so bad. He needs him because right now, the Sceptre is nothing but a fancy stick. Maybe he thinks if he kills Sergel Tuteron, he can somehow inherit the juice to supercharge the Sceptre. Or maybe he can force Sergel Tuteron to give him the secret."

Geof tried to make sense of the goulash of information. "I think I understand the mission. You want us to go to Mu-jin and snag the Sceptre. But what good is it if Sergel Tuteron has headed off into the sunset?"

"You must understand that the important thing is that Bu-usah does not have it. There is an inscription on the Sceptre which may unlock its secret. Even the Eruds do not know the translation. If Bu-usah stumbles onto its meaning, it is the end of our world, and maybe yours. The Sceptre must be returned at all costs."

The discussion continued into exhaustion. The next few days would be jammed with information on Mu-jin weaponry, Mu-jin customs, and most importantly, detailed diagrams of Bu-usah's castle. The Lantucians did not know the exact location of the Sceptre. Their best guess was near the base of the highest tower where they believed lived the giant two-headed snake. Although no one from Lantuc had actually seen the snake, Jok-imo swore that Halb-ean saw it and reported that it was very real and very terrifying. Jonster the Monster and the Bear, for the first time in their academic history, found it prudent to pay close attention to their lessons.

Andi addressed the Searchers. "It must now be clear how perilous our situation is and how ill-equipped we are to deal with it. We have taught you everything we can, and now we shall learn from each other on a more specialized basis. Constantine…"

"Uhh, before we go… wherever, I have a DQ," Geof said. "If you know so much about this Sceptre and where it probably is, why don't you just send in one of your own homeys and get the stinkin' thing? What do you need a bunch of kids who don't know… well don't really know anything?"

"A fair question," Andi answered. "You must understand that Vandun knew many people in Sergel-tuteron. Only a true outsider can be completely safe from recognition."

Constantine took over and pointed at Clark. "You are to go with Edgal."

"Lucky dog," Debbie winked to a giggling Pat.

Geof overheard his beloved's annoying adoration of Edgal. He squinted his eyes at Edgal and curled his upper lip like Elvis, but he wasn't thinking, "Thank you very much."

"Debbie, you are to remain with the queen. There is much she wants to learn from you."

This really confused Geof. What, in the name of Lantuc, could the queen of this snazzy place think she can learn from a sixteen-year-old farm brat like Debbie? The one consolation was she wouldn't be getting lessons from Edgal.

"Geof, Jon and Patricia, please accompany Uriah and Stevloyd."

With that, Andi left the room followed by Constantine.

The Bear grabbed Clark's trembling arm and momentarily separated him from Edgal. "Remember the Superman inside you," he winked.

Clark straightened his back and said, "Thanks."

Debbie turned to wave at her friends as she exited. "See you all soon," she chirped, blowing a kiss.

"Bye, bye, bye."

CHAPTER 21

Clark

Edgal led Clark down a large stone ramp where two horses were waiting.

"Oh no. Not horses again."

"You need to get used to this, my friend," Edgal laughed.

A horse dutifully lowered his head to facilitate Clark's unsteady mount. "You see? Already it becomes easy for you," Edgal said, still laughing.

"Haha," Clark whimpered.

After a short ride, Edgal dismounted in front of a large building with a square front embellished with the same gold trappings as other buildings. It boasted two enormous statues of warriors on either side of the front door, men of battle who seemed out of place in peaceful Lantuc.

Clark slid awkwardly off his horse but managed to land on his feet. He followed Edgal into the building and was greeted by an enormous room filled with an impressive assortment of military paraphernalia. In the middle was a twenty-foot square table boasting models of buildings with a castle on one end. On the felt surface were models of ships and miniature armies. This was Clarkland as he never imagined. "Wow," Clark was giddy as he walked around the table. "This looks like a macro version of get-a-life night in Sheridan."

"I am sorry. What night?"

"Oh," Clark explained. "Every Friday night, a group of us get together to stage wars and replay historical battles. We call it war night, but the anti-nerd crowd calls it get-a-life night."

"I do not understand."

"Doesn't matter," Clark said. "This... this is fantastic."

"There are many wars in your world, is it not so?" Edgal asked.

"Countless," Clark answered sadly.

"Do your people like war?" Edgal asked with childish innocence.

"Well, uh, no. No, no, no. Everybody hates war. But we seem to be pretty good at it." Clark's voice trailed off when he realized he was mired in ironic quicksand.

"That is why you were sent. You are to use your skills to defeat the Mu-jin army."

"What do you mean sent here?" Could it be peaceful Lantuc was seeking military help from a nerd kid who would be kicked out of boot camp the first hour? And now it sounded like they recruited him.

Edgal picked a piece of the model off the floor and carefully set it back on the table. "You know. Sent by the Song."

"Yeah, I keep getting reminded." The Song again. The musical bible of Sergel-tuteron hung around Clark's neck like a millstone.

"Over here is Mu-jin," Edgal pointed. "And these are the Mu-jin ships. If their ships are able to enter our harbor, we will be destroyed. They must be stopped before the Gates as Sergel Tuteron did before."

"The Sergel Tuteron plan worked fantastically. Why not do it again?"

"No Sergel Tuteron. No Sceptre. And we think the next attack will come during the lumen. Besides, we do not know how it worked."

"Hmmm."

"You said you play war games. Can you show us some games that might help us?"

OMG, Clark thought. *He doesn't know the difference between real war games and my games. He must think I am some kind of military genius. I have to tell the truth before I get everyone killed.*

Edgal missed Clark's distress. "So, if this was your war game, what would you do?"

Clark's mind was in a panic. *I can't do this. I wish I could just fly away.* Wait... Flying. Clark was reminded of one of his favorite movies, *Flight of the Phoenix.* A group of doomed men saved themselves by geeking-out a crashed airplane and making it fly. But the thing was, a model airplane designer, not an airline engineer reassembled the plane and made it fly. This was the same principle. Clark just had to imagine that he was strategizing for get-a-life night. These weren't real people, just models. And if it worked on the table, it should work on land. That is how generals do it anyway. See it, be it.

Clark decided to be it. "I don't suppose you have any bombs or torpedoes?"

Edgal shrugged.

"Didn't think so." Clark's fingertips tapped the frame of his glasses. "Think Clark, think." He studied the table and asked, "Is this the real shape of the sea? What about the harbor?"

"That is the harbor right here," Edgal said, pointing at a piece of blue felt surrounded by steep cliffs near the shores of what Clark assumed was the Secret City.

"Is that what it looks like?"

"Not exactly," Edgal answered as he massaged the blue felt sea to proper dimensions.

There was a very narrow strip of blue between the sea and the harbor. "How many warships can come through this harbor opening side by side?"

"We call it the Gates. One ship. Two if they are small."

The solution jumped out at Clark. "We can crash the ships as they reach the mouth of the harbor. This would block other ships. Sailors on the wrecked ships would be sitting ducks for Erud archers on the cliffs above. But even if we block the harbor, couldn't they just land near a beach somewhere and get to the city that way?"

"The Secret City sits high in the cliffs. There is no beach. The creators of the Secret City built it that way."

"So, the waterway through the Gates is the only way in?"

"It is the only way that would not be certain death. The land of Mu-jin lies on one side of the Great Canyon while Agron and Erud are on the other. But of course, they are far apart. The Great Canyon has many dangers and would claim any army that dared to cross it."

Nice world, Clark thought. *Everything is great. Great Sea, Great Hall, Great Canyon, and below-average general.* "Let me ask you something," he said. "How is it you have all this cool stuff in here when you have no army?"

"We have had visitors from your world before, and they provided us with information to build these models."

"And where are these people now? Can't they help you?"

"I do not know. They were from long ago. Queen Alma knows much. But she knows little of war machines. Others came long before, but their knowledge in matters of war was ancient compared to you, General. We do not know how to make war. We are creators and thinkers, artists, and scientists."

It was true. The ship models, intricate and impressive, were all sailing ships. Whoever brought these plans had no concept of modern warfare at all.

Clark cleaned his glasses with this shirttail. "How do we block the harbor so it can't be cleared from the Mu-jin side?" This was the kind of problem Clark would love under normal circumstances. A riddle, wrapped in a mystery, inside an enigma. The Eruds had no weapons to speak of, limited personnel, and no military training. He needed something

with very little human involvement. Clark thought hard and waited as the answer faded in like a sunrise.

Clark smiled at Edgal. "Have... you... ever heard of Archimedes?"

"No."

"Well, I like to think of him as the original nerd, and I say that with the utmost pride."

"I don't—"

"Let me tell you a story."

Edgal leaned back against a display table, folded his arms across his chest, and listened.

"There was this powerful civilization called the Roman Empire. They were conquerors of pretty much the whole world in their time. They were in one way very progressive but in another way, very cruel and backward."

Edgal raised his eyebrows at the contradiction.

"Anyway, the Romans, for some reason, and they never really seemed to need a reason, decided to conquer this city called Syracuse. Syracuse was much like the Secret City, except instead of cliffs, they had high walls guarding the city. And these walls were quite near the edge of the sea just like your cliffs."

"So what does this Archim... Arkimmee..."

"Archimedes. Well, he was like Sergel Tuteron, the most brilliant man in a time of many brilliant men. One of his many talents was to devise weapons which were far ahead of his time."

"What weapons?"

"One was the Claw which could accomplish exactly what we want in the harbor... IF you can build it."

"Claw? Like on a bird?"

"Exactly." Clark found some drawing paper. "Can I use this?"

"Yes."

Clark took the paper and drew a respectable rendering of the Archimedes Claw. "It was a simple but ingenious device that, employing proper use of levers and pulleys, enabled a large crane to reach over the walls of Syracuse, grab the bow of a large ship with a gigantic iron claw, lift it partway out of the water, and capsize it. We could build these on the cliffs and clog the entrance with their own ships." Clark reached across the table, fashioned his hand like a claw, plucked a ship a few inches off the table, and dropped it on its side.

At that moment, Geof, Jon, and Pat walked into the armory accompanied by Uriah and Stevloyd.

"Greetings, Earthling," Geof called out jovially to Clark. "We come in peace."

"Good," Clark responded. "I was just telling Edgal that I think the Archimedes Claw could work to defend the Secret City from a sea attack."

Jon and Pat looked at each other and shrugged. Geof, a fellow Archimedes fan, walked up to the battle panorama and looked it over closely. "Interesting idea," he said to Clark's honor. "Where would you put them?"

"I was thinking on the cliffs above the harbor."

"How do you know the ships would get close enough for the Claw to get them? And, do you know if the Eruds have the means and materials to build them?"

"Those are good questions, Geof. You'd make a good nerd."

Jon chortled at the comment and received the snake eye from his big friend.

"Of course, I haven't seen it, but from what Edgal says, it would be sufficiently close. And the cliffs are layered so we wouldn't have to put them all the way on top."

"What about materials and time?"

Clark looked out the corner of his eye. "These are large machines, but they are simple machines."

"It would be difficult, but possible," Edgal said.

"That means you shouldn't waste any time," Geof counseled.

"We must leave for the Secret City with haste," Edgal ordered.

Clark looked up at Geof. "Whatever happens, thank you. Nobody ever gave me the chance to do something special before. In fact, nobody ever gave me the chance to do anything."

"No worries…"

"But I'm scared to death."

Geof slapped Clark's back. "Always remember what my dad says, the geek—"

"Shall inherit the earth. I know." He took a lingering look at three friends who looked back at him and smiled. With his back a little straighter, and his head a little higher, Clark whirled and followed Edgal out of the building, leaving Jonster the Monster and the Bear wondering if they would ever see their unique new friend again.

CHAPTER 22

Debbie

Debbie followed Andi to a room dripping with luxury. Maximillian and Crystal lounged on a round platform covered with pillows. Debbie instinctively went over to pet the two cats, but Crystal's icy white eyes froze her in her tracks.

Debbie stepped back and looked at Andi. "What is the deal with these kitties anyway? They're always hanging around you. And that Crystal, I've never seen eyes like that. It's like she's looking right through me. She scares me."

"Maximillian and Crystal are my most trusted friends."

"You mean there is somebody in Lantuc who is not your friend? This place makes Disneyland look like a den of thieves."

"Disneyland?"

"It's just a place. So why am I here anyway? It sucks that my friends will be in danger while I'm in the safety of... wherever I am."

Andi paced around the room before answering Debbie's question. "You are... you have... the qualities to accomplish things of greatest importance to Lantuc and Sergel-tuteron."

"Qualities? What qualities?"

"You are aligned with Maximillian and Crystal and their people. It is a bond born at the beginning of your life. We must all have patience. But your destiny will soon be revealed as it is with all of us."

"And right now, it's me and the cats? Whoopee! I get the cats! What do they have to do with anything?"

"I met Maximillian and Crystal long ago. It is from them I learned of the cave your friends will take to enter Mu-jin. They are fortunate that the entrance is very well hidden in both Lantuc and Mu-jin."

"*They* are fortunate... ?"

"The hidden entrances are for the protection not only of Lantuc but also for Crystal and Maximilian. The cave must remain the most sacred secret."

"Protection? Are the kitties in danger?"

The word "kitties" was foreign to Andi, but as Debbie had used it twice to refer to the felns, she decided it was no insult. "I am afraid you do not understand, my dear." Andi's voice took on a more serious tone. "Maximillian and Crystal did not find the cave. They *came* from it. I was out walking near the cave and fell into a hole. Maximillian and Crystal left the protection of Dorotel, their home in the cave, and rescued me. They put their lives in danger to save mine."

"Dorotel? Is that a Karroll? You mean there is another place we haven't heard of?"

"My child," Andi said, hopping up on her bed, "there are places *we* have not heard of. We know there is a world below the surface of the cave and may even be below Lantuc itself. It is called Elstrom. Elstrom has many lands of its own such as Dorotel, and in them live creatures we have never seen."

"But if Max and Crystal came from Elstrom, couldn't they tell you all about it?"

"Only what they know. Maximillian has told me that Elstrom has many worlds. It is like a honive."

"A honive?"

Andi thought for a moment and made a buzzing sound. "Bzzzzzzzzzz."

"Oh. Oh!" Debbie cried. "Bees. Like a beehive." She drew a crude picture of a beehive with her finger on the table.

"Yes, bees… stigs," Andi said. "The Rodarts live not far below the surface of the cave in Sydtel. The felns live below them in Dorotel. Crystal has also seen unknown divisions in the corridor that connects the cave to Sydtel and Dorotel. She says they live below Dorotel."

"So how do the kitties survive with all these crazy creatures running around?"

"The entrance to Dorotel is small and hidden. The Rodarts cannot enter."

"Okay, if the Rodarts are between Dorotel and the cave, how did Crystal and Max get by them? And how will Geof get by them?"

"Felns are fast and can evade the Rodarts with ease. The Rodarts no longer try to catch them."

Debbie's brown eyes lit up. "That's why Stevloyd is going with them," she said excitedly. "He's going to stop the Rodarts, isn't he? So how do we get to the Secret City?"

"There are three cave entrances to Lantuc. One brought you here, and there is the one which the Searchers will take to Mu-jin."

"And the third?"

"The third links Lantuc and the Secret City. It is the journey you shall take. It is safe."

"Are there Rodarts in that cave?"

"There are no Rodarts," Andi answered calmly. "As far as we know, the Rodarts live only in the two caves. The third cave is on the other side of Lantuc. It allows us to move freely between Lantuc and the Secret City undetected."

"Queen Andi, that is some story, but I still don't know how I can protect Max and Crystal, especially if I am cooped up in a castle somewhere. They seem pretty safe here without me."

The queen's reply was unexpected. "I want you to take them with you to your world when you return."

Debbie stared at the queen, her emotions pulling her in a thousand directions.

"Maximillian and Crystal are the critical link with Elstrom. If they were lost, the consequences would be catastrophic."

"I would be honored to host them, but I can't even get close to Crystal. I don't think she has any intention of going anywhere with me."

"It is true you need time to adjust to each other. But it is crucial. You will do what is needed. Of this, we are certain."

Debbie figured the term "adjust" was Lantuc-speak for bond. "And you're not going to tell me why it is so important?"

"In due time. For now, look within yourself, and you will see that you are a Lantucian."

"What does that mean? Can I see my friends before they, or we, leave?"

"Of course, dear. We will be with them shortly."

Debbie smiled at Andi, bucked up her courage, and went to sit next to the cats one more time. She slowly reached out her hand to touch Crystal on the head. This time, Crystal did not resist but closed her eyes and purred. Max scooted next to Crystal. Debbie grinned at Andi.

"You see?" The queen smiled.

CHAPTER 23

Of Beauty, Sceptres, and Cats

Queen Andi shepherded Debbie down a long, statue-embedded hall to a room a short walk away. They arrived at a typically large wooden door with a life-sized carving of a human figure holding a spear in his left hand. Andi stopped short of the door and stood motionless. The gnarly right hand of the figure reached out and released the lock. The built-in doorman smiled kindly at Debbie and motioned for her to enter.

She was relieved to see Geof and Jon standing a few feet inside the door. Pat was not in immediate view, but the quiet manner of the boys assured her that all was well, but not normal. They were dressed in Mu-jin style tunics. Each was fashionably attired in a white, knee-length kilt with the classic Mu-jin two-headed snake on the front.

The guys fixed their eyes on Debbie, expecting approval. Something along the lines of "you look great" or "great legs" would be nice. Although such thoughts attempted to navigate their way past Debbie's lips, they were intercepted by uncontrollable laughter. Debbie sniffed, wiped laughter tears from her eyes, and managed a weak "sorry."

Jon squinted his right eye. "Laugh it up. We feel like a couple of refugees from a battle of the bagpipe bands."

"I think you look very handsome. Both of you. It's just a little, you know, surprising."

"Awww, don't worry about it," Jon dismissed. "We think it's kinda funny too."

"Speak for yourself," Geof grumped. It was *his* heartthrob that was laughing, not Jon's. "Wait till Pat gets a load of this."

It was a short wait. A door at the farthest end of the ornate room swung open to introduce a large woman dressed conservatively in a below-the-knee skirt and matching blouse. Her hair was gray and was short-cropped above her ears. She walked directly toward them. As she got closer, the woman smiled broadly at Queen Andi and said, "I hope you approve, Your Majesty."

With that, the woman stepped aside to reveal a girl who strongly resembled Patricia Chamness. She was dressed in a midriff-revealing white tunic skirt. Her arms were sleeveless from the shoulder, and her neckline was a smart V-shape, dipping just below the collarbone. Her light blonde hair cascaded around either side of her neck and fell perfectly over her shoulders. Her short skirt, also pure white, was accented by slits up either side, reaching halfway between her waist and knee. On each arm, a gold bicep bracelet in the shape of a snake completed the picture. She looked like she was born to wear this tunic.

"Hi guys," she said.

"Msoib dnob fmonir," Jon flummoxed.

"I'm... I'm sorry, Jon. I didn't understand you."

"Mmmmfgmmmm."

Geof pushed Jon forward. "He bit his tongue and can't talk."

Debbie giggled at the crude face-saving measure. Pat pretended to accept Geof's cryptic explanation without question. "Sorry, Jon. I know that hurts."

Jon nodded thank you. "Smooooth pal. Some lady's man," Geof smirked. But he had to admit she looked devastating.

The large woman broke up the Pat Adoration Society by grabbing Jon's arm and examining his costume. Her assessment concluded with a nod of approval, followed by a similar appraisal of Geof. "They are as ready as I can make them, Your Majesty."

"Well done, Artemenk," Andi nodded. Artemenk was a close confidante of the queen and had served as Royal Clothier since Andi's crowning. The responsibility to make the Searchers indistinguishable from Mu-jinians fell to her, and she was flawless.

"My friends," Andi spoke softly but with authority, "the time has come."

Artemenk made a graceful exit at the same moment Constantine and Uriah entered the room. Constantine surveyed the room with approval. "I apologize to you that we have not had more time to prepare you. Jok-imo tells us that King Bu-usah is readying his armies and ships as we speak. If we hope to be successful with our defense, we must act now. The choice is yours. Are you with us?"

Uriah, Constantine, and Andi waited for a response from the teenagers, but none came.

"*Qui tacet consentire videtur,*" Geof said with a nod.

"Say what?" Jon said, miraculously recovered from his phantom tongue injury.

"Oh, sorry. It's Latin. It means he who is silent is assumed to consent."

There was a group "aha" nod, and Geof gave the Lantucians an "it's all good" wave-off.

Jon smacked Geof on the arm and whispered, "Hey, I just thought of something."

"What? Why are we whispering?"

"They didn't understand."

"Come again?"

"They didn't understand what you said. This Uni thing doesn't work with Latin."

"Hey. You're right. Well, I guess if we want to talk behind their backs, all we have to do is talk Latin."

"Yeah, good idea."

Geof laughed. But it was curious. "Maybe Uni didn't work because Latin is a dead language. And why didn't Constantine the brainiac say something about it?" Definitely curious.

Uriah circled the Searchers like he was about to give a pregame speech. "As you know, Clark has gone to the Secret City. His task is great. I will be accompanying Geof, Jon, and Pat to Mu-jin."

Andi grimaced at the thought of her brother defenseless in a land where dogs were food. There was surely no soul in Sergel-tuteron who could match the courage in Uriah's tiny heart.

"Debbie and Her Majesty will soon be in the Secret City along with Maximillian and Crystal. There will be no second chances for any of us. Each must fulfill his destiny as prophesied by the Song for Tomorrow, or we all fail."

No one moved an eyelid. Geof looked at the strange friends he never knew existed a few days ago and felt honored to be in their presence. "Do you mind if we have a few minutes together?"

Everyone knew what he really wanted and dissolved into the background leaving Geof and Debbie alone in the center of the floor. "Uhhhh... so can you tell me why you're going to the Secret City?"

"I guess so. The queen tells me I am to protect Max... uh... Maximillian and Crystal."

Something was off. "Excuse me," Geof motioned to Andi.

"It's none of my business, but—wait a minute, it *is* my business. I got her into this," Geof said. "If she is supposed to be protecting these cats... er... felns, it seems to me that they would all be safer in a place nobody knows about like Lantuc than in the Secret City, which is, by the way, the worst-kept secret of all time."

"Your questions will be answered in due time. Know now that this is the way it must be. Debbie is of incalculable value to me, Crystal, and your success." Not allowing for further questions, Andi turned and rejoined Constantine and the others.

Geof frowned. That "in due time" thing again. That must be the Lantucian version of the "we'll see" comment he always heard from his dad when he wanted something his dad did not want to give. "Forgive me, Debbie. But I'm just worried about you, and this thing just seems so rand... weird."

"I know. But I still don't know why she chose me for this. She said I was a Lantucian, and you would know why she would call me that."

Geof scratched his head. "Amazingly, I think I do know. I actually do think I know. You are a Lantucian because you have a kind and unselfish heart, and you have a special bond with animals. She knows that you will stop at nothing to protect those cats, whether you understand their importance or not. I don't know how I know this, but I can tell you one hundred percent that without you, we all will fail."

"Really?" Now her face turned red.

"That's how I see it, and, hey, I'm *the Searcher.*"

They looked at each other and laughed. Debbie grabbed Geof's neck and pulled him down to normal person height. She gently kissed him on the upper lip and whispered, "Pity I don't get to wear one of those cool outfits like Pat, isn't it?"

"Tragic," Geof thought he said. His heart was beating so fast he could not hear his own voice. He could only look at Debbie and smile. She smiled back.

Sensing the Geof and Debbie Show was about over, Jon and Pat joined them to offer their farewells. Debbie hugged Pat, then Jon, and turned to leave before things degraded to Kleenex level. "Hey," Geof rebounded enough to yell at her. "Keep an eye on Clark, will ya? Somehow the thought of him building weapons scares the crap out of me."

Debbie smiled and winked. "Take care of yourself." In an instant, the queen and Debbie were gone.

"Are you ready?" Constantine asked.

"Bring 'em on. Bring 'em all on," Geof said. Bolstered by the Debbie kiss, it was he who was now Superman.

"You are the heroes promised in the Song," Constantine said with humility. "I believe it. Capturing the Sceptre could be the single most important act in the history of Sergel-tuteron."

"Oh, good. No pressure," Jon cracked.

"And what about you?" Pat asked.

"I must stay here. I have my own battles to fight. Be safe, my friends."

"Come on," Uriah beckoned. As they left to meet Jok-imo and Stevloyd, Constantine nodded, and the door between them closed itself.

Uriah led the Searchers to a room not far from their previous meeting. Inside they found Stevloyd and Jok-imo, who was comfortably fitted with his blindfold. It seemed unfair. He gave every appearance of being a decent guy. But this was for all the marbles, and there was no room for error. Jok-imo did not like it, but he accepted it.

CHAPTER 24

The Forbidden Garden

The journey out of Lantuc began with a ride on the trusty elevator. It slowed to a stop without sensation. Jok-imo was told he was on a platform where horses would come to take them to Mu-jin. Any subtle movements he might detect were explained away as normal traffic in and around the platform. Geof thought it was a silly explanation, but he closed his eyes, and it actually worked.

It came as no surprise that two grizzly dogs were waiting for them at the top. In fact, it was THE two grizzly dogs. Pat immediately hid behind Geof. "Those guys scare me," she shivered.

"Hello again. We will be accompanying you to Mu-jin," the large grizzly dog said.

"Awesome," Jon shouted. "It will be nice having you watch our backs when we are in Bu-usah's face."

"We are not allowed to enter Mu-jin. Too dangerous for you and for our kind if we did," the smaller grizzly dog said sadly.

"Too dangerous for YOUR kind?" Jon gulped.

"Regrettably, yes. Our division was exterminated in Mu-jin shortly before the Great Sorrow," the large grizzly said, trying to control his emotion. "Once we were the proudest and bravest in all of Mu-jin. We built Mu-jin into a wonderful civilization. But that was before Bu-usah. When we refused to join the unjust assault on the Secret City, Bu-usah sent his killers into our cities and poisoned our water. It took several passes of the lumen to learn what he had done. When it was revealed to us, it was too late. Of all our people, we know of only twenty or so that escaped to Agron. My wife and I were secretly brought to Lantuc, where we now offer our lives to protect the queen. We do not know the fate of our family and friends. We were able to save only three children of Fidoa's sister who now live with us."

"Did you live near the castle of this Bu-usah guy?" Pat asked timidly from the protection of Geof's back.

"No. Most of our people lived in the forest regions near the Great Sea, far from Bu-usah's castle. We only know Bu-usah through his treachery to our people and to Mu-jin."

"I'm so sorry," Geof consoled the grizzlies. "Do you have—I mean, would you tell us your names? You're Spoto, right?"

The big grizzly said, "Yes, I am honored to be called Spoto, and she is Fidoa."

Geof and Jon's eyes locked in amusement. "Spot and Fido?" Jon said under his breath. "They're putting us on."

"Those are honorable names," Geof said before Jon could offer a tasteless comment.

"We were shamed by our Mu-jin names and were given Lantuc names by Queen Alma herself. To be given a name by Queen Alma is a great honor."

"You said you got Fidoa's sister's kids?" Jon asked courteously. "What are their names?" Politeness aside, Geof knew this was a set up for a Jonster the Monster zinger. He shot him a narrow look that warned, "Don't go there."

Spoto replied, "Roveran, Lassing, and Rexe."

"Lovely," Geof smiled.

"Yes, I can see the queen put a lot of thought into them," Jonster added.

Spoto looked at Jon and nodded thanks. Geof stepped up and said, "You know Spoto, there are many of your kind where we come from with very similar names. And those names in our world mean loyalty, love, friendship, and courage. You have every right to be proud."

Jon's embarrassed ears singed, and he took a quick inventory of the situation. He was looking like a jerk to Pat. The grizzlies were there to protect him. The math was pretty simple. "Geof is so right," he said in retreat. "Most people have no control over their names. But yours have been earned."

The landing platform was in an open area that was not larger than fifty feet in diameter. They mounted their horses, and Uriah casually hopped onto the rump of the horse carrying Geof, his head rigidly forward.

"Forward," Stevloyd said. Spoto and Fidoa advanced toward a solid cave wall. They stepped into it without breaking stride and disappeared. The wall still appeared to be there, but it wasn't. Stevloyd entered the wall guiding Jok-imo behind him. Geof followed and held his breath as he glided effortlessly through a swirling gray portal that morphed into cascading colors of increasing brilliance. The clock stood still, as forever and instantaneous fused into one impossible time warp.

Geof fell under the spell of the breathtaking vista that lay before him. The lime green sky bathed its soft light on a jungle garden that stretched to the horizon in every direction. Trees and flowers of every imaginable shape and color invaded Geof's eyes until he thought they were going to explode. The Bear flashed a "glad you made it" smile as his friends appeared. The floral brilliance was everywhere. The entrance back to Lantuc was no longer visible. Seconds before, they were in the portal, and now there was not even a hint that an entrance ever existed.

Inside the garden, Stevloyd removed Jok-imo's blindfold freeing him to drink in the beauty that had mesmerized his companions.

"Is this... is this... the Forbidden Garden?" Jok-imo said, his voice trembling with excitement.

"Say what?" Jon smacked. "Did he say *Forbidden Garden*?" Stevloyd nodded.

Jon grunted, "I really hate to ask why it's forbidden."

Uriah hopped from the back of Geof's horse to Jon's with a dexterity that would make a cat envious. "The Forbidden

Garden protects the Secret City from approach by land. In the garden live the noblest and bravest people ever to inhabit Sergel-tuteron, the Chyn. The Garden is sacred to the Chyn, and it is almost certain death to enter without an escort."

"What the hell are we doing here then? Who is our escort?" Jon asked.

"I am," Uriah replied, jutting out his small chest.

"Oh dear," Jon moaned.

A happier Jok-imo looked around the garden in awe. "It is beyond beautiful. Thank you for letting me see this."

Stevloyd shrugged. "The Forbidden Garden is no secret." He knew this would tip Jok-imo off that he was no longer on the Mu-jin side of the Great Sea. But Stevloyd did not think it mattered now.

"We must proceed with haste," Spoto said with a growl that got everybody's attention.

Jok-imo slid from his horse and walked alongside the grizzlies so he could feel as well as see the beauty. Not knowing what piece of sense-delighting flora might be poisonous, prickly, or flesh-eating, Geof, Jon, and Pat elected to stay mounted.

Geof trotted up alongside Jok-imo and tapped him with his foot. "Jok-imo. Can you tell me about this snake?"

"I am told he is about six of you in length and maybe the girth of your horse."

"So, it's forty feet long and fat. Any ideas how we can defeat a thing like that, Jon boy?"

"With a head on each end, it will be impossible to kick its butt, that's for sure."

Geof and Jon laughed. Uriah grimaced. How difficult it was to understand these people from the land of Sheridan.

They rode on silently for hours, trying to concentrate on the majesty of the garden. It was more pleasant than thinking about a forty-foot, two-headed snake. Jon rode up next to Geof and said, "You know, we've been in this garden for hours, and nothing's happened. I just know that pretty quick, one of these guys will say they·saw something move in the bushes, and all hell will break loose. It's in every movie."

"You and your movies," Geof grunted. We're in real life now... or... well... sort of."

Suddenly Uriah and the two grizzlies stiffened and stopped cold.

"Hey," Geof started to say.

"Quiet," Uriah commanded. "We just heard something."

"There it is," Jon said under his breath. "There it is. Boy, I hate being right all the time."

"You weren't right," Geof countered. "You said they would say they saw something, and they said they heard it."

Pat looked sharply at them. "Will you two fools silence?" She glared. "Some*thing* is out there."

Geof and Jon forced a queasy, sorry smile. Spoto and Fidoa silently motioned to the horses to draw close to each other. Everyone surveyed the surrounding area with caution. They reached a spot where there was about fifteen feet of open space between the trail and the edge of the garden, providing a second or two to react to an attack.

Suddenly, Fidoa let out a howl. An arrow was protruding from her right shoulder. Seven blond warriors dressed like Geof and Jon charged out of the dense garden brandishing swords. The two-headed snakes on their kilts danced wildly as they attacked. Pat dove behind Geof and covered her head with her arms.

Geof's horse reared, forcing him to lean forward to keep his balance. His hand felt the ornate handle of a sword attached to the saddle which he instinctively drew and held before him.

The Searchers had only a split second to learn hand-to-hand combat. Neither boy had ever touched a real sword before, let alone used one in battle. When Geof felt the sword in his hand, it was like he had been born holding it. It was not instinct. It was not experience. Someone was giving him on-the-job sword training, and it was graduate-level instruction.

The Mu-jin assassins were within inches of the band when the smallest of the travelers stopped them in their tracks with his patented wide-mouthed roar. The Mu-jinians' momentary disorientation was sufficient for the grizzlies and Stevloyd to act. Spoto charged the ambushers and flattened two of them. Geof jumped from his horse and engaged the closest blond warrior with the skill and aggression of an experienced swordsman. His adversary was quickly dispatched with a swipe that cut him severely on the upper arm. Geof's attention immediately turned to his friend. To his surprise, Jon was holding off two Mu-jinians with his trusty staff, wielding it like the most expert kendo master. Geof ran to help Jon but

was knocked off balance by Fidoa. In her zest for payback, she clamped her jaws around the neck of an unlucky Mu-jin combatant and tossed him flailing helplessly into the garden where he lay motionless.

Spoto took out two more of the attackers with one crushing blow of his powerful arm, and Stevloyd vanquished the last of the Mu-jinians by slicing the back of his calf with a well-aimed thrust. The man tried to disappear into the garden but stopped short and started limping back toward Stevloyd.

Blocking the injured man was a menacing figure astride a tall horse. He had no shirt and cloth pants that dipped just below his knees. Around his neck were several necklaces that looked like they were made of stone and wood. He stood about Geof's height, and slung across his broad shoulders was a bow. His back was covered with arrows placed horizontally, one on top of the other, their method of attachment not visible.

The man was joined by twenty look-a-likes who closed a ring around the Mu-jin soldiers, now cowering in their presence. The Sheridanites were shocked by the facial features of these scary people. They looked just like Donald Deernose, a map of the Wyoming great plains written all over their faces.

Jon drew close to Pat and Geof and looked questioningly at Uriah. Were these familiar-looking-warriors friend or foe? The slightest breath might unleash a series of events that could obliterate the prophecy promised by the Song for Tomorrow.

The ring of braves parted, and a man came forward astride a striking white horse. He was dressed as the others, but more ornately, and his face and body were marked with painted symbols. He was obviously a man of great importance in the garden. He surveyed the scene with a stern and foreboding look that gave little comfort to the strangers. Uriah positioned himself on the back of Jon's horse so that he could be seen by the newcomer.

Uriah spoke with the familiarity of an old friend. "Broken Rope, we greet you with gratitude."

"Broken Rope?" Geof said to Jon. "Like the artist? What's going on?"

"It is I who give thanks that you are unharmed, Prince Uriah. I suffer great shame that these murderers make way into Forbidden Garden and make danger for you. We will deal with them." With that ominous comment, Broken Rope made a slight head gesture, and the Mu-jinians were whisked away.

"What will happen to them?" Pat asked.

"What do you care?" Jon shot back.

"Just wondering."

"My friend Fidoa is injured," Uriah told the chief.

"Come. We shall tend to her wounds and give you rest."

"You are most gracious as always, my friend," Uriah nodded. "Sorry to say, our time is limited."

"I know this. The sacred skins have prepared us for your coming. Your rest will be brief, and we will promise you safe passage to your destination."

Uriah nodded.

"Sacred skins?" Geof and Jon said to each other.

Emerging from her shell, Pat said boldly, "Perhaps some introductions might be in order."

"May I present Broken Rope, chief of the great Chyn people. Chief Broken Rope, I present the Searchers."

The Searchers all waved stiffly, and Broken Rope bowed slightly in recognition. Whoever he was, he seemed to know who they were. Spoto made a gesture to Stevloyd, which resulted in Jok-imo being refitted with his blindfold, an indication that they were about to enter yet another not-too-fun place.

"I am amazed how well Jok-imo accepts that blindfold thing," Geof said. "I don't think I would roll over so easily."

Jon shrugged. "He has no choice."

Uriah horse-hopped again, this time joining Broken Rope. The two engaged in a serious conversation loud enough to be heard, but in a language that was, like Latin, another Uni failure. Uriah did most of the talking, and Broken Rope listened intently, rotating his gaze between the Searchers and the Prince. Broken Rope said something in his native language, and the braves closed ranks in front of Fidoa, leading her off the trail into the garden. Fidoa's shoulder looked bad, but she moved stoically forward as though nothing had happened. None of Broken Rope's men moved to help her. It was a sign of respect, not indifference.

The Chyn guides veered off the trail into a tangle of foliage where visibility was but a few feet. The Chyn navigated their way with ease, mystically finding pathways with sufficient clearance to safely admit a horse and rider. The garden soared above them to a height impossible to gauge because of its density. The canopy was so thick, the sky was only visible in small patches. With such a blanket, the forest should have been dark, but it was comfortably lighted. It appeared the lumen was seemingly not the only source of light for this wondrous place. Some of the plants appeared to give off their own light.

Forced into single file, the group found little opportunity for conversation. Pat was riding directly behind Stevloyd with Geof following her and then Jon. Geof twisted toward Jon.

"Pretty impressive work with that stick, buddy," he said.

"Staff."

"Oh, I forgot... staff."

"Yeah, it's funny. I had no idea what I was doing, and yet I felt like that staff was part of me, like it made me the perfect weapon."

"Yeah, that's how I felt with my sword," Geof beamed.

"Huh? Sword?"

"Ummm, hmmm. Just like the one you have hanging from your saddle. I would rather have that than a big stick in a fight, but that's just me."

Jon looked down and the sword reflected in his eyes. It was impossible to miss now that it was no longer needed. It had slipped down to a position in front of the horse's front leg, and in all the excitement, was not on Jon's radar.

"Oh," he said sheepishly. "Yeah. Sword. Maybe I should use it next time, if there is one."

"Yup. Next time."

The Chyn guided their guests through miles of foliage that, over time, became more forest than garden. The plants and their striking flowers gave way to pine trees. The aroma of pine permeated the air, filling Geof with a feeling of home. Home. It had been only a few days, but it seemed so far away, like maybe Sheridan was the dream, and this craziness was real. Actually, this was real, as real as it gets, at least for now. And home, precious as it was, would have to wait its turn.

Pine needles on the forest floor made a pleasant crunching sound as they were crushed below the horses' hooves. Gradually, a clearing came into view. In it stood a host of pitched teepees... thousands of teepees with thousands of Chyn milling about as far as the eye could see. Aside from the rustic nature of the setting, the community was no different than what one would expect to see in any city in the natural course of a busy day.

The horses were quickly surrounded by what must have been the entire Chyn nation. Happily, their faces were smiling, or at least most of them were. They seemed particularly interested in Uriah, bowing slightly or nodding their heads as he rode by.

"Look at these guys licking Uriah's boots," Jon sneered.

"Yeah. I see that. I guess he really is royalty."

The procession passed endless teepees and came to an abrupt halt in front of a structure that looked more like the longhouses of the northeastern Iroquois than the teepees of the western Plains Indians. It appeared the Chyn utilized the best architecture of more than one Native American tribe.

"Look how many different Indian influences there are in this place," Geof said. "Do you think it's possible that these guys are descended from a bunch of different Native American cultures?"

Jon nodded. "Could be. Or maybe these guys were there first and they are the ancestors."

"Interesting idea. I don't know. The way things are going, I don't imagine we'll ever find out."

Uriah hopped off his horse and motioned for his friends to follow him. Broken Rope bent down and entered the low opening of the longhouse. Uriah stood to one side and ushered the Searchers inside.

"What happened to Jok-imo?" Geof asked.

"He has been taken to another place. He cannot be part of what we will share this day with the Chyn," Uriah explained.

CHAPTER 25

Medicine Man

Broken Rope escorted the Searchers into his home. "We wait," he said.

"Chief Broken Rope…"

Broken Rope turned to Geof. "Do you question me?"

"Actually, Chief, I am wondering if you have news of Queen Andi and the young girl who was traveling with Her Majesty. They were on their way to—"

"The Secret City. Yes. It is well."

Geof smiled with relief. "One other thing. I believe my mother may live somewhere around here. Have you ever heard of a woman from the, uh, other side living in Sergel-tuteron?"

"I do not know of such a woman. Why do you think I would know of her?"

"All I know is that she is here somewhere. Actually, I don't really know that. I suspect it. I have to ask everybody."

"If Broken Rope learn of this woman, he will find you and give you peace."

"Thank you," Geof smiled.

Broken Rope sat erect before them. "We know prophecies in Song for Tomorrow. By authority of Uriah, we believe you are the Searchers. We accept your word is straight."

"I—well—" Geof squirmed.

"Evil Bu-usah threatens Chyn," Broken Rope continued. "We see him destroy Mu-jin. Mu-jin was land with gardens, many gardens like here. Now Mu-jin gardens sand. No life. If he make Sceptre his slave, he destroy Forbidden Garden. My people die. All die."

"It cannot be. It just cannot be." Uriah said.

Broken Rope bowed to Uriah. "I invite Walking Horse." Walking Horse was the Chyn Medicine Man. He enjoyed a status nearly equal to Broken Rope, if not greater in some respects. Walking Horse's age was not known. His origin was not known. All the Chyn knew was that he was a man of mythical powers.

Uriah explained the many legends of Walking Horse to a fearfully impressed Geof, Pat, and Jon. Jon pondered, "He sounds cool. I wonder if he's going to come through the door in slow motion surrounded by fog like they always do in the movies."

"Wouldn't doubt it. This place…"

Geof was interrupted by a sliver of light bayonetting between his legs. A large figure stood silhouetted in the slowly opening doorway. He dropped his head to negotiate the low door frame. The first glimpse of the legendary medicine man was two or three feathers intricately woven

into an impressive head of long silvery hair. Walking Horse was boiling over with charisma. There was no slow motion and no fog, but such Hollywood trappings were not needed to enhance the aura of Walking Horse. He was nearly seven feet tall, and though along in years, was powerfully built. His muscular chest was bare, except for several strands of beads that hung about his neck and draped neatly to the midpoint of his diaphragm. He wore long pants made of cloth with beaded decorations running up the outside seams. A heavy rope belt with several bulging pockets hanging from it was tied around his waist. Outside of his size and belt, he did not look much different than any Chyn brave. But something was definitely different.

"Another Donald Deernose," Geof mumbled.

"What a shock," Jon said. "Donald Deernose is for sure mixed up with these guys somehow. He knows a lot more than he told us."

Geof shrugged. "I think everybody here does. We should be used to it by now."

Walking Horse's clothes resembled those commonly seen at All-American Indian Days, but there was not a stitch of leather anywhere. Everything was woven fabric except his moccasins, which looked like leather but had a faint greenish tint.

The Chyn Medicine Man looked intently at each of the teenagers, his dark eyes dissecting them with eerie precision. Without a word, he walked up to Geof and held out a sinewy hand. "Come," he said brusquely.

"Nice to meet you too. Where?" Geof gulped.

Walking Horse led an apprehensive Bear to the middle of the room where Broken Rope waited. The chief stepped back and motioned for all to circle around Geof and Walking Horse.

Geof nervously stood facing the medicine man. "Soooo, what are we doing here—in the middle of the floor... alone?"

Walking Horse stood Geof erect, grabbed his forearms, and looked him squarely in both eyes. "Road before you long with many turns. Strength lives within you, and your heart is pure." Geof stared into his eyes like the medicine man had hijacked his senses. "But your strength not alone defeat Bu-usah. You must open heart and receive gift from my people." Geof appeared oblivious to everything. His eyes followed Walking Horse's eyes, and his body moved in unison with the medicine man.

A low hum emanated from the throat of Walking Horse and increased in intensity and volume. As it grew louder, the hum formed into distinctive sounds. Broken Rope and Uriah joined Walking Horse's mantra. The sound was familiar to anyone who had lived a long time in Sheridan. Geof's father many times regaled the boys with stories of the wonderful times he enjoyed as a child at All-American Indian Days. During a parade to mark the annual summer event, flatbed trucks would slowly drive up Main Street with Indians from different tribes outfitted in full authentic costume, dancing, and singing to appreciative onlookers.

Small puffs of smoke formed at the highest point of the fifteen-foot wall. The intensity of the voices swelled along with the clouds. Blood rushed so furiously through Geof's veins that it was visible beneath his skin. The chanting intensified, and guttural sounds became names, Indian names from long ago. As the roll call of hallowed warriors was chanted, the brilliantly colored image of a face with Native American features formed in the fog. Its lips moved in unison with Walking Horse's words. The face exploded like a horizontal Roman candle and, with a whoosh, shot straight at Geof, a comet tail blazing behind it. The face rocketed through Geof's body and turned into a violent rainbow. Colors inhabited body and soul as the face passed through Geof. When the face exited from his back, it was gray, stripped of its life energy in the unsteady body of the Bear. Job done, the face floated to the opposite end of the ceiling where it dissipated as quickly as it formed. Jon jumped to protect his friend, but the iron forearm of Spoto put him back on the floor.

As the face evaporated, another formed and repeated the electrifying journey. The Bear jerked violently as hundreds of faces passed through him and dyed his body every imaginable color. Face after animated face created a kaleidoscope as it interacted with the chants and the blood raging through Geof's veins. Jon ached to do something but had no idea what, or even if he should.

The parade of ethereal faces finally came to an end, but the chants, which had continued unabated, grew even more forceful. The ground convulsed beneath their feet, and the walls of the lodge shook violently. Another face was forming, but it was not like the others. It had the same Native American features but was framed by a huge headdress. Whoever this ancient was, he was of enormous importance. The rhythmic chanting escalated to a wail and electrified the great face. Uriah, Broken Rope, and Walking Horse continued to chant, but the mouth of this face did not mirror their words. His lips were moving but saying something else. The more the mouth moved, the more intense the chanting became. This time the face whooshed through the onlookers before slamming through the body of Geoffrey the Bear.

The fury of the face knocked Jon and Pat to the ground. It blitzed through Geof's body, turning it bright red until the spectacle was itself consumed by the ceiling. As the mist gave its last breath, Geof returned to his normal color. He collapsed into the unyielding arms of Walking Horse. The medicine man lifted him up and carefully placed him on a pile of blankets.

"Is—is he okay?" Pat asked.

"He must sleep now," Walking Horse said. "He received wisdom and strength from ancients. His body and mind rest now to accept that which has been given him. Leave him and find for yourselves rest you need."

"Come," Broken Rope commanded. "We prepare place of rest for you."

Stevloyd and Spoto led Pat and Jon from the longhouse. Jon glanced back to see his friend sleeping peacefully on the blankets, his face relaxed, but far away.

CHAPTER 26

The Return
of the Bear

Jon and Pat were led to a longhouse divided into two rooms, which nicely accommodated any boy/girl privacy concerns. Standing in the middle of the room was an attractive girl about their age with long, dark, straight hair, and flashing dark eyes. She was dressed in a simple black dress with beaded trim around the collar and hem. She looked like the photographic negative of Patricia.

She greeted them sweetly, "I am River, daughter of Broken Rope. My father has entrusted you to me."

"To do what?" Jon asked.

"Help if you need something. I am here for help. I stay with you."

"That is very nice, River," Pat graciously smiled. "How do we find you if we need you?"

"Here. I will be here."

"You're staying here? With us?" Jon asked casually. His fantasy of being locked up alone with Pat went quickly down the drain. On the other hand, River was intriguing.

"Yes. It is forbidden for Chyn guest to stay alone. I must accompany Pat at all times."

"Well, okay by me," Pat agreed. "And I'm sure it is okay with Jon too. Is it not, Jon?"

"Ooooooh yeah," Jon answered.

Pat narrowed her eyes. "I might have known this situation would appeal to you."

"Well, not really. It just kind of reminds me of an old Beach Boy song, or was it Jan and Dean?... 'Two Girls for Every Boy'."

Pat tapped her finger on her chin. "Maybe. But I think Elvis said it better."

"And how's that?"

"'Are You Lonesome Tonight?'"

"Well done," Jon laughed. "I didn't know you were a classic rock fan."

"It is good cultural education."

"Yeah, well, I think that's my cue to say good night," he smiled as he walked to the room nearest the door. Morning came too early, and without any news of Geof. Jon assumed he had been asleep about nine hours. It felt good. Spoto popped in with a woman from the tribe in tow. She spread a sumptuous breakfast on the table in the corner of Jon's sleeping quarters. Spoto offered no information on Geof other than he was fine and would be joining them when he was ready. Ready turned out to be two days.

The fun of being cooped up with two gorgeous girls surprisingly got a little boring for Jon. There was no TV, no video games, and no phone. As the hours passed, the long conversations shared by the three were tantalizing. River's stories of her tribal history were fascinating and, at some point, might shed light on what was going on with Geof. But to Jon, it became routine, like being stuck on a desert island with the girl of your dreams and discovering you still wanted to go fishing.

About noon on the third day, the door swung open, and everyone expected to see the figure of Spoto silhouetted in the door. But this time, the outline was Geof. Pat ran up and hugged him while Jon waited patiently to pay his respects. "Are you okay? Do you feel all right? Did it hurt? Do you remember anything?" The questions peppered Geof like buckshot.

"Why wouldn't I feel all right?"

"Because of everything that happened to you, Bro," Jon gasped.

"Happened to me? Nothin' happened to me."

"You... you don't remember anything?"

"Remember what? We just got here, and I was talking to Broken Rope. Where did you guys go anyway?"

Jon smacked his forehead. "Are you kidding me? You just downloaded Walking Horse 10.1, Ancestor Version, and you don't remember anything?"

"Downloa... What are you talking about?"

"I think you better sit down," Pat said, taking his hand.

Geof sat on a blanket with his two friends and River. Jon took the lead and described all that had happened the past few days. It was unbelievable to the Bear, and yet...

Geof scrunched up his face and closed his right eye. "If I heard that story from anybody but you, I might believe it."

"Every word Jon said is true," Pat confirmed. "Do you remember Walking Horse?"

Geof nodded, "Yeah. He came into the longhouse, said hello, and left. I don't know what the big deal is about him. I mean, he's cool and all that, but I don't see where he's such a rock star."

"Oh my God. Bearman, for once, I'm not bagging you. I'm really not. You won't believe the stuff Walking Horse made happen. All these dead guys came out of thin air and zoomed right through you. It was like the attack of the fog zombies or something."

Geof looked up at the ceiling, "Ahhh. I think I remember something, but—I guess I should believe you. But if what you say really did happen, why?"

"I think they gave you something," Pat said. "Strength... power... wisdom... magic. I do not know what. But it was something."

"I don't know what it could be. I feel pretty much the same. I certainly don't feel any better."

"You don't look any better either," Jon smiled.

River said, "When the time comes, you will know."

The door opened, and Spoto entered the room with Uriah.

"We must go," Uriah said. "Are you ready?"

"Oh sure. Yeah. Definitely," they lied.

"Then let us depart."

Jon grabbed his trusty staff, Geof took a deep breath, Pat smiled, and off they went.

CHAPTER 27

What's in a Cave Anyway?

The group assembled in a small open area where Stevloyd and Jok-imo awaited them on horseback. Stevloyd sat on a pure white horse with Spoto and Fidoa on either side of him. Fidoa looked perfect, no wound in sight. Broken Rope stood nearby in his finest regalia, including a headdress that reached down to his calves. Necklaces adorned his burly chest. High-top, pale green moccasins from the mesyan tree laced nearly to his knees. Behind Broken Rope, the entire village stood in rank.

Broken Rope's right hand grasped a lance decorated with feathers and beads. When the teenagers mounted their horses, the Chyn chief raised his lance, and a cheer broke out. Broken Rope dropped his lance, the crowd grew silent, and Stevloyd nudged his horse forward. The tribe stood respectfully as the group passed.

It was not long before they traveled the length of the village and moved toward the thick growth of the garden. On his left, Geof observed a longhouse silhouetted in the distance. A solitary figure stood in the open doorway. Geof could not see him clearly, but he knew it was Walking Horse. The figure raised his right hand, and Geof reciprocated. Jon also saw Walking Horse. He was awed by the talents of this unusual man but felt pity for him. With all his powers, Walking Horse was a sympathetic figure relying on a handful of wisecracking kids to save his people. He did what he could. He gave Geof all his magic and power. But now he must wait, just as people throughout the centuries waited when their loved ones went off to war.

Stevloyd led the procession onto a narrow path, and the house of Walking Horse disappeared. Geof looked back and recognized nothing. His heart felt strange... like he had more than one beating inside his chest. He felt strong.

The trek through the garden was uneventful, but its density challenged their progress at every turn. It was beautiful, captivating, and creepy. As they moved forward, the path narrowed, but Stevloyd held steady. One hundred feet from the wall of greenery, the plants, branches, and flowers came alive and politely withdrew, creating an open pathway. The plants, not Stevloyd, were now in command. Stevloyd moved ahead, knowing there was no way to turn back. As soon as the procession passed, the path closed behind them.

On the morning of the third day, Spoto awakened Jok-imo and brought the dreaded blindfold. It had been enhanced with two cups that covered his ears. Stevloyd again led the way, with Uriah sitting comfortably behind him. Uriah wrapped the leash of Jok-imo's horse around his right foreleg and held it firmly as the colorful floral hosts continued to provide a red carpet for the adventurers. As the day went on, the path opened into a small clearing. Beyond the clearing, the garden thinned, and they were suddenly on the outside. Looking back, they could see the path was no more. The red carpet was rolled up, and the show was over.

In time, they found themselves on a high bluff looking down on the Great Sea. It looked like an ocean with angry waves crashing violently at the rocks below. Stevloyd led the unsteady group down a rocky path guarded on either side by what looked like Joshua trees. The path was a few hundred yards long to the bottom of a valley and then reversed course to rise steeply up the other side. "Now you must all do exactly, and I mean exactly, as I say. Stay on your horses, touch nothing, and stay away from the walls."

Stevloyd stopped in front of a soaring rock wall and sat motionless as Spoto and Fidoa approached it. Spoto looked back at Stevloyd and motioned for him to come forward. Stevloyd obliged. Spoto turned, walked directly into the wall, and passed through it like nothing was there. Fidoa followed. Stevloyd turned to his wide-eyed companions and said, "Come."

"Man, they really know how to make an entrance AND exit in this place," Jon admired.

"This is the easy part. There are dangers just ahead," Geof said.

"How do you know that?" Pat quivered.

Geof looked at her. "I... I don't know how. I just know."

"I think that Walking Horse app is running in the background," Jon said.

By this time, nobody second-guessed Stevloyd, and certainly not the grizzlies. One by one, they breached the wall, entered a cave, and said goodbye to the tentative security of the Forbidden Garden and Sergel-tuteron.

"I totally hate caves," Jon whispered.

Geof smiled. "It's what's in them that sucks. And stop low talking. What do you think those things on Jok-imo's ears are for?"

The cave was too familiar. Dark and dreary it was, but not completely black as the familiar light-giving crystals randomly dotted the walls. Somebody from Erud had been here before.

They had gone only a few hundred yards when Stevloyd abruptly stopped. Instinctively, Spoto and Fidoa leaped in front of him and pulled their swords.

"Get behind me," Stevloyd said calmly.

"We must protect you," Spoto growled.

"You already have. Now get behind me and protect Uriah."

Fidoa snatched Uriah from Stevloyd's horse and placed him with Pat.

"Everyone stay well behind me," Stevloyd ordered. The group stood in frozen silence, awaiting the inevitable encounter with everyone's favorite slimebag, the Rodart. Stevloyd studied the tunnel before him.

"Is he looking for the butt-uglies?" Jon asked Uriah.

"Not looking. Sensing."

"Sensing?"

"Yes. He will sense the Rodart before they are aware we have entered their home."

"Why doesn't he just stick his nose up in the air," Jon sniffed. "You could smell those things underwater. In fact, I do right now. Oh crap. I do right now!"

"This is their home. Why would it not smell like them?" Uriah scolded.

Jon felt like he was standing in front of the entire student body with a toilet paper tail. "Well, yeah."

Spoto and Fidoa quietly closed ranks in front of them. Jon noticed their change in posture and said, "It's showtime."

Stevloyd's horse rose up and whinnied, kicking his forelegs in defense. Stevloyd did not pull his sword but raised his right hand, palm forward in the direction of the tunnel before him. The unforgettable rumbling of the Rodarts filtered through the cave and grew louder by the second.

Stevloyd opened his mouth and sang. He sounded like an angel as both he and his horse became bathed in a soft light. The light engulfed him, and the color of the horse began to darken.

Within seconds, Stevloyd, his horse, clothes, adornments, and halter were transformed to jet black. Stevloyd and his horse tripled in size as they blocked the way between the Rodarts and his friends. The light around him grew brighter, washing out all colors within its reach. Man and horse no longer looked real as they were submerged in the brilliance

of the light. Jon and Pat stared wide-eyed at each other. Geof stood by quietly, confident, and undeterred.

The rumble of one... or many Rodarts grew louder. Stevloyd's voice grew deeper and resonated off the walls with indescribable beauty. His hand stretched out and pointed down the tunnel toward the outline of the all-time gross-out king, a Rodart. It was rolling forward in a nauseating collage of lips, teeth, and eyeballs.

Jon jumped in front of Pat and made sure he was between her and Big Ugly. He didn't know what he was going to do if the Rodart got past Stevloyd, but it looked heroic. Geof sat on his horse, watching passively.

The Rodart slowed as it got closer to Stevloyd. When it was only feet away, it stopped. Stevloyd and the Rodart stood eye to eyes while Stevloyd continued to sing. The song subjugated the Rodart and forced it to spew gas from an infinite number of orifices placed throughout its repulsive body. The Rodart vibrated violently and bounced from wall to wall, propelled by the noxious vapor squirting in every direction. The smell was horrific. Jon and Pat started gagging and retching violently to the amusement of the grizzlies.

"I... I think I'd rather be eaten than smell this any longer, gaggg, hack ghji moj," Jon choked.

The rotund frame of the Rodart slowly lost its shape. Resembling a deflating balloon, it jetted crazily around the cave. Geof grinned as his friends searched for something to shove in their noses. Somehow Walking Horse's self-improvement program made the Rodarts smell like crushed lilacs to Geof.

The world's most potent stink bombs self-propelled into the small crowd forcing everyone except Geof, Jo-kimo, and Stevloyd to dive for cover. Curiously, Jok-imo could not smell them either, which made awkward explanations unnecessary.

The Rodart deflated completely, floated onto a pile of rocks, and lay draped on them, still watching but unable to move. The Searchers saw that not one, but five Rodarts suffered the same fate at the hand, or voice, of Stevloyd.

Jon raved, "Yes! Elvis is back in the building!"

He looked at Jok-imo, who sat motionless and calm, astride his horse. "Look at that," Jon griped. "Geof and Jok-imo don't even smell these things. I don't know why they couldn't have stink-proofed us while they were at it."

"For once, I agree with you," Pat said, holding her nose.

Jon surveyed the eerie scene of the feared Rodarts lying helpless on the rocks. "You know," he said, "those things look like that Picasso painting... you know... the one with the floppy clocks."

"Dali, not Picasso," Pat corrected. "It's called *The Persistence of Memory*. But I am impressed. Did you see that painting in the CheatNotes for famous art museums?"

"Cute," Jon twitched. "Whoever painted it, this looks like that. I gotta get a closeup of these things."

Either forgetting or ignoring Stevloyd's instructions, Jon hopped off his horse and skipped to the nearest Rodart. Spoto yelled for him to stop, but it was too late. As Jon got within two feet of the flaccid creature, a glob of stinky, gooey, crud shot out of one mouth of the Rodart and blasted Jon square in the face. It was the color of cucumbers mixed with beets, with little lumps the size of marbles in it. And it stunk. The normal smell was bad enough, but to have Rodart stew shoved up your nose was cruel and inhuman punishment.

"Iiiick," Jon cried as he franticly wiped slime from his face with his hands. Unfair as it is, bad things can be funny when they happen to somebody else. Jon's mess was hilarious to Pat and Geof. He stomped around in a circle, franticly wiping his face, with no luck.

Stevloyd was returning to normal but was wiped out and under the care of Spoto and Fidoa. Thinking things were under control, Pat forgot herself, dismounted, and rushed to help Jon. His eyes were closed, and he jumped when she touched him.

"Jon! It's me."

The sound of Pat's voice soothed the Monster but did nothing to release him from his predicament. "Can you see anything?" she asked.

Jon wiped what gunk he could from his eyes and saw the outline of Pat's face, most pleasant evidence that his fears of blindness were premature. "Yes," he pouted.

"Follow me. Up ahead, I see some water coming out of the wall just past where that, that thing is."

Jon nodded and followed obediently, his hand in hers. They tiptoed around the occupied Spoto and Fidoa and found that water was seeping from the cave wall but did not wet the floor. It dripped off a ledge and disappeared into a dark hole cut back into the wall. Pat filled her hands with the cool water and washed Jon's face. His eyes cleared, and he was able to enjoy the cleansing feel of the water, and even more, the soothing touch of Pat's hands. Jon maneuvered around Pat and cupped his hands to immerse himself in the friendly water.

Stevloyd and his horse returned to a tired version of themselves, which freed Spoto to check on everyone else. Jokimo was in place and sat motionless, the reins of his horse still wrapped around the arm of Uriah, who continued to sit calmly on the rump of Pat's horse.

Spoto expected Jon to be back on his horse by now. But he was not. And neither was Pat. What was that kid up to now? Spoto heard voices a short distance away and zeroed in on Jon with his face in the stream of water and Pat standing a foot or two behind him.

Spoto's eyes widened, and he yelled, "*No!* Get back from there!"

Jon turned to see what the excitement was but was only able to see a flash of Spoto's fur when his feet were yanked from under him. He fell against Pat, knocking her to the ground, and landed on his face. He screamed and clawed the ground furiously, but his hands found nothing to grip. Spoto and Geof ran toward him, but they were too late.

Pat lurched forward and grabbed Jon's hand but could not hold on. In an instant, Jonster the Monster disappeared into the hole. Geof charged the hole and shoved Pat out of the way as he dove headfirst toward the blackness. But he did not make it. He felt the steel grasp of Spoto's arms wrapped around him. Geof struggled frantically to free himself from Spoto's unyielding grip, but the grizzly was too strong.

"You... can't... go.... .after... him," Spoto growled into Geoffrey's ear. "That is the entrance to Elstrom, and he is gone."

Geof went limp. Pat stared at the hole in disbelief. Jon's foolish act could cost Geof his best friend, any chance to find his mother, and destroy the prophecy of the Song for Tomorrow. For the first time in his life, Geof resented Jon for being Jon.

Geof was submerged in despair, but from somewhere deep inside, he gained strength. The power of the ancestors rushed through him with such force that he threw out his arms and tossed a shocked Spoto several feet in the air. Geof yanked Pat away from the opening and dove headfirst into the hole. Fidoa ran to help Spoto restrain him, but Geof was gone.

"Stevloyd, do something!" Spoto howled.

"I can do nothing," Stevloyd said. "They are gone. Our mission has failed. I have failed. We must return and alert Queen Andi. The Rodarts will soon awaken."

Uriah was not to give up so quickly. Maybe it was because he was the brother of Queen Andi. Or maybe it was because he understood more of the spirit of the Chyn than anybody else. "Hold your ground," he barked sharply. "Do you have so little faith in the Song? Do you have so little faith in Walking Horse?"

Stevloyd faced Uriah. "Nobody has ever entered Elstrom and returned. Nobody. But I will go after them if you so order it."

"Wait," Uriah said simply.

The room fell silent, and everyone watched Uriah as he walked to the hole. He stared into the darkness for an eternity.

"Do you see anything," Pat sniffed.

Uriah turned from the hole and faced his heartbroken friends. "We must go on without them."

"What?" Pat shrieked. "We can't!"

"We must. We must secure the Sceptre at all costs."

"I knew there was a cold heart beneath that fuzzy exterior," Pat sniffed.

Uriah accepted her indictment. "We do not know what the outcome of this event will be. But we must trust the Song. The Rodarts are stirring. I command we all go now."

"I obey, Prince Uriah," Stevloyd deferred. "Everyone, follow me."

Stevloyd and Uriah walked past the moaning Rodarts. Pat walked behind them, straight, poised, and highly agitated. They navigated past the Dali-esque landscape of limp Rodarts, very mindful to stay out of crud-spewing distance.

The somber group rested for the night. Stevloyd went off alone to keep a watchful eye for unwelcome visitors. Pat huddled against a wall, trying desperately to process her predicament. "Spoto, do you think they are gone forever?" Pat asked.

"I hope they are not. I have to believe they are not."

Pat struggled. "But it does not make any sense. Why would all that stuff happen with Geof and the Chyn if it meant nothing? There must be more to this than we realize."

"It did not happen for nothing." Uriah came up and sat next to them. "We must have faith in the Song. I believe Geof will find his way back to us."

"Well, I'm not giving up, not one little bit," Pat said. "But in case they don't come back. What then?"

"You all have proven your strength and courage. I believe in you. If they do not come back, we must do it without them," Uriah said. He stood and began to walk away. He looked back over his shoulder and affirmed, "We will do it without them."

"We will," Pat said.

Travel continued for two days without further incident. In time, the cave took on a completely different ambience. It grew lighter, and splotches of color could be seen intermittently on the walls. There was no sign of Rodarts or any other impediments. Every few miles, a small sub-cave or indentation could be seen along the base of the cave wall. The first time one appeared, Stevloyd checked on his charges to make sure they were staying clear. The beauty of the cave increased with every mile. In some places, it bore a striking resemblance to Lantuc, which granted a measure of peace. The horses also found comfort in about two inches of white, powdered sand beneath their hooves.

In the near distance, a small pond came into view. Beautiful crystals and multicolored translucent rocks surrounded it. "We rest here," Uriah said.

Still angry at Uriah for leaving Geof and Jon, Pat isolated herself beside the pond.

Uriah sniffed the ground as he walked from one side of the pond to the other. He would stop, raise his nose, and continue.

"Why don't you sit down," Pat snapped. "Or better yet, try to find Geof and Jon."

"That is my mission," Uriah said. "I feel them to be close. Look for anything unusual."

"You must be kidding," Pat smacked. "Everything here is unusual."

Stevloyd joined Uriah in his search. "And what are *you* doing?" Pat demanded.

Stevloyd put his hand up to shush her. "Listen. Look around," he said.

Pat huffed. Her eyes darted around the cavern in a totally unconvincing and haphazard manner. Stevloyd put his hand up again, and everyone fell silent. "What is it?" he asked Uriah.

"I smell something. I smell Jon."

Pat followed the curves of the rocks that formed a wall behind the pond. A faint unholy shriek startled her. She cried, "Did you hear that? There, in those rocks," she pointed at the wall and scanned it feverishly. Out of the corner of her eye, she saw movement and shoved her hand into a crack. When she pulled her hand out, it came with a hand clasped around her fingers. Pat was able to pull a bruised and bloody arm free to the elbow but no farther. Stevloyd ran to the wall and called into the hole. "Geof, do you hear me?"

"Yes," came the welcome reply.

"Let him go," Stevloyd told Pat. He placed his hands on the wall and concentrated. The stones around the hole slowly melted into a gaping hole. The head and shoulders of Geof slid out. Stevloyd pulled him through the hole and onto the ground. Geof's left arm came last. Vice-gripped to his hand was the right hand of Jon, who fell out of the hole and onto Geof.

Pat pulled Geof to his feet and hugged him, but not Jon. "I was lost too, you know. Am I chopped liver?" Jon pouted.

"You stink," Pat gagged. "Only a Rodart would hug you right now."

Stevloyd grabbed Jon by the shirt and dragged him toward the pond. "The scent of the Rodart stays with you. It is most unpleasant, and you must wash yourself and your clothes."

Shamed and embarrassed, Jon slipped into the pond as everyone discretely looked the other way.

Geof found a comfortable sandy spot, and Pat sat down next to him. Something bothered her. "Geof, I need to ask you something,"

"Okay," Geof panted, still short of breath.

"What happened in that hole? What got Jon, and how did you free him?"

"I—I really don't know what got him. I couldn't see much. It was almost completely black, except way down below I could see some kind of orange light. I flew… I mean, I crawled down until I ran into him and grabbed onto him."

"That's just it. You just said you flew."

"I didn't really mean fly, fly. I meant went really fast, you know, by my standards."

"I saw you when you went into the hole, and you were flying. You were actually flying, but I was afraid to say anything. And you didn't just go down a few feet. I looked into the hole, and neither of you was anywhere in sight."

"Well, it was dark."

"Where were you the past two days?"

"I was able to find Jon. Something had him. Something big and evil. I found a rock and hit it. It let go of Jon, and we were able to get away. But it was very dark, and we did not know where we were going. Jon still could not see very well, so I did the only thing I could think of and led him to the blinking lights."

"Did they help you?" Pat asked.

"It was the strangest thing. We got close to the lights, and I felt something tug at my clothes. I looked down and could see the outline of a yellow cat with my tunic in her teeth, pulling me away from the lights."

Pat's ears perked up at the introduction of the cat. "What did it want?"

"I don't know. It was very dark, and I heard somebody or something say the word *danger*. It may have been the cat. I grabbed Jon and followed her. We traveled for a long time in a direction away from the hole where Jon fell. We made it to here and saw a sliver of light coming from that hole in the wall. It was where you were. The hole produced a glow bright enough to illuminate the cat, pointing toward the light. But then something happened." Geof leaned back and buried his face in his hands.

Pat put her arm around him. "What's wrong, Geof?"

Geof's chest heaved. "There was a noise behind us. The same kind of growl I heard from the thing that had Jon. But it was around a corner, so I don't think it could see us. Then the cat… The cat…" Geof's voice trembled. He closed his eyes and shook his head. Pat patted his shoulder. "The cat ran toward the sound and led the creature away from us. After a few minutes, I heard a loud scream, like the sound of a cat when somebody pulls its tail. Only worse. Then I heard nothing. I put my hand through the crack in the wall and found you."

Geof slammed his fist on the floor. "It's killing me. That cat sacrificed itself to save us. Why would she do that?"

Uriah overheard the conversation and came up to Geof. "Do not blame yourself. The feln did what she needed to do. And felns are very clever creatures. Do not abandon her future so quickly."

"Uriah is right," Pat said. "And besides, you saved Jon, and that cat helped you for a reason. I am beginning to think you really are the hero from that song thing."

His mind and body spent, Geof changed gears. "Hey, Spoto," he yelled. "What happens when we get out of this cave?"

Spoto dropped his head. "We cannot go with you. You three, Uriah and Jok-imo, will try to get to the castle and reclaim the Sceptre. Now you need to rest. We are about to enter Mu-jin." With that, the grizzly dog got up and rejoined Fidoa.

Geof looked at Pat for a long time. "Maybe it's just me, but you don't seem concerned at all about going into Mu-jin with its two-headed snake and nasty ruler. What's the deal?"

Pat looked at his forehead. "It is just too much. I cannot feel anything."

Uriah deposited Jok-imo on a rock where he could not hurt himself and ambled over to where Geof and Pat sat quietly. "The time is short," he said. "You must prepare yourself for a most arduous journey."

"Prepare ourselves how?" Geof asked. "And I don't understand your definition of arduous. We haven't exactly had it easy so far. I don't think I'm the hero you think I am."

"Yes, you are. Yes, you ARE. Remember why you are here and how important it is. You have the chance to save an entire civilization. You must remember this when times seem darkest. Promise me you will."

"But..."

"You must promise."

"Okay, okay, I promise."

Uriah relaxed. "Now, I know you will do it. I believe it."

Looking to get the Bear off the hot seat, Pat asked, "What is the deal with Jok-imo anyway? Surely, he realizes he isn't on a ship or something. I don't think we are fooling him at all."

"He thinks he is traveling on the cliffs above the Great Sea."

"Seems reasonable. Why aren't we doing that?"

"Faster this way, and we are hidden."

"But Jok-imo..."

"Jok-imo thinks there is a secret trail through the Great Canyon from the cliffs into Mu-jin, and that is what we are hiding. He thinks he is sitting on a rock somewhere on that trail right now."

"That is most interesting..." Pat was interrupted by the entrance of a wet, clean Jon. His eyes were sad as he, too, felt guilt over the cat who saved them. "I'm ready to go," he said glumly.

Pat went up and hugged Jon. "Welcome back."

"Yup," Jon said.

Seeing that the rest period had done its job, Stevloyd rallied the troops to move on. In two hours, the end of the cave would be in sight. At the exit of the cave, Stevloyd dismounted and stepped gingerly into the light of the lumen. He carefully surveyed the landscape and found it without movement. Satisfied that it was safe to summon the others, he motioned to Spoto to bring them out. Once outside, Uriah took the reins of Jok-imo's horse in his teeth and walked about two hundred yards to the base of the cliffs.

"I am sorry. This is where we must leave you, my friends. Our hearts will be with you," a tearful Spoto said. Fidoa joined Spoto and laid her head on his shoulder. She knew it was torture for him to sit back and watch someone else go off to fight. But this was the way it had to be.

Geof, Jon, and Pat sat on their horses and faced the cave's entrance, which was completely camouflaged from even a few feet away. Stevloyd stood in front of them. "Your training is inadequate, but your courage is infinite, and your hearts are pure. Go now and fulfill your destinies. Walk with honor." With those words, Stevloyd bowed to his friends and retreated with Spoto and Fidoa into the cave.

On their own, the three joined Uriah, who waited with Jok-imo. Geof took a deep breath. "Let's go," he said. "We have work to do."

CHAPTER 28

Debbie and Clark Cook

Debbie awakened at mid-morning and exited her lavish room. Queen Andi gave her free rein to explore the castle as long as she did not go outside. There was plenty of castle, and Debbie was anxious to get to it. Without a plan, she walked casually down wide hallway after wide hallway with Maximillian and Crystal in tow. Andi's matchmaking skills were evident as the two cats now seamlessly attached themselves to Debbie.

Earlier she reiterated to Andi her guilt about being safe while her friends were in danger but received no absolution. Andi advised that not being in danger made her role no less important and to enjoy her temporary bed of roses. "Each has a time of fear and a time of comfort," Andi counseled. "It is unwise to regret your times of comfort just as you should not lament your times of fear. You will find that they are brother and sister, and you must be prepared to conquer both." Debbie looked at Andi through optics that changed the queen from black and white to the pastel complexion of a multi-faceted leader imbued with the wisdom required to lead a country. Andi was queen of Lantuc for reasons beyond just finding a cave.

As she walked down the ornate hallway, Debbie's eyes drank in every inch of its beauty. Beautiful paintings and gold trim on the ceilings, walls, and doorways overwhelmed her, especially in light of the fact that the part of the castle where she stood seemed nearly deserted. Where is everybody? Who built this magnificent palace? How did they do it? Why did they leave? Did they leave?

She occasionally met a person scurrying up or down the halls. They all seemed to be in a hurry and paid little mind to her. They were dressed in white, not very tall, and all had long hair. Most of the men had a small bald spot on top. Debbie could not help but wonder if some disaster had largely wiped out the Erud civilization. Maybe they were victims of the Great Sorrow plague after all, and that was the true secret of the Secret City.

Debbie and the two cats spent an hour or two wandering from doorway to doorway and peeking inside room after room. Large or small, they were luxuriously furnished... and mostly deserted. Nothing about this place made sense. It should be full of people living it up in the lap of luxury. But it was for all intents and purposes, deserted. As beautiful as everything was, the sameness began to bore the simple girl from Sheridan. She decided it was time to see what Andi was up to. She stopped and realized she had no idea where she was. Debbie felt panicky but held herself. She knew she was in a safe place, at least for now. When she looked around to get her bearings, Max sprinted past her leg, followed closely by Crystal. The grand tour was over. She refocused on her job, which was to protect the very cats who were now running away from her.

Debbie knew there is no way to catch a cat. She hoped to stay close, but lost them when they whipped around a corner, tails sticking straight up in the air. She ran to the corner just in time to see the black tip of Crystal's white tail disappearing inside a lighted doorway. She followed her inside and found herself face to face with Clark and Edgal. Debbie flushed at the sight of Edgal, ran to Clark, and gave him a hug that turned him several shades of crimson. The closest thing he ever got to a hug from his parents was when his drunken stepfather picked him up and threw him against a wall. To get a real, heartfelt hug from anybody was a new and wonderful experience.

Clark reluctantly extricated himself from Debbie's pleasant clutches and pointed toward a series of large tables covered with models and construction paraphernalia. "These people are beyond amazing," he gushed. "Come look."

He dragged her by the arm to an open window that overlooked the bay. The Secret City was built high above the cliffs, and from the window, they could watch the activity on the bluffs below. Bordering either side of the bay were large numbers of workers constructing the very claw mechanisms described by Clark and Geof a few days before. They were not finished but were well on their way.

Debbie surveyed the scene with wonder. She gawked at Clark and said, "I'm speechless. How did you do this?"

Clark let out a deep breath and said with a giddy smile, "I didn't. Or, well, I don't know. These guys are miracle workers."

"But how did they do this so fast?"

"No clue."

Debbie knitted her brow and stared at him.

"No. I mean, I really don't know. I just drew up a plan, and the next day the claws were going up. I don't know where they got the materials or anything. It's like they conjured them up or something."

Debbie shook her head. "You know... I don't know much about the Mu-jin army, but I wouldn't write these guys off so fast... General."

Clark blushed again. He looked at Debbie for a long time, but words failed him. Debbie could see he was conflicted and waited for him to open up. When he did not, she asked gently, "Are you okay?"

Clark turned his back to her, walked a few steps, and wiped his eyes. Edgal discretely walked to the other end of the room. Clark's body shook, and though he tried to hide it, she could see he was crying. She walked toward him, hesitated, turned away, and turned back to place her arm around his shoulder.

"What's the matter?"

Clark stiffened his upper lip and turned to face her. "I'm no general," he whimpered. "I'm nothing. These people are all going to die because of me."

"Wait a minute—"

"Don't try to make me feel better. Don't you think I know what I am?"

"And what is that?"

"A loser. A dweeby, laughingstock, loser! What do I know of war? These people believe in me, and I know nothing."

"From the look of things, you know a lot."

"I know how to play games with plastic armies against other people like me who have no life. My role models are forty-five-year-old guys still playing war against kids. There's got to be a better person for this than me. I'll just screw it up."

"You know what? You're right. There are probably thousands of people better suited than you to do this."

"Exactly. That's what I—"

"And you know what else? They're not here."

"They should be."

"But they're not. And you are. And from what I can see, you're doing a fantastic job. Look at the hope you're giving these people."

"Hope. Big deal."

"Is there a bigger deal? Look, these people are like the Sergel-tuteron version of you in Sheridan. Long on brain and short on brawn... no offense. But you're giving them hope... a chance to save their way of life. You're right. You're not the best person for the job, but in my book, you are by far the best person in Sergel-tuteron."

Clark raised his chin. "Do you really think so?" he asked, his lip still quivering.

"Yes."

"I… I just don't know what to do. Surely everyone must see I'm scared out of my mind."

"Ya think? So am I. I bet everybody else is too. Fear is going to save this civilization."

"I think it's courage that will save it. And I don't have that."

"Just as courage imperils life, fear protects it."

"Huh?"

"Leonardo da Vinci. One of the most advanced military contraption inventors of all time said that. I bet he was considered a nerd when he was young."

"You have to be kidding. Leonardo? You can't compare me to him. He was a great man, maybe the greatest of men."

"He didn't start out that way."

"That's easy for you to say. You've probably always been… well, you."

"You think it is so easy being me? I have to put up with slimeballs like Snively Asstead all the time just as you do, only in a different way."

Recognizing that Debbie was also victimized by the Snively Assteads of the world was a shocker. So, no life was perfect. But in some strange way, it felt good. They had something in common. "I never thought of it like that."

"You've got to pull yourself together. This isn't the best circumstance for anybody. But check it out. A few days ago, you were picking up books knocked out of your hands by some butthead bully, and now a whole world believes in you. I believe in you. So I suggest you quit whining and get on with it."

Clark nodded his head and stood up straight. "I suppose you're right."

"I'll do all the supposing around here," she smiled. "Now get back to work, will ya?"

She patted him on the chest and turned to find the kitties sitting in the doorway. Debbie got the feeling that they had brought her here for a reason, and it was mission accomplished. She joined the cats at the door and turned to Clark. She waved her hand and called out, "Good luck, Leonardo."

Clark nodded, turned to walk back to where Edgal was now waiting at a table but stopped dead in his tracks. "Edgal," he yelled excitedly. "Tell them to stop work on the claws."

Without hesitation, Edgal motioned to a man standing near the window. His blending-in skills were so great that Debbie never noticed him. The man pulled out a long horn and blew three blasts in the direction of the bluffs. All motion ceased immediately.

Clark ran to catch Debbie before she was far down the hall. "Debbie, you're a genius. A genius, I tell you," he said, jumping around like a puppy about to go walkies.

"Me?"

"Leonardo! Leonardo and Archimedes! What a combination!"

"What on earth are you talking about?"

"I watched this documentary about the Leonardo museum in Florence and—"

"Wait. You did what?"

"Okay, okay. I watch documentaries. Sue me."

Debbie suppressed a laugh. "Please continue."

"Anyway, they have all these cool machines invented by da Vinci. They even built them according to his plans."

"I'm sure it was very entertaining, but how does that make me a genius? Not that I'm arguing the point."

"The revolving crane."

"The what?"

"The revolving crane. Don't you see? It was similar to the Claw, but with other purposes."

Debbie managed a half-smile to hide her confusion.

"Look… look. Da Vinci invented a crane on a 360-degree swivel. Right now, our claws are fixed to one spot. But put them on a swivel and booyah! It will be impossible for the ships to outmaneuver them." Clark skipped back to the table already being cleared by Edgal so he could work his magic on it.

"If you need anything else, don't hesitate to ask," she called out, feeling pretty good about herself. "Just think of yourself as the chef and me, your sous chef."

"You have some great recipes," Clark shot back over his shoulder. He then went back over the rainbow and immersed himself in another design challenge, totally insulated from the natterings of mere mortals.

Seeing the show was over, Debbie threw a quick appreciative glance at Edgal and left the room. Once again, Maximillian and Crystal dutifully followed her.

CHAPTER 29

What Do You Mean, Qualifications?

Geof, Jon, and Pat rode along the rocky hillside to reconnect with Uriah and Jok-imo. Uriah directed Geof to remove Jok-imo's blindfold, which he did with some difficulty. Jok-imo shut his eyes to the bright light and rubbed his ears. When his senses adjusted to their natural environment, Jok-imo recognized their location, straightened up, and said, "We must quickly get out of sight."

The area was dangerous. Not far from where they stood, dozens of ships were being readied to attack the Secret City. They followed Jok-imo through a valley of rocks, dismounted and settled in a shady area to await instructions. Jok-imo stood and surveyed the countryside. Geof shook his head. "One hour ago, prisoner. Now leader. What a world."

Pat pulled the hood of her garment over her head and buried her face in her knees.

"Are you okay?" Jon asked.

"Yeah, but my skin is fair, and for all I know, this lumen has ten times the UV rays of the sun."

"Yeah, there's a ton we don't know about this place. And now that I think about it, Jok-imo doesn't know anything about us."

"You are right," Uriah said. "Jok-imo, this is Geof, Jon, and Pat."

Geof waved, and Jon uttered the valueless "Whassup." Pat acknowledged him with a twittering of her fingers but did not look up.

Jok-imo paced back and forth for a few moments. "I think… I know who you are. Mu-jin needs you."

"What do you mean?" Geof asked.

"There are only remnants of our once-great forests. Our farms are nothing but blackened ash, incapable of growing anything. Our people live in rotten clothes and fight each other for what food there is. You, my little friend," he said to Uriah, "are in the gravest danger, and we must keep you out of sight."

Uriah nodded. Jon looked at Uriah and said, "I guess capturing an Agron prince would be a big bargaining chip for Bu-usah."

"That is not what I meant. Nobody cares about that but Bu-usah. To these people, Uriah is food."

"What?" Jon blurted.

"They told us about this kind of thing before, remember?" Geof reminded him.

Jon looked at Uriah and shook his head. "Why are you doing this then?"

"Why are you?" Uriah countered.

"I don't seem to have a choice."

"Nor do I. Just as you have your destiny, I have mine."

Jok-imo looked at his new friends, the imprint of his blindfold still visible on his forehead. "We will do our best to keep you safe, as you have done for us so far."

"Thank you, Jok-imo. Thank you," Geof said. "The fact that you have gone through so much and still are willing to take such chances shows you are a man of great character." The Bear's friends nodded.

"So, where is Bu-usah's crib?" Jon asked.

Jok-imo gave him a puzzled look.

"That is a name for castle used by the uneducated where he comes from," Pat said without looking up.

"It is two passes of the lumen inward from the shipyards. But first, we must find out about the ships and how close they are to sailing against the Secret City. We may be too late."

"Isn't that dangerous?" Jon asked.

"Duh!" Geof snorted. "Can you think of an un-dangerous part of this deal?"

"Well, yeah... well, no. So, what do we do?"

"Those who stand against Bu-usah, we call them the Protectors of the Sacred Territory of our Forefathers, have found places where we can go and not be noticed by Bu-usah's guards."

"Let us begin then," Uriah said, taking the lead.

Jok-imo joined Uriah as they wound their way through rock-lined gorges bordering the Great Sea. The journey only covered half a day before the sound of work was audible from the sea. They arrived at the base of a hill that rose two hundred feet above them. Jok-imo motioned for all to follow him to a small clearing. From the rocks, a group of Jok-imo look-a-likes armed with swords surprised them from behind. Geof was the first to see them and whirled to warn the others. Pat screamed and threw her arms up, protectively covering her face as Jon jumped in front of her. They were surrounded.

"It is okay," Jok-imo said, holding his hand out to the Mu-jinians. "My friends. We must get to Bu-usah's castle quickly."

The Mu-jinians embraced Jok-imo, unconcerned that Geof and Jon posed any threat. They looked strangely at Uriah, but he held his ground.

Geof said, "Any chance you might tell us what in the heck is going on here?"

"This is De-shal and my friends. They are the Protectors of the Sacred Territory of our Forefathers I told you about."

"Can't we just call them the good guys?" Jon asked, looking at his fingernails.

De-shal looked like a mirror image of Jok-imo with long blond hair, fine features, and a soiled white tunic. "We feared you would never come back. We feared you were dead."

"Never mind that," Jok-imo dismissed. "We need to know about the ships."

"Warships are stretched from the shoreline far into the sea. Thousands of Mu-jin workers are working on those ships."

"What does that mean exactly?" Pat asked.

"Bu-usah has the only navy in Sergel-tuteron," De-shal explained. "They will smash through any defenses the Eruds can employ. The Secret City will be taken with little resistance. Once Bu-usah controls the Secret City, all of Sergel-tuteron will soon fall under his bloody hand."

Jon closed his eyes and shook his head. "Clark's screwed."

"Debbie is with him," Geof moaned. "We have to stop this."

"It may not be possible," Pat said.

"It is possible!" Uriah barked. Looking at Geof, he said, "You have the power of the Chyn ancestors within you. You are the hope of the Secret City."

"I don't know what power I have. But I know that Clark and Debbie need me. Just tell us what we need to do."

"You must stay here while the lumen rests," De-shal said. "In the time of light, we will travel the safest passage to Bu-usah's castle."

Jon scratched his head. "Don't you guys have a name for things like day and night? Seems like it would be easier."

Uriah said, "What you call day, we call *antanauticanus*. And night is *atramentron*."

Jon shook his head. "I like day and night better."

Uriah nodded. "I do too."

As night fell, Jon smiled at Uriah and walked over to check on Pat. She appeared to be asleep, her head still covered by the white hood. He tiptoed back to Geof. "She's sleeping."

"That's good," Geof smiled. "She's acting kind of weird lately, don't you think?"

"A little. But I think we all are."

"Fair enough." Geof directed his attention to Jok-imo. "Do they have some kind of underground railroad here to the castle?"

"Underground... ?"

"Sorry. I just mean do they have friends along the way that will help us?"

"Yes. Most of the way, we hope. We have information for you now."

"What information," Jon asked.

De-shal began. "We believe we know where the Sceptre is."

"How does he know about the Sceptre?" Jon asked suspiciously.

"It is not such a secret," Jok-imo reminded them. "People in Mu-jin have heard. But nobody knows what it does. There are many stories, but..."

"Well, at least if we know where it is, it's a start," Jon said.

"Cool," Geof grinned. "All we have to do is waltz right in there and get it," he added, fist-bumping Jon.

De-shal was not used to such cockiness and looked at Jok-imo for guidance, but he was equally baffled.

Jon continued, "I think we already heard where this Sceptre is, and it's guarded by a gigantic two-headed snake, right?"

"Yes, Joneva," De-shal affirmed. "My people are deathly afraid of him."

"It is not just his size," Jok-imo sighed. "It is said he has other... qualifications."

"Uhhh, what do you mean qualifications?" Geof asked.

"He has the power of magic."

"Magic?"

"Yes."

"Heh, heh. A giant snake with magic powers."

"Yes."

"Magic. Like magic?"

"Yes."

"I hate to ask what kind of powers... but what kind of powers?" Geof swallowed.

"No one knows for sure. But legend has it he can melt a person just by looking at him. And maybe other things too."

"Melt? Did you say melt?" Jon gasped. "Personally, I think that Sceptre is fine right where it is."

"Where did the snake come from?"

"It is said that Vandu-un brought him to the castle—"

Jok-imo interrupted his friend. "Vandu-un stole the Sceptre from the Secret City and swore his allegiance to King Bu-usah. The Sceptre was locked away in the very place it is now."

"And the snake?" Geof asked. "Can't forget the snake."

"Vandu-un expected to be rewarded greatly for bringing the Sceptre to Bu-usah. But the riches and power Bu-usah gave him were not enough. In revenge, some say he found the snake and somehow forced its loyalty to him. With the snake guarding the door, only he could enter."

"Clever boy," Jon smirked.

"How do you know this?" Uriah asked, annoyed that he had never heard any of it.

"My father, Halb-ean, told me. He was one who had access to such knowledge. Soon after the snake was in the place it still resides, Bu-usah bestowed upon Vandu-un the offices and powers he holds to this day."

Uriah abruptly sat straight up like a lightning bolt had just gone through him. "And no soul has seen the Sceptre since the arrival of the snake, not even Bu-usah?"

"That complicates things. We now have two scary powerful adversaries," Geof moaned.

"You mean Bu-usah and the snake?" Jok-imo asked.

"Duh. He means Bu-usah and Vandu-un," Jon snarked. "I think Bu-usah is—"

"Afraid of Vandu-un," Uriah said. "That is one reason why Bu-usah hasn't learned the power of the Sceptre. He cannot get to it. It certainly explains how Vandu-un got to be Bu-usah's most powerful advisor."

"Sooo, let me follow this," Jon mused out loud. "Bu-usah can't get the Sceptre that might give him great powers because this Vandu-un guy won't let him get at it. So why doesn't Vandu-un just take the Sceptre and make himself king?"

"He does not know how," Uriah shrugged.

"Wait a minute. Just wait a minute," Geof broke in. "Do you suppose all this stuff about capturing or killing Sergel

Tuteron is just a smokescreen and the real reason to attack the Secret City is to find the secret of the Sceptre? Because if the Sceptre is such a bad toy, who needs Sergel Tuteron or anything else?"

"Your idea has merit," Uriah nodded.

"Maybe that big armada is just a red herring to occupy the Eruds so a smaller force can sneak in and find the secret to the Sceptre. You said Vandu-un worked with Sergel Tuteron, right?" Jon's conspiracy-theory brain was kicking into high gear.

"So, who is behind this attack? Bu-usah or Vandu-un?"

"My father thought both," Jok-imo answered for Uriah.

"This is really twisted," Jon beamed. "Two guys, who are friends but aren't, go off to kill thousands of innocent people in a game of 'let the best sicko win when he finds the Sceptre.' In the meantime, one of them sneaks into the Secret City, unlocks the Sceptre, and badabing, badaboom, gets to rule the world while the other guy loses his head. I love it."

De-shal said, "So you are saying that killing Bu-usah may get us no closer to controlling the Sceptre than we are now?"

"And I thought this was going to be easy," Geof groaned.

CHAPTER 30

Your Highness

De-shal rousted everybody early and moved inland from the bay area. The landscape of Mu-jin looked like a bad dystopian movie with locusts the only survivors. The land was stripped of vegetation save for a few solitary green soldiers struggling to taste a bit of lumen before being discovered by some starving Mu-jinian. As the terrain of Mu-jin shifted from large boulders to depleted farmland and stripped forests, hiding places became scarce, and the vulnerable band of Searchers was forced to travel in plain sight. Occasionally they did encounter a Mu-jin native. But those wretched souls were more concerned with their own survival than this unobtrusive group of travelers. It might be different if Uriah were visible. De-shal explained that the average Mu-jin citizen abhorred the idea of eating dogs, but starving people will do anything to survive. Anything. The Searchers understood that fact, as tragic as it was. Sheridan was certainly not the vegetarian capital of the world, though

Geof never was a meat eater. But his father had beaten into both Geof and Jon that if animals were to be used for meat, they should at least enjoy a cruelty-free existence while they were alive. Such concepts were unknown to Bu-usah.

Dawn broke on the third day, and the landscape changed as they closed in on the castle. The charred remains of this blighted Eden showed hints of fertility, at least by current Mu-jin standards. With that change of scenery came increased numbers of curious people forcing the Searchers to abandon the wide-open spaces and travel on a less-secure road. The choice was not an easy one. Members of Bu-usah's army were more likely to be on the road. But in the fields, they were conspicuous. With any luck, the group would not encounter Bu-usah's security forces. If they did, they were just a few harmless Mu-jinians on the road going somewhere equally harmless. There would be no cause to detain them.

"I hate these people looking at me," Pat grumbled from under her hood. "They give me the creeps."

"So what?" Jon shrugged. "They're just looking. Probably never saw anybody as good-looking as me before."

"Just act like you belong here," Jok-imo advised, staring intently at the back of Pat's head. "They know no different. My people are overly mistrustful. You would be too if you lived here."

They walked in a slow and relaxed fashion, purposefully paying little attention to anyone around them and happily receiving little in return. As long as they stayed under the radar, all was well.

There was something about this setup that puzzled Geof. He rode up next to De-shal and asked, "If there is such a lack of food here that cains are not safe, why are our horses not in danger?" Geof's horse paused momentarily, looked back at him, snorted, and continued on his way.

"By royal edict, King Bu-usah has placed all horses within his protection."

"Well, if he's a horse lover, he can't be all bad."

"Lover? You do not understand. Bu-usah wants the horses for his army. He intends to attack the Secret City by sea AND by land."

Jok-imo reined in his horse sharply, reached out, and grabbed De-shal by the shoulder. "What do you mean by sea and land?"

"Yeah," Geof said. "I thought that it was impossible to attack the Secret City by land."

"Not impossible. Difficult. Bu-usah thinks that the Eruds are so focused on a sea attack that they will have minimal defenses on land. It is said that Bu-usha's finest soldiers, the Eternals, have already begun the journey through the Great Canyon."

Jok-imo scratched his head. "Makes no sense. The cliffs leading to the Secret City are so treacherous that Bu-usah would lose half his army before even being challenged by the Eruds."

"Yes," came the simple reply.

"Yes?" Geof asked with amazement.

"Half would die, maybe more. But half might live. Bu-usah would let half his men die if it meant he could gain control of the power of the Sceptre."

Geof and Jon looked at each other and then at Pat, who shook her head underneath the hood. "We must warn them. We must warn Debbie," Geof said, his voice shaking.

"There is no time," Jok-imo said. We will reach Bu-usah's castle before the lumen goes down."

"NO! We must warn them now." Geof forcefully turned his horse only to find his way blocked by Uriah."

"Get out of the way, Uriah," Geof growled.

"No. You are making a mistake. Even if you warn them, they will have no chance to do anything about it. The best way to stop Bu-usah is for you to capture the Sceptre and wield its power against him."

"Wait a minute," Geof interjected. "Wield its power? I thought only Sergel Tuteron could make the Sceptre do its thing."

"The power of the Sceptre shall flow through hands from another land. This is foretold in the Song. Who else but you?"

"Is this another part of the Song you never told me about?"

"Yes. We thought it necessary that no one know."

"You mean the Sceptre might obey me and not Sergel Tuteron?"

"It is a possibility."

"Oh man…"

"Listen to him, Bear." Jon rode up next to his friend. "Our best shot is to stop the whole thing. If you want to help Debbie, Bu-usah's entire gig must be stopped. Not just part of it."

Geof sat, his soul in conflict. "All right," he grumbled. "Let's go get the damned thing."

"SEARCHER!" De-shal cheered along with Jok-imo.

The journey was progressing smoothly when they came to a fork in the road. De-shal and Jok-imo rode a few paces in front of the others for a private pow-wow which quickly became an argument.

"What's going on?" Geof butted in. "Is there a problem? I mean, you know, outside of the million or so problems we already have."

Jok-imo pointed his fingers in opposite directions. "There are two roads to the castle. The main road is on the left. The road on the right is longer but less traveled."

"Which one do we take?" Geof asked.

"De-shal thinks we should take the main road, and I think we should go the other way."

"And the winner is?"

De-shal and Jok-imo resumed their debate ignoring input from anyone else.

"Just do what Yogi Berra would do," Jon said.

"Huh?"

"You know... Yogi Berra. He said, when you come to the fork in the road, take it."

Geof looked at Jon and grinned. "You know what, man? Yogi's right."

Jon nodded. They approached De-shal and Jok-imo together and demanded a solution or let them in on the discussion.

"We are sure to encounter trouble on either road. I just think the small road will provide less resistance."

"How much longer will it take?" Geof asked, his mind still on Debbie and the Secret City.

"About half a . . . um… day," came the reply. "But if we take the main road, we will most surely encounter Bu-usah's elite guard and will have to trick our way past them. Not so easy."

"We can do it," De-shal said plainly.

"I was never any good at these fifty percent things," Geof said. "There is no educated answer, so let's rely on women's intuition. What do you think, Pat?"

"Why me?"

"Why not? You're the only girl. Maybe you will be good luck. Is that okay with you guys, or do you want to stand around and argue for the rest of our natural lives?"

"Well, the right road seems like it could be safer," Pat squeaked, afraid to look anyone in the eye.

"Let's do it," Geof said forcefully.

Realizing their winless argument would last forever, De-shal and Jok-imo agreed.

"Bear, I hope the right road *is* the right road, but I have a bad feeling there isn't one."

The road made a lazy curve to the right and seemed inviting, as visibility was clear for many miles. Farmers were working in their fields, and there was no sign of hostile forces. Maybe the road to the castle would be a cakewalk. But this was not Sheridan, and things did not tend to tilt toward the effortless in this land of two-headed snakes and evil kings.

Geof joined De-shal and Jok-imo, thinking that now would be a good time to learn some things about Mu-jin omitted by Constantine and Queen Andi.

"You guys have seen your homeland smashed by this wacko king, and yet he is still king. Why has there been no revolt?"

"There was resistance… at first. But any who opposed the king were brutally murdered along with their families. Many were betrayed by their friends and slaughtered. The unlucky ones were sent to the University."

"Torture?"

"Yes, Geof. The worst kind. Their bodies were ravaged until their minds failed them. When they were released, they were supporters of Bu-usah and would report on their own families. Everybody lives in fear of everybody else."

"That's it?"

"People hate what has happened to their country. But…"

"Same old story," Geof said. "We've seen this before in our world."

"And what happens in your world?"

"Usually, the people prevail."

"Then, there is hope?"

Geof shrugged. "Often, it takes many lifetimes. But they never had a game-changing Sceptre lying around. That oughta speed things up considerably."

Uriah positioned himself on the back of Pat's horse, where such depressing talk was only faintly detectable. The less he had to think about where he was and what he was doing, the better.

For miles, Geof, Jon, and their Mu-jin guides commiserated about the injustices of today and the glory that was Mu-jin. After a time, a band of mounted horses appeared in the distance. Follow the plan... hide Uriah, no eye contact.

The riders came into view. They were all women of great beauty, a surprise that brought a short-lived smile to the faces of the two boys. They wore the standard Mu-jin tunic, but these were snow white. There looked to be about twenty of them, and as they got closer, their movie-star faces projected the bearing of someone who meant business.

Geof drooled to Jon, "I think we're on the wrong side."

"Yowza," he leered.

De-shal led his party off the road to let them pass. But pass they did not. Four of them confronted De-shal, forcing him to stop.

De-shal said calmly, "Greetings, sisters. May we assist you?"

A guard broke ranks and circled the Searchers. She was particularly interested in Geof, as he physically did not fit the mold of the perfect Mu-jinian. "I am Ren-te, and we are the Royal Guard. Identify yourself," she commanded.

"I am De-shal, of the outer provinces. I wish you strength and unity."

"And you?"

"I am called Jok-imo."

Ren-te reared her white horse. "I thought so." Turning to her small army, she decried, "It is our lucky day. We have captured the traitor, Jok-imo."

"Traitor? My loyalty to Mu-jin is without question."

"We have learned you are the son of the traitor, Halb-ean. That makes you a traitor. That makes all of you traitors, even you," she said, reaching out and stiff-arming Pat, who nearly fell from her horse. Pat's displacement revealed the tiny tail of Uriah, who tried in vain to conceal himself.

"Ahhhhh. And we shall eat well tonight," Ren-te gloated to her gleaming troop. "Detain that cain, and let us take these traitors to the king and claim our reward." A woman rode from behind Ren-te intending to nab Uriah and prepare him to be the main course at tonight's dinner. Uriah opened his mouth to engage his fearful growl but was struck from behind by an unseen sword handle. He fell, dazed to the ground below. His attacker emerged from behind Pat with a cloth sack and grabbed Uriah by the scruff of the neck. Geof moved to help his friend but, like Jon, was stopped by a sword to his throat.

The alluring captor lifted Uriah to put him in her sack but was diverted by a charging De-shal, sword in hand. The Mujinian guards drew their swords and descended on De-shal. A gleaming sword touched De-shal's neck when a blinding white flash separated De-shal from his executioners. It was Pat.

Her horse reared powerfully on its hind legs and snorted at the woman with the sword. Jon's mouth flopped open as he watched the no-horse-skills Pat handle her mount as if she were Debbie. Pat threw off her hood and shook her long, blonde hair until it cascaded over her back and shoulders. "Stand down!" came a forceful voice from the lips of Pat Chamness. "Sheathe your weapons."

Ren-te leaped from her horse and fell to one knee, her eyes firmly focused on the ground. "Princess Trixi-lyn," she said humbly. Her action was mirrored by all in her charge, including the one who snatched Uriah. As she fell to her knee, she dropped Uriah on his head where he lay quietly to ponder his next move.

Jon and Geof looked at each other without word or thought. Where did that come from? Jok-imo nudged his horse around the two boys and rode up to Pat, grabbing Jon's trusty staff from his hands in the process.

"What?" Geof and Jon both cried.

Pat turned to them with an icy stare. "Be silent if you want to live."

She turned to the leader of the Mu-jin force. "I will make certain my father knows you served him well. Be honored that you will be my escort the rest of the way."

"Your Highness," twenty voices said.

"But Pat..." Jon whimpered. "You can't be this... this princess."

"You fool," she snapped. "Even the obvious eludes you." Turning to De-shal, she hissed, "Watch this traitor closely."

Trixi-lyn looked cryptically at Jok-imo, "You have suffered much. Was it for your king or for yourself?"

Jok-imo bowed. "Your humble servant. I am forever at your service."

Geof's eyes shot daggers at Jok-imo. "That piece of crap was fooling us the whole time."

"Everyone was fooling us," Jon whimpered. "But why is she buying Jok-imo's story so easily?"

"No idea. Very weird."

Trixi-lyn looked down at a defiant Uriah. She laughed, "You should have listened to your wife." Uriah stared back at her but said nothing. He was on the thinnest ice and needed time.

Jon's spirit broke as though all of his friends had died on the same day. "I... I can't believe this."

"Do your eyes lie?" Trixi-lyn laughed. "Your Song for Tomorrow fantasy will be crushed before the end of the first verse. Did you seriously think four kids from that hick town of Sheridan could topple a great king like Bu-usah?"

Jon lurched forward to strangle this new princess but was held back by Geof. "Not now, my friend. Not now."

CHAPTER 31

Princess Trixi-lyn

A leash was put around Uriah's neck as Geof and Jon were tied to the reins of their horses. Geof tried to muster some Walking Horse magic to free them. But nothing came to him. Whatever powers the Chyn gave him were either gone or hiding. The usually animated Jon was withdrawn and distraught, realizing that his crush was not the girl he believed her to be. She was the loyal daughter of a murdering, evil king.

Geof knew he had to shock his partner back to reality if they were to stay alive. He needed Jon now more than ever.

"Come on, dude," he chided him. "You need to get back in the game."

Jon raised his gloomy eyes. "I don't think we were ever in the game."

"As random as it sounds, an entire world is depending on us."

"That's not random. It's—it's random."

"We can't let a little thing like Pat being a lying, traitorous, double-crossing, backstabbing, little witch derail us, can we?"

Jon's eyes turned fire engine red. "She will pay for this; I swear she will."

Geof looked down at Uriah, who was being half dragged to keep up with the horses. "Are you okay?" he asked.

"Degrading and humiliating. That is what this is. Degrading and humiliating."

"Yeah, but you are alive, and we intend to keep you that way. We have to let things come to us right now. Our moment will come. I feel it."

Knowing the power of Chyn medicine, this last sentence comforted Uriah. Geof was right. Their time would come.

Turncoat prisoner Jok-imo was riding free alongside the sparkling but treacherous Pat. The boys continued to be perplexed at the Trixi-lyn/Jok-imo dynamic. "Jok-imo gave an Oscar-worthy performance of being anti-Bu-usah," Geof said. "So why did she buy his story now without question? It doesn't seem like she knew him from before. Something doesn't add up."

The Royal Guard drifted ahead unconcerned about Jon and Geof. Jon, like Geof, was perplexed by Jok-imo. "I agree with you about Jok-imo. He acts like he was a spy all long. But I'm confused."

"The math is not right," Geof said. "At least we know why Pat kept her face hidden. It wasn't from fear, but to hide from anybody who could recognize her."

"Like Jok-imo?"

"Yes, like Jok-imo."

Jon struggled to regain his balance. "We have to do something before Pat spills the beans on that cave to her father. That will be the end of the Secret City, Lantuc, and the whole shooting match. I'm afraid I don't have any great ideas right now. Even if I did, we don't know where this castle is or anything else. This way they will take us right to it—"

"Yeah. Right to it. Interesting. Hey Princess Trick-see-lyn," Geof yelled. "Would it kill you cretins to let Uriah ride with us? I mean, he gave you dinner."

Pat pirouetted her horse and charged back to get in Geof's face. "Don't expect me to return the favor," she laughed. "Ren-te, put the cain on the horse with the small invader," she commanded.

"Wait a minute," Geof said. "I don't get it. How did you get to Sheridan? What about your parents?"

"Why should I tell you?"

"Who are we gonna tell?"

"For once, you are right. You will never have the chance to tell anyone. At the Secret City, Vandu-un heard rumors of your world, and it was decided that I should be the one to enter and learn what I could to protect us from people like—well, like you."

"People like us? We're about as threatening as cottage cheese."

"Really? I had plenty of opportunity to learn about your endless wars and your cruelty, not only to each other but even more to every other creature in your world. And you condemn us for being the same?"

"We would fight against cruelty and torture in your world or ours. Your father is a heartless savage. And while we're talking about dads, what about your parents in Sheridan? Are they part of your little spy team?"

Trixi-lyn laughed. "They are no parents of mine. They found me shortly after I entered your world. I must have looked lost to them. They took pity on me as a poor, homeless child. Your people are incredibly weak and embarrassingly easy to fool. They took care of me and said it was okay to call them mom and dad. I just became what they wanted me to be. No person in Mu-jin would be so easily fooled."

"You must have been very brave to go there alone," Geof said, attempting a flanking movement.

"My people are smart, and they are brave," Pat replied, not taking the bait.

"Looks to me like lots of them are starving too,"

"You see nothing," she snapped.

"I may be naïve, but you are blind. And what about Bloomingdales? Art museums? How did you know about all that?"

Pat laughed wickedly. "Television. Internet. Music. I learned all about those things in a short time. While you were avoiding your schoolwork, I was studying you—easiest subject in the world. Hee Heeeee!" she cackled, dumping Geof and retaking the lead of the procession.

"Oh my God, Geof." Jon gulped. "If we don't stop her, she'll bring guns and fast food... and tattoos... and, and, and other stuff like rap music to Sergel-tuteron."

"We'll stop her," Geof said in a most solemn tone. "I swear we will."

"Oh man, you don't mean kill her, do you?"

Geof paused for a long time and said nervously, "At any cost. Right now, only she knows about that stuff. Nobody here can find out... Nobody."

Prince Uriah looked stoically at Geof. "I agree with you."

"Huh?"

"Some in our own royal family know about your weapons, and they must be kept out at any cost."

Jon attempted to hold up his bound hand. "Are you shitting me? If you guys knew about them, why didn't you— you know—smuggle a few in and blast Bu-usah back to the Stone Age?"

"That decision was made by Queen Alma."

"The phantom Queen Alma again," Geof grunted. "What is so great about her, anyway?"

"She is most wise. She said that if we brought those weapons, we could not keep them a secret from Bu-usah forever. In no time, he would get them too, and Sergel-tuteron would be like your world. We choose to preserve our way of life in victory or defeat."

"That is the stupidest thing I ever heard of," Jon said bitterly. "Now that tramp princess will spill the beans to her father, and you'll be spitting Uzi marbles through what's left of your teeth."

"I don't know why, but I hate either of us talking about her like that," Geof frowned.

Jon ground his teeth. "Man, if I could, I would drive a sword right between her lying shoulder blades."

"Choose your time for battle, my friend," Uriah counseled. "It will come."

Jok-imo rode back to break them up. "Stop talking," he ordered. "It will only make matters worse for you."

"Congratulations," Geof sneered. "You fooled everybody, you lying piece of garbage."

Jok-imo looked deep into Geof's eyes and said in a quiet voice. "We are all sailors, and sailors must tilt their sails to the wind. Do you understand?" Geof felt Jok-imo could be trying to tell him something, But what? Jok-imo held Geof's gaze for a few moments and rejoined Trixi-lyn.

"What do you s'pose he meant by that?" Jon whispered.

"Unknown. But I think we should follow his advice."

The two boys were left to their thoughts as the parade wound its way past field after field. In the distance, they could see the outline of Bu-usah's castle. Lush patches of greenery were strategically placed in front of the castle to give the illusion of healthy farmland to any visitors.

Trixi-lyn again trotted back to rub a little salt in the festering wounds in the hearts and egos of Jon and Geof. Her blue eyes pierced every defensive veil and frayed what was left of their burgeoning manhood. She motioned to one of the Marilyn Monroe-style guards to put a collar around Geof's neck and affixed the other end to his saddle with a chain. Jon was left alone.

"Look familiar?" she laughed. "The king has heard the little stories of your Song for a long time. I will show him that there is no truth to them. That image from the Song is real because I choose to make it real. You soon will recognize what a pathetic illusion that Song for Tomorrow is. You have been tricked into thinking you are something you are not and that you have abilities you could never possess." She drew her face close to Geof's to put an exclamation point on her assault. "Your little Chyn experience is nothing but a cruel trick played on you. I almost feel sorry for you."

Jon's red face burned at Trixi-lyn. "You saw it was no trick. I suggest you save your sympathy for yourself. Tyrants are always defeated by people they underestimate."

"Maybe in your world but not mine. Again, I tell you. Be silent if you want to live." Trixi-lyn spun her horse with a flourish and left Geof once again staring at her back.

"I guess you told her," Jon smacked.

"Yeah. I guess I did." Geof stared ahead at the former Pat, and the soupy concrete that had been his will began to harden. "We may have a surprise or two in store for her and her father." He bent down and tugged at the annoying collar around his neck. He looked over the top of his glasses and glared at the princess. "Soon you will be wearing this, not me."

"For once, I really want to believe you," Jon nodded thinly.

"So do I," Uriah said.

"Me too," Geof sighed as he rode ahead. "Me too."

CHAPTER 32

So Near, and Yet So Far

The humiliated Searchers stood before the castle of Bu-usah dwarfed by its grandeur. Constructed of huge blocks of carved stone, it looked like an impenetrable fortress. Opulence dripped unapologetically from every gargoyle, column, and statue, a spectacle of carved excellence that rivaled the great stone masterpieces of Europe. If the wealth of Mu-jin flowed downhill, the castle of Bu-usah was at the bottom, gobbling it up with insatiable greed.

"How do you s'pose they built this thing?" Geof asked Jon. "I saw no rocks within miles of this place, and they have no machines."

Jon leaned in closely and grinned, "Just like the pyramids... aliens."

Geof chuckled. But in his reality-based mind, slave labor, tons of slave labor, was more likely, and more frightening.

As they approached a massive rock arch that outlined the entrance to the outer courtyard, the road narrowed, revealing a fifty-foot deep moat, complete with a mammoth wooden drawbridge that dropped on cue when Trixi-lyn came into view. As the princess advanced, she shook her head, and her sunlit hair descended over her shoulders like a waterfall. Her back straightened, and royalty oozed from her pores. The drawbridge fell into place with a thud, and the Marilyn Monroes briefly reined in their horses, leaving them fifteen feet behind Trixi-lyn.

As Trixi-lyn entered the archway, the stone walls shook from the shouts of people assembled inside the wall. People were throwing flowers and crying as they hoped to glimpse, or even touch, the princess.

"Get the bucket," Jon choked. "I'm going to throw up for a week."

"Yeah," Geof nodded. "One second she's our friend, and the next she's such an uber-star she makes Princess Di look like an untouchable. The only catch is, she's the bad guy. Man, you reeeealy know how to pick 'em."

"You liked her too, Bud," Jon shot back. "But look at her. I haven't seen this much adoration since junior high when I accidentally walked into the girl's locker room without my shirt."

Geof laughed.

Uriah growled at them. "I am beginning to think my initial impression of you was right."

"What impression?" Jon asked.

"That you are fools."

"Now wait just a darned minute—"

"Calm down, Jon." Geof leaned close to Uriah. "Sparring with Jon keeps me sharp. It's what we do."

Ren-te turned and said, "Move forward, stay close to me, and do not make any sudden moves."

"Sure, baby," Jon cracked.

Ren-te gave him a toxic stare. "The king will silence your insolent mouth."

"I think she likes you," Geof winked.

"It'll never work. She's geographically undesirable."

The procession crossed the drawbridge, and adoration turned to hate. The Marilyn Monroes pushed the people back as they rode through. Citizens who threw rose petals under the hooves of Trixi-lyn's horse now threw venom and had to be physically repelled.

With the view in front of them blocked, Jon and Geof could not see Trixi-lyn gallop back toward them. The only evidence of her presence was the change in the crowd, which collectively dropped to one knee and lowered their heads.

"Touch not the prisoners," she admonished in a loud voice. "They must be preserved for the king's pleasure."

The multitude obligingly backed away, providing clear passage for two defiant teenagers and one stiff-necked dog. The people either held unwavering respect for Trixi-lyn or lived in complete fear of her. Either way, her word was law.

The trek from the moat to the castle entrance seemed to take forever but was only a few minutes. Inside the cavernous opening to the castle was an area filled with stalls and the smell of livestock. Trixi-lyn dismounted and handed her horse to a stable hand. She gestured for the others to do likewise, and they dutifully did. "Follow me," the princess ordered. Geof picked up Uriah as the Marilyn Monroes led him down a straw-covered walkway leading to an unfriendly hall with doors every twelve feet. Each door had a ten-inch square window with bars on it. Geof and Jon looked at the doors and knew that they would presently be on the wrong side of one. Ren-te stopped in front of a door and opened it.

"I do not know why, but the princess has pity on you," she said. "Prisoners like you are usually sent to the University."

"That's too bad. I'm a fast learner," Jon sneered.

"You will learn very fast. I requested the honor of being your guard, and the princess granted it. I can make the stable cells very persuasive."

"I told you she liked you," Geof smirked.

"Can you blame her?"

"Be silent and get inside," Ren-te commanded.

Geof quickly entered, hoping no one would notice Uriah in his arms. Ren-te made no mention of him, which was strange. Jon followed Geof, and the door slammed behind them.

Trixi-lyn peered through the bars. "Do be comfortable. When I see you again, you will call me Trixi-lyn, Princess of Mu-jin."

Geof walked to the window and stared into Trixi-lyn's eyes. "Don't do it."

"Don't do what? You are hardly in a position to give orders."

"Don't do it," Geof said again firmly.

"What is it all you crazies keep talking about? Destiny? Well, I have mine too. Let us see who fulfills their destiny first." She tossed something onto the straw floor, spun away from the door, and disappeared.

Geof and Jon dropped to the ground to search for whatever it was Trixi-lyn threw inside. It was a small key. Jon inserted the key into the collar around Geof's neck. The collar popped open.

"Feel better?" Jon asked.

"I guess a little."

Jon sat down next to his friend, and Uriah joined them. Jon shook his head. "This ain't right. We're supposed to get that Sceptre, defeat Bu-usah, become heroes, and get the girls. I saw it in a movie."

"Yeah," Geof said, his eyes firmly closed. He gently banged the back of his head against the wall. "What would my dad do?"

"Well, I know one thing. He'd never give up. Never."

"You know, Jon? For once, you're right. And we won't either. No matter how long it takes, we're gonna get out of here, we're gonna kick that snake's nonexistent butt, and we are gonna get that Sceptre. In fact, I can't wait to get my hands on it and cram it down that lying Pat's throat."

"A poor use of the Sceptre, my young Searcher," Uriah said.

"You have to start somewhere. Consider it a warmup. And yet—"

"And yet what?" Jon asked.

"And yet, I am confused with this whole Trixi-lyn thing."

"It seems pretty clear to me," Jon growled. "She's as evil as her father."

"But why did she give me this key? Why did she let us keep Uriah from harm? And most of all, why did she so easily accept Jok-imo as being on her side? I mean, he was pretty convincing that he hated Bu-usah."

Uriah did not know the answers to those questions. But despite his dilemma, he felt he truly was in the presence of the legendary Searcher, and he felt proud. He held his paw out. Geof grabbed it, and Jon laid his hand on Geof's knuckles. "To the Searcher," Uriah said, looking Geof squarely in the eye.

"To the Searcher," Jon said.

"To Walking Horse," the Bear said defiantly. "We're gettin' outta here."

CHAPTER 33

Castle Bu-usah

Princess Trixi-lyn readied herself for a triumphant return to the court of her father, King Bu-usah of Mu-jin. She stood straight and tall, chin slightly canted upward, Artemenk's faux Mu-jin clothing perfectly in place. The panorama of the great hall opened to her like curtains parting before a Broadway play. Trixi-lyn strode into the hall, her aura of nobility casting a spell on all those who looked upon her. An adoring public lined both sides of the hall and bowed slightly as she passed. Several feet or so in front of her sat King Bu-usah on his gaudy throne, and between the king and his daughter stood the ever-present Vandu-un.

Vandu-un shuffled up to meet the princess and bowed with enough panache to make Cyrano blush. He straightened up, his signature Cheshire cat grin plastered on his face in all its counterfeit splendor.

"Your Majesty," he purred. "Let me be the first to exult in your safe return home. I do not believe the kingdom could have borne another day without your presence."

"Thank you," the princess said coldly.

Sensing his schtick was bombing, Vandu-un slipped smoothly into plan B and turned to announce her return to the court proudly. "Your Majesty, it is with joyous and humble gratitude that I present the return of Princess Trixi-lyn." After another overdone bow, Vandu-un strategically withdrew from the limelight, leaving the king and princess to greet each other. Bu-usah stood up and descended to the long red carpet upon which his daughter stood, his craggy features disguising what was really going on in his head. "My beautiful Trixi-lyn, you have returned."

Trixi-lyn bowed slightly and said mechanically, "I am happy to be back, Father."

"Your country eagerly awaits the information you have for us, but first we must celebrate your return... and I am told you bring guests. How strangely you treat them."

"I bring prisoners, Father."

"Prisoners? Bring them before your king."

Ren-te discretely slipped from the hall and proceeded to the stables. She reluctantly unlocked the door and led the three prisoners before the throne. Bu-usah circled them, looked at Ren-te, and then at Trixi-lyn. He threw back his head and laughed. "Why, they're children. Your prisoners are just children."

"Do not be influenced by their innocence, Father. The tall one is believed by the fools in Sergel-tuteron to be the Searcher from that Song for Tomorrow nonsense."

King Bu-usah directed himself to Geof. Geof shot his most disrespectful glare. After everything he had heard about the king of Mu-jin, it took all his willpower not to strangle the king then and there.

Bu-usah looked at Uriah and Jon and smiled at Geof. "So, young man, we have heard such sad tales of a Searcher forever. Am I to believe that the Eruds are so desperate that they are now trying to convince a mere child such as yourself that *you* are this phantom Searcher?"

Geof shuffled his feet. "I have to admit it seems a little silly."

Bu-usah reached up, put an avuncular arm around the fidgety Geof, and patted him on the shoulder. "Come with me."

A guard stood rigidly as the king directed them to a small but elegantly furnished room behind the throne. Several matching chairs were scattered haphazardly around the room, leaving everyone unsure of what they were supposed to do. King Bu-usah took the lead by turning one chair to face the others and deposited himself casually into it. Uriah found comfort between Geof's two large feet and rested his chin on Geof's left sandal. Trixi-lyn sat next to the king and glanced at Jon, her icy gaze stabbing one more hole in his Swiss cheese pride. Jon looked away, unwilling to waste another second of precious vision on this beautiful, but deceitful, female. Most guys his age dealt with the humiliation of being turned down for a date to the movies—kid's stuff.

Geof and Jon looked at each other and back at the king, who smiled at them with the beneficence of a pope about to bless kittens on St. Francis day. He stroked his chin and

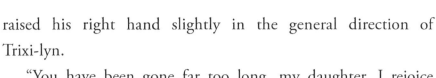

raised his right hand slightly in the general direction of Trixi-lyn.

"You have been gone far too long, my daughter. I rejoice in your return and await your report."

Vandu-un leaned toward her, his green-teethed grin grossing out everyone in the room. "Yessss, Princess. Tell us about your travels."

Trixi-lyn looked Vandu-un square in the eye and replied, "A waste of the princess's life. The stories you told me about some secret land are fairy tales."

The king looked up in shock, and Vandu-un's demeanor immediately changed. He jumped out of his chair, a vein in his forehead visibly throbbing. "What do you mean fairy tales? Do you humor us now, or are you just lying?"

The conversation had taken a sharp left turn from what the boys expected. "What is she doing?" Geof whispered.

Trixi-lyn sat with the confidence of a princess and replied, "They are fairy tales. Dreams."

"Sergel Tuteron himself spoke to me many times of this other world. And what about them?" Vandu-un demanded, pointing a bony finger at the perplexed teenage visitors. "Did they just fall out of the sky? Hmmm? Hrmmumpfh!"

Trixi-lyn laughed and faced down the infuriated Vandu-un. "I brought them here to put to rest once and for all the silly rumors of magic kingdoms and undiscovered lands. These so-called Searchers are nothing more than simple farmhands from Agron. They have been duped by the Eruds, as have you." She turned to face her father directly. "There is no magic hindering your destiny. Tell the king the truth," she ordered the boys. Her blue eyes penetrated their brains, which were at the moment, completely cross-threaded.

Geof and Jon had no idea where she was going with this, but right now, the smart money was on going with the flow. They both nodded weakly. "Yeah. Farmers... errr, farmhands. People who live on a farm. You know, farm..."

Vandu-un's upper lip curled wickedly as he mounted another attack on the princess. "And where have you been all this time?"

"Chasing your phantoms."

"And this is what you bring us?" The king finally joined in. "These two..."

"Farmers," Jon muttered.

"Yes, farmers," Trixi-lyn confirmed. "And what is worse, they are so low they are in the employ of this cain. They are simpletons, just playthings for the Eruds."

Vandu-un stomped around the room like a two-year-old who was just told it was bedtime. "You were sent on the most vital mission, and this is what you bring us? Two... two..."

"Farmers," Geof said proudly

"Insolence!" Vandu-un cried. "I will expose you as the liars you are... And you too, Princess... you... you... you..."

The king leaped from his chair and admonished his number one subject. "Do not say such words to the princess. I will send you to the University."

Geof and Jon cringed, but at the same time, hoped these two madmen would destroy each other on the spot. Vandu-un walked defiantly up to the king and said in a low voice, "I don't think so."

With that, he swirled and left the room, glaring at Trixi-lyn for effect. With Vandu-un's exit, Trixi-lyn lowered her head and spoke contritely to her father. Her demeanor was that of a girl who was busted for taking the family car without permission. "I have failed you. I am sorry."

The king looked at his daughter and thought for a long time. He said, "You have not failed, my daughter. Exposing false Searchers is equally important as defeating real Searchers. If these two—what did you call yourselves?"

"Farmers," Geof and Jon again mumbled simultaneously.

"Yes," Bu-usah bellowed gleefully. "Farmers. Of course. What else?" Still laughing, the king again put his hand on Geof's chest. "You represent no threat to me," he laughed.

Geof and Jon laughed uncomfortably with him. "Who us? No chance."

Bu-usah's smile darkened. "Still, you cannot be too careful," he said with a steely stare. "I will turn you over to Joneva, beginning with you," he gnashed at Uriah. Uriah sniffed defiantly.

Bu-usah raised his hand to call for the expulsion of his so-called guests but was checked by Trixi-lyn. "Where is Irishka-ru?" she asked sweetly. Bu-usah stopped in his tracks and backpedaled.

Geof raised his right eyebrow. "Who's Irishka-ru?"

"Sister," Uriah said.

"Where is Irishka-ru?" she repeated with more emphasis.

Bu-usah turned his back to her and said, "In the chapel."

"What?" she bristled. "Why?"

"Treason," he said simply.

"Impossible," Trixi-lyn panted. "She is as loyal to you as I am."

"She was," he said.

"How could you imprison my sister?" she wailed. "I want to see her."

"Of course, in due time."

"No! Now. Now or I will give you no more information."

"My dear, you needn't threaten me. Of course, you may see her." Bu-usah called the guard. "Take them to Joneva," he waved.

"And I thought we were gonna be friends," Geof said sarcastically.

"A king has no friends." Bu-usah turned his back and walked away.

Guards grabbed the three interlopers and spirited them from the room. Out of the corner of his eye, Geof thought he could see Pat, not Trixi-lyn, watching them go.

The door closed behind them, leaving Trixi-lyn and her father alone.

CHAPTER 34

Irishka-ru and the Broom Closet

Trixi-lyn looked her father straight in the eye. "What happened with Irishka-ru?"

Bu-usah stared into space. "She plotted insurrection against me."

"What?"

"Oh, the pain of being a trusting and benevolent king," Bu-usah wailed. "I learned that she was secretly involved with the traitor, Halb-ean."

"Halb-ean, a traitor?" Trixi-lyn asked, feigning surprise. She heard the story of Halb-ean from Jok-imo but was torn. Years of obedience to the king directed Trixi-lyn to spill the beans on Lantuc, but her sister's incarceration made her pause.

"Yes. Halb-ean tried to raise the people against me. Like my own son betraying me. And his co-conspirator—my own daughter. Why? Why?"

Trixi-lyn could name several good reasons why anyone would betray him, but her mind was on her sister. She would ignore the Halb-ean issue for now. "I must see her, Father… to hear for myself."

Bu-usah feigned dejection by cradling his forehead in his right hand. "Then go. Your heart will be broken too."

Trixi-lyn left without a word. Her father's hollow display of emotion did not mesh with the image of a father who, in a fit of paranoia, was rumored to have murdered her mother.

The climb to the chapel was not an easy one. During the reign of Bu-usah's father, the chapel was home to high-level weddings and ceremonies of honor. The three hundred steps were three feet wide, with the only light coming from a small window every twenty steps. Circular, with a huge stone pillar in the center and no crystals, the dark and musty stairway was unwelcoming. The chapel had been a playroom for the child Irishka-ru but was now her lonely jail cell. There was a small anteroom directly at the top of the stairs occupied by a single guard. He was nearing the end of a long, boring day and could barely keep his eyes open. His chair leaned back against the wall, the front legs eight inches off the ground. Startled by the sound of Trixi-lyn, he jerked his body erect and banged the back of his head on the wall with a thud. He jumped to his feet and came to attention before the bemused Trixi-lyn.

"Your Royal Highness," he flustered. "I was just—I—"

"Your name, guard?" Trixi-lyn answered, pretending to be unaware of his lapse in diligence.

"I am Ranpaz, your loyal servant. Welcome home, Your Highness."

"I grant you your leave, Ranpaz. I will alert the king to your dedicated service."

Her simple directive made Ranpaz feel like he had one foot stuck in quicksand and the other in a bucket of rattlesnakes. Either way he moved, he was in big trouble. His orders came from the king himself and specifically forbade anyone to see the Princess Irishka-ru. But, to disobey Princess Trixi-lyn would mean certain death. If Bu-usah learned he quit his post without being properly relieved, he would meet an equally unpleasant end. This was a high wire act not normally encountered by a man of his stature, and Ranpaz felt frozen in his own skin.

Trixi-lyn sensed his discomfort. "I am here on orders from my father. You are to wait in the anteroom to guard against any who might attempt to harm me."

This was the best offer Ranpaz was to get today. How could he be held guilty if he obeyed the princess's orders to protect her? To let something happen to the king's favorite daughter would not only mean death but a slow and painful one. As the princess was present and the king was not, he had no choice.

"Your humble servant." He stepped aside.

Trixi-lyn opened the door to the chapel and quietly went in. The chapel was beautiful. Rich tapestries and beautiful paintings adorned the walls and ceiling. Several stained-glass windows displayed scenes of high-level everyday life. Rows of chairs with ornately carved backs faced a stage area on which sat three even more ornate chairs. At the far end of the front row sat a small figure, her back to Trixi-lyn. She was hunched over, and her arms were crossed in front of her stomach, the picture of defeat.

"Ishka," Trixi-lyn said softly.

Irishka-ru raised her head slowly, swirled around, and managed a smile with the effort of someone who had forgotten how. She rose to her feet to see her sister running to her. They hugged, and tears flowed freely.

Irishka-ru was, like Trixi-lyn, a beautiful young woman, several years older, but very much her sister. Hair not as blonde as Trixi-lyn's, eyes more green than blue, but with her high forehead, pronounced cheekbones, and flawless skin, she was a kindred classic beauty by any standard.

"Ishka," Trixi-lyn sobbed. "The king told me such horrible things."

Irishka-ru turned away. "He is mad, you know. Completely mad. He starves our people while sending you on silly journeys to find make-believe adversaries."

"Our father told me you had a relationship with Halb-ean, he who has been executed for treason."

"I—I can't say. I don't know if I can trust even you, my dear sister."

Irishka's comment shot a poison dart into Trixi-lyn's heart. The sisters grew up being each other's gold standard for loyalty. "You cannot mean that," Trixi-lyn gasped. "You can trust me with your life."

"That is exactly what I would be doing," her sister answered, still looking the other way. "Our father keeps me alive for information. If he thought I had nothing more to tell, I would be dead already."

"Do you really think our father would kill you?"

"You know it is true."

Trixi-lyn did know it was true. He was father in name only. The warm, nurturing touch of an affectionate father was a foreign language to the girls. When passing through streets lined by adoring commoners, the princesses looked with envy upon the poorest children who were cuddled by loving fathers.

"Ishka. Tell me what happened. Your secrets are safe with me."

Irishka-ru paced the floor. To survive, she knew she must once again place her heartbeat in her sister's hands.

"After you left, Father became increasingly unstable. And there is something between him and Vandu-un that is even more frightening."

"There has always been competition between Father and Vandu-un."

"This is different, Trixi. I don't think it is just competition. It is just... just... evil."

"Ishka, what can I do?"

"Nothing, I am soon going to die."

"No," Trixi-lyn shouted. "I won't let them. I will—I will get you out of here."

Ishka forced a smile. "That is not possible. The king's eyes are everywhere."

"I can get you out. We can run away from the castle."

"Away? There is no away. The king will reward any citizen who betrays us and kill any who help us. Even if you could get me out of here, there is nowhere to go."

"There might be," Trixi-lyn said carefully.

Unaware of Trixi-lyn's adventures as Pat Chamness, Irishka-ru could not believe that her baby sister could pull off anything as bold as an escape from the king. To her, she was just a sheltered kid.

"I can take you to the Secret City," Trixi-lyn blurted.

Irishka-ru looked at her sister and shook her head. "The Secret City? What do you know of the Secret City? Besides, soon there will be no Secret City."

"No, no, no," Trixi-lyn corrected. "I need to tell you something. But now, I require your trust."

"You have it."

"The Eruds know the king is going to attack them. The king's fleet will never make it to the Secret City, not all the way anyway."

"The fleet?"

"Yes, the Eruds know of the attack, and they are preparing for it. With their superior intelligence, they—"

Ishka's piercing eyes stopped her sister in mid-sentence. "You don't know, do you?"

"Don't know what? I just got back. What should I know?... What should I know?"

"Stopping the fleet will not save the Secret City."

"What do you mean?"

"Before his death, Halb-ean told me he learned the Secret City would be attacked by both land and sea. While the Eruds are distracted by the fleet, they will be set upon from the rear and destroyed."

"I heard this. But the Great Canyon is impenetrable."

"I thought that too. But from my window, I have seen the royal condors carry Vandu-un and the king toward the Great Canyon and back again."

Trixi-lyn's heart raced. "That means... the condors... the condors must... know a way."

The royal condors were favored even above horses among creatures in Mu-jin. They were huge and graceful and afforded the king the gift of flight. Their nesting areas were high along the walls of the Great Canyon, at least they were until they were enslaved by the king. "Perhaps the condors provide a view from above that reveals a safe avenue through the canyon," Irishka-ru said.

"Come. We must find our way to the condors," Trixi-lyn panted.

"But..." Her voice failed her as Trixi-lyn dragged her to the anteroom where Ranpaz waited nervously.

"Your Majesties!" Ranpaz exclaimed, jumping to his feet. "What are you doing?"

"We are going to see my father," Trixi-lyn said.

"But—but—Your Majesty. The king—"

"The king will reward you handsomely for keeping us safe from those who have framed the loyal Princess Irishka-ru," Trixi-lyn said, determined not to break stride.

Ranpaz dug deep within himself to muster the courage to challenge the princess. "I—cannot let you do this. I have my orders."

Trixi-lyn stopped. "Perhaps you are right, loyal servant of the king. I will produce the king, and you can hear from his own mouth. Return the princess to the chapel."

Ranpaz breathed a huge sigh of relief. "Your obedient servant."

Ranpaz guided Irishka-ru back to the chapel, turning his back on Trixi-lyn. She grabbed a small statue and whacked him across the back of the head. Ranpaz fell forward and struck his forehead on the stone floor. Trixi-lyn knelt by his motionless body and was relieved to find he was still alive. She shoved Irishka-ru out of the chapel and locked the unfortunate Ranpaz in.

They hurried blindly to the circular stairway in a near panic. The realization that two princesses would have little chance to go anywhere unnoticed in suspicion-riddled Mu-jin brought the sisters to a halt. Once they got to the bottom of the stairway, a guard would still be at the door, and this would be the shortest escape on record.

"What are we doing?" Irishka-ru trembled. "We will never get out of here."

"Yes, we will. Let me think." Trixi-lyn stared at the door. A few minutes before, her impetuous rescue attempt seemed like not only a good idea, but the only idea. But now it had the feel of a plan without a plan, and Trixi-lyn felt like she was leading her sister from the frying pan into the fire.

Trixi-lyn's despair was Irishka-ru's inspiration. She clapped her hands excitedly and said, "Trixi! The broom closet! Remember?"

Trixi stared at her older sister and smiled. The broom closet offered freedom only a few feet away inside the hollow pillar. "Do you remember the first time we found it?" Trixi smiled wistfully. "We thought we got locked in and would starve to death, and nobody would ever find us."

"Yes. I remember. That was many epochs ago." The two girls looked in each other's eyes and, for a few soothing moments, drifted back to their childhood.

"Look Irishka-ru. Look," eight-year-old Princess Trixi-lyn said. "I banged my elbow against that thing that looks like a man's head, and this little door popped open. Can we go inside and see what is in there?"

"Of course." The door opened three inches from the wall. With some difficulty, Irishka-ru wiggled the stone door open and peeked inside. "This is extraordinary," Princess Irishka-ru said in a tone that validated her standing as a well-educated and refined royal. "I see a little room and another stairway. Help me get the dirt out of the way so the door will open more easily."

Adrenaline pumping, the two sisters cleaned epochs of gunk from under the door, making it operate so smoothly that even young Trixi could work it with ease. They went inside, and without thinking, closed the foot-thick door behind them. The door was masterfully built and fit so snugly into the wall that no seam was visible.

Total darkness terrified the girls, but within a few seconds, the stairway was dimly lit as multiple crystals delivered much-needed light. The light was dim but sufficient enough for Irishka-ru to find another carving in the shape of a man's head near the top of the door. It clicked when she pushed it, and the door opened again. Realizing they were not trapped, the girls closed the door again and excitedly descended the stairway. At the bottom, the stairs came to a dead end, along with their adventure. There was no landing after the bottom step. The steps ended abruptly against the wall. "This is so strange," Irishka-ru said. "The stairs end at the wall. Why do you think they would do that?"

"I do not know," Trixi shrugged. "Maybe whoever built this decided not to finish it." She ran her fingers over the craggy wall and found a head-shaped carving identical to the others. She pressed it, and again she heard the sound of a latch. A sliver of light pierced the doorway. This door did not move easily, but in time revealed a neglected and overgrown outdoor garden obscured by a large hedge. Irishka-ru was puzzled. How could they exit the center of the stairway without stepping smack into Bu-usah's royal hall? She walked around the stone structure and realized that the doorway into the garden was beneath the level of the throne room. Nobody of any importance would waste their time in what was essentially a place for lowly workers. It was the perfect hiding place.

"Look at this. Look at this," Trixi-lyn squealed. Irishka-ru stuck her head through a hedge and got her first look at normal Mu-jinians struggling to get through another day. "Watch them with me, Ishka."

Spying on average Mu-jinians became the best television show the girls could ever hope for. Whatever interesting things they could find in their daily activities, there was always the specter of their father looming in the background. Bu-usah was the ultimate control freak, and his daughters were not immune to his tight fist. Every brain cell told them not to disobey their father, but the excitement of real life was irresistible. "I want to go out and meet some of those people," Irishka-ru said.

"I am a little scared," Trixi answered. She was still a long way from the age of required teenage rebellion. Even so, she idolized her big sister and felt safe doing just about anything if she were in the shelter of Irishka-ru's wing.

Irishka-ru held out her hand, and Trixi took it. The princesses parted the hedge and took their first steps on a road destined to change their lives in ways they could not imagine. Outside of the hedge was a forbidden world where people worked, and struggled, and starved. In this watershed moment, two sheltered girls came face to face with the consequences of their father's iron-handed rule.

"Let us not go too far from the castle," Irishka-ru said.

Trixi held her sister's hand as they walked. Everyone in the fields stopped their work momentarily to size up these pretty strangers. The princesses were used to being the center of attention wherever they went. After all, they were the princesses adored by all. But these people were not supposed to know who they were. Trixi squeezed her sister's hand. "Why is everybody staring at us."

"I do not know. We look no different from them."

The precocious Trixi looked at her sister and back at the workers toiling in the fields. "Yes, we do. Look at their clothes."

Irishka instantly saw the Mu-jinians through Trixi-lyn's eyes. They were all dirty. Very dirty. She looked down at her spotless, bright white tunic. "We are too clean. Quick, Trixi. Lie down and roll around in the dirt."

Trixi obeyed, and the girls did the most un-princess-like thing ever, getting filthy dirty. When they got up, they pointed at each other and laughed uncontrollably. Their clothes were dirty. Their faces, arms, and legs were dirty. "This is fun." Trixi-lyn giggled like a child for the first time. "Look, nobody is looking at us anymore."

They boldly ventured forth, strolling hand in hand along a narrow road as they studied the work habits of the ordinary Mu-jinian. Their happy-go-lucky demeanor was tempered by the sad faces of the people in the fields. "Why do they look so unhappy?" Trixi asked her big sister.

Princess Irishka-ru looked down at three gold rings on her right hand. She removed them and stashed them in her pocket. "Better hide your rings, Trixi." Trixi-lyn dutifully obeyed. Unsure if their jewelry shielding efforts were seen by anyone or not, Irishka-ru decided the best course of action at the moment was to return to the castle. "Let us go back," she said. "The next time, we will be better prepared."

They reversed course and headed back toward the castle. As they passed by the people in the fields, Trixi shuddered and looked at Irishka. "I feel like someone is following us. Do you think Father knows?"

The realization came upon them that they may have been too quick on the draw to leave the safety of the castle without considering potential dangers. A pang of guilt shot up Irishka-ru's back as she realized that she might have put her young sister in danger. "I don't think Father knows. Just keep walking."

Irishka turned her head slightly and heard the unmistakable sound of footsteps right behind her. Trixi was right. "We must go faster," she whispered.

The girls were nearly back to the castle when Trixi felt something touch her shoulder. She stopped and screamed, "Ishka, help!"

Irishka-ru pivoted into a defensive posture but dropped her arms immediately. "It is okay, Trixi." Trixi turned and was relieved to see a young girl staring at them. She was in between Irishka and Trixi in age, very dirty, and dressed in tattered clothes. She was smiling at them.

"Hi. I am Robinh. I do not remember seeing you before."

Trixi smiled. "Hi. I am—" Irishka-ru flashed her hand to Trixi's mouth.

"I am Iris, and my sister is Teris," Irishka said politely. It was not allowed for anyone in the Kingdom of Mu-jin to have the same name as the royal princesses. Giving their real names would instantly blow their cover.

"Would you like to play with me?" Robinh said, her sunny disposition hiding her desperate situation.

"Sure," Trixi said. "We would like to make some new friends."

"Why have I not seen you before?"

Irishka-ru took the floor. "We live on the other side of the castle. Our mother and father came here from far away."

Robinh looked around. "If they are looking for work, there is little work here. We are lucky to have enough food to eat after we pay the king's tribute."

Irishka and Trixi looked at each other. "What is the king's tribute?" Irishka asked.

"We must give two-thirds of what we grow to the king. Did you not have such an arrangement where you lived before?"

"I do not know. My father handles those things," Irishka-ru sidestepped. "He is an officer in the king's legion, so we do not work in the fields." The back of her neck burned with shame. These people would hardly have enough to eat if they got to keep it all. Irishka thought about the mountains of food placed before them every day. They could eat to their heart's content. When they were full, the remaining food was thrown away.

"My father allows me to play before the lumen goes down," Robinh gushed. "He says it is very important that children play. He says it helps them to grow up to be good citizens."

"What do you do the rest of the time?" Trixi-lyn asked hesitatingly.

"I work in the fields, of course. What a silly question. Is that not what you do? Oh yes, you already said you did not."

Irishka-ru looked more closely at Robinh. She was a pretty girl with brownish hair. At least it looked brown. Irishka figured it might be much lighter if all the dirt were washed out. She had a very slender build consistent with being on an excessively restrictive diet. Still, she did not appear to be sickly.

"As I said, we do not work in the fields. My little sister and I, uh, work with the horses in the castle. That work gives us much free time."

"Ooo, that sounds so exciting. Horses work in the fields with us, but just before the lumen goes down, the king's men come and take them back to the castle. You might work with some of the same horses as me."

"Robinh! Robinh!" came a call in the distance. Robinh turned and saw a man running toward them.

"That is my uncle, Vladal. He is the leader of my family."

Vladal was quickly upon them. "Robinh. What are you doing here with these two strangers?"

"We were just going to play. My father said it was allowed."

"Sometimes your father is a reckless fool," Vladal snapped. "You do not even know these girls. They could be spies for the king. If they tell the king you take time out to play, he may think we do not work hard enough and punish us."

Irishka-ru stepped forward. "Do not be unhappy with Robinh. She just wanted to play. We will not turn you over to the king. We could not. Why would he listen to us? We are new here and want to be Robinh's friend. Will you not let Robinh play with us?"

Vladal crossed his arms and grunted. "Be careful. And you must be back in the field well before the lumen goes down."

"Yes, uncle."

Trixi grabbed Robinh by the hand. "I know a safe place we can play." She guided Robinh to the hedge and pulled her inside. The area inside the hedge was not large, but there was ample room to play in complete secrecy.

"This is wonderful," Robinh smiled. "Do you want to play imagine?"

Irishka and Trixi looked at each other. "Ummm. What is that?"

"Teris, you mean to tell me you do not know how to play imagine?"

"Not really."

"It is really simple and fun. All you have to do is imagine you are somewhere else, doing something else. I like to imagine that I live in the castle and have lots of servants and all the food I can eat. It makes my life so much easier."

Princess Irishka-ru could not bring her eyes from the ground. "Yes. That sounds fun. But what then?"

"Then, we imagine we are riding horses and playing with all the fun toys the princesses must have to play with. Don't you think it would be fun to be a princess and have toys?"

"Yes. That would be a lot of fun," Trixi said quietly.

The girls had fun playing imagine and other games suggested by Robinh. The princesses did not know how to play games of any kind. There was no room for such foolishness in the castle of Bu-usah. As the lumen began to descend in the sky, Robinh said her goodbyes. The time they spent together was so wonderful, it was agreed they would do it again the following day. Robinh entered the hedge but was pulled back by Irishka-ru. She rummaged in her pocket and pulled out one of the rings she had hidden. She handed it to Robinh. "We found this in the stables. I think it might have belonged to someone of importance. Please take it as a token of our friendship. It is likely you can buy a lot of food with it."

"I... I cannot accept this."

"You must accept it. It means our friendship is real and everlasting. Do not insult us by refusing this gift."

Robinh closed her hand around the ring. She said goodbye with tears in her eyes and promised to meet again tomorrow. Then she was gone. The princesses looked at each other helplessly. It was a rough initiation to the real world, and one they had a hard time processing. They had been taught by their father that he was a benevolent king, beloved by his loyal and happy subjects. The things he said clearly were not true. They did not understand.

"We need to hide until we can change our clothes," Irishka cautioned. "If the king sees us like this, we will be in a lot of trouble."

Trixi nodded. The girls successfully sneaked back into the castle, changed clothes, and no one was the wiser. The king demanded much from his daughters, but at the same time, paid little attention to them. To Bu-usah, the princesses were an asset to parade before his subjects as the picture of the perfect family of the perfect king.

"We will see Robinh tomorrow," Irishka-ru said. "But tomorrow, we will be prepared with extra clothes."

"And can we bring her some food?"

"Yes, little sister. That is a great idea."

Tomorrow did come. The girls got together for many tomorrows, and Robinh's family enjoyed their first full stomachs in a long time courtesy of the princesses. Playing together was a carefree recess from three unhappy lives. One was desperately poor and always hungry. And two who were never hungry but even poorer. Neither princess knew the joy of spontaneous laughter or the tender touch of a doting father. As pleasing as their time with Robinh was, it was destined to be short-lived.

The girls rendezvoused at the agreed-upon time and place. It was the usual carefree escape from two radically different prisons. Field hands pleaded, coaxed, and begged the land to work with them and bring forth new life. But years of abuse made the soil stubborn and defied the axiom that the oxen are slow, but the ground is patient. Robinh could see her uncle Vladal keeping one eye on her as he worked, protective family head was he. Knowing he was there gave her peace. Her father was forced to work an even harsher piece of farmland some distance away. It was decided that Robinh should stay with her uncle in a safer environment.

The stirring of dust in the distance was ominous. It could only mean that a substantial contingent of the king's men was on the way. Such an occurrence was not unheard of based on the proximity of the castle. The main road was not far from the small road bordering the farms and would usually host the members of the king's army. Not this time. They were on the small road, and that was generally not good news for the farmers.

As the dust cloud approached Vladal, the workers went into double time. If the king learned from his eyes and ears that farmers were dogging it, retribution would be swift and severe. The king's cavalry surrounded Vladal and his co-workers.

A look of horror crossed Robinh's face. "I must go back."

"What is it?" Princess Irishka-ru asked.

"They are going to take us."

Trixi held Robinh's arm with both hands. "Take you where?"

"To another place. The land has given up. We will be taken to another field to work. It will be hard. We will be blamed for the failure of this field."

"That is ridiculous," Irishka-ru frowned. "No one could blame you for this."

"King Bu-usah will. You do not know him."

Irishka-ru felt her spirit collapse. "I think you are right. Will we see you tomorrow?"

"I do not know. I do not know where we will be taken. I will try."

Robinh hugged her two cherished friends. They had given her affection, companionship, food, and, most of all, temporary liberation from her sad life. "I must go before they see where I am coming from. I must protect you. I love you, my friends." She crashed through the hedge at a full run. As innocent as playing with friends was, she could easily be blamed for the decline in food production. Playing instead of working would be the perfect excuse for Bu-usah to use Robinh's family as a warning to others that such frivolous departures from their assigned duties would be dealt with as only Bu-usah could.

"Wait," Irishka-ru screamed. But Robinh was too far away. The princess opened her hand and stared at the two rings in her palm. She had planned to give these to Robinh if her visits were ever in danger of stopping. It would not happen. Robinh left so fast there was no chance.

The princesses watched from the safety of the hedge as their friend and her family were herded away to a destination unknown. What happened to Robinh would become a somber mystery. She never came to play again.

King Bu-usah would be furious if he ever learned of his daughters' extracurricular activities. And thus, was born a sacred pact to forever guard their secret place. They had no way of knowing that faithfully honoring this covenant as children would prove to be their salvation years later. The sisterly bond allowed them to continue using the broom closet and the garden for playtime. But it was never the same after Robinh disappeared.

The sound of rapid footsteps and swords banging against the walls outside the broom closet brought the two princesses back to their present predicament. Reminiscing about Robinh was pleasant, but it was over. There was little time to flee from the palace. They opened the secret door to the garden and established their new realities as hunted fugitives.

Outside, they were temporarily out of peril. But new dangers that would never have threatened the girls behind the castle walls were all too real now. There were no protective guards, no food tasters, and no nannies. They were on their own without a friend in the world.

Finding temporary security in the secret garden, Trixi implored, "You must stop the legions before they all die trying to cross the Great Canyon."

"It is not possible," Irishka-ru said, sounding curiously distant.

"Not possible? You are the heir to the throne. They will listen to you... or maybe enough will to stop the others."

Irishka-ru hung her head. "You do not understand, Trixi. The legions marching to the Secret City are not the King's Eternals."

"Not the Eternals? They are the king's finest soldiers. Who else... ?"

"The Unborns," Irishka-ru choked.

A cold silence gripped the two sisters. Trixi-lyn gasped, "The Unborns?"

Irishka-ru nodded.

"The Unborns are only legend," Trixi-lyn said, desperately looking for any reason to make this horrific truth untrue.

But they did exist. The Unborns were an outcast group living in the far reaches of what was once the densest forest of Mu-jin. Little was known about them. Legend was that they had no mother or father but sprang from the earth fully grown, consumed with hatred for all those not of their own blood.

Bu-usah's assault on his own country's natural resources spread outward from the castle grounds until the Unborns' forest was in his sights. Bu-usah sent an army to throw the Unborns out of his coveted forest, but they were easily repelled. Bu-usah was stung by the defeat, but only until he realized that the Unborns could be the X factor he was looking for to destroy the pesky Eruds once and for all. At that moment, the prospect of the Unborns as friends was very appealing. He would make peace with them. The Unborns and their suspicious King Alwes wanted no friends, but Bu-usah was undaunted. He called upon the cunning and guile of the crafty Vandu-un to bring them to his side.

Vandu-un was not excited about this mission as people entering the forest of the Unborns never exited alive. But his apprehension was overcome by the tantalizing prospect of using the Unborns against the Eruds and their annoying Secret City. Vandu-un had his own motives for conquering the Secret City, motives he chose not to share with his king.

Vandu-un managed to arrange a meeting with Alwes. It took three messengers to accomplish it. Two did not return at all, but the third, shaking uncontrollably from fear, gave Vandu-un the invitation to an audience with Alwes. The Unborns were the Mu-jin Bigfoot. But they were very real and very dangerous. Nearly eight feet tall, their shoulders were huge and easily accommodated two muscular arms jutting from each. They had the basic pattern of a human face, but the addition of two large canine teeth and a massive square jaw gave them the appearance of deformed saber-tooth tigers.

They wore a thigh-length black tunic that was held up by a single strap over the right shoulder. On their feet were leather sandals laced up to the knees.

"They are real, too real." Irishka-ru sighed. "And what is worse, Vandu-un convinced them to join forces with our father."

"How?"

"Halb-ean told me that Vandu-un promised them all the forests in Sergel-tuteron if they helped secure the Secret City."

"You know that is a lie," Trixi said.

"Yes. The stupid Unborns do not know those forests have already been destroyed. That is the real reason I believe Father is attacking the Secret City. We have nothing left to build with. Nothing left to feed the people. And the king fears they will rebel against him."

"He thinks attacking the Secret City will prevent this?"

"Trixi... the Secret City is only part of it. He wants Agron and their food. You know he has always tried to convince the people that the Eruds and Agrons stole their food and caused them to starve."

"That makes no sense." Trixi-lyn closed her eyes, trying to understand Bu-usah's logic. "If he wants Agron, I still don't get why he is attacking the Secret City. Why not just attack Agron?"

"I do not know, but I overheard Father and Vandu-un arguing. Vandu-un insisted they conquer the Secret City first. He said the Eruds could protect Agron, and they needed to be eliminated. I don't think that is true, but Father believed him.

And it was a good enough story to convince our people that the Eruds and the Agrons were the cause of all their problems."

"None of that matters. We must stop the Unborns before they reach the Secret City. If we can convince them the king lied to them, they might abandon their attack."

"I agree, Sister. We must get to the condors. We must get to the Secret City. You can warn the Eruds, and I will attempt to stop the Unborns."

"That is much too dangerous," Trixi-lyn admonished. "I will go with you."

Irishka-ru stiffened her back. "I am the eldest, and it is my responsibility. If royal blood truly runs through my veins, I must put my people first. And if my life is to forfeit, so be it. I will go to the Unborns. You go to the Secret City. Come. We must waste no time."

The girls turned to make their way to the cages where the condors were held, but Trixi froze. She grabbed her sister by the arm and stopped her. "I cannot."

"What do you mean? You, too, have royal blood. Now is the time to honor it and help me undo the horrors of our father."

"I would not dishonor my heritage. But I brought friends here. And I know they will soon be thrown to Joneva to provide sport for the king."

"If they are with Joneva, you cannot save them. But you can save the Eruds."

Trixi-lyn shook her head. "I put them in danger. I cannot let them die with Joneva. Besides, I think they are the Searchers."

The Searchers? Irishka-ru knew of the Searchers from Vandu-un, and the possibility of their existence intrigued her. Now, two girls whose most difficult decision in their pampered lives had been to choose what to eat for dinner, had to pick between two pure and noble actions, neither of which offered much chance of success, or even survival.

"Okay, Trixi. Help me with the condors and go to your friends. I will try to stop the Unborns."

"How do you plan to do that?"

"I have no idea."

CHAPTER 35

They Are Here Somewhere

Princesses Irishka-ru and Trixi-lyn crept from the garden and slipped unnoticed past fields of sad Mu-jinians forever toiling to create an agricultural miracle in the exhausted soil of Mu-jin. The condors were kept in an elaborate enclosure about fifteen Sheridan miles from the castle and hidden in the highest mountain range in Mu-jin. Irishka-ru's mind raced as she considered what might give her leverage with the Unborns. She could come up with nothing. Her ability to properly appraise the situation was muddled by Trixi's plight. Her duty pulled her to the Unborns. Her heart pulled her to her little sister. "Trixi," she said, "We will go to your friends first, then to the condors."

"But the Unborns—"

"I cannot abandon you. Neither can I abandon those who have earned your devotion. These friends of yours—they are truly the legendary Searchers from the Song of Tomorrow?"

Trixi-lyn shrugged. "I do not know. I think they are."

"Then they must come first. Follow me. Halb-ean showed me a hidden way into the tower arena." They turned and headed back to the castle and the tower that held her friends, Joneva, and the future of Sergel-tuteron.

Jon and Geof sat staring at each other on the stone floor. They were in a round pit, eighty feet in diameter with craggy walls all around them. At the top of the walls was a viewing area a few feet deep, sufficient to accommodate ten to fifteen people, the king's guests, to watch Joneva play with his human treats. Facing the viewing area from the floor level was a huge wooden door eight feet wide and twice as tall. A two-inch-thick ring, eighteen inches in diameter, was attached to the front of the door. Bu-usah would stand on a slightly raised platform to afford a better view and set him apart from the other attendees. Four feet below the platform area, a bas relief in the shape of a crown bulged out to bestow a figurative coronation for anyone who walked under it. One-inch jewels accented the crown and it's surroundings. Some were set several inches into the wall, while others jutted purposefully out. If the jewels themselves formed an image, it was not discernible from either the viewing area or the floor level.

While the boys sat on the floor, Uriah paced the wall of the pit, carefully inspecting every nook and cranny. He circled the arena like a caged lion, occasionally stopping to paw at the wall before moving on. This went on for some time until his repetitive dance sent Jon off the deep end. "Sit down, will ya? If you think you're going to find a way out of here, you're nuts. The only way out of here is through that door—"

"Where the Sceptre is," Uriah interrupted.

"Where *Joneva* is. I don't know about you, but I'm not all that anxious to open it just yet."

"I am not looking for a way out," Uriah squinted. "I am looking for weapons."

"Seriously? In the wall? What do you think you're going to find?"

"I thought I might find—" Uriah cocked his head. "I do not understand. I do not understand," he repeated over and over.

"Understand what?" Geof asked.

"You should have a weapon."

"I know. I can't believe I forgot my hand grenades."

"No, no, no, no, no. Do you not remember the image of Joneva from the Song for Tomorrow?"

"Yeah, yeah, I remember," Geof dismissed. "I was supposedly fighting this two-headed snake with a sword..." Geof paused and repeated himself slowly, "With a sword."

"Hey, I remember that too," Jon said, hopping to his feet.

"If this is the lair of Joneva, there must be a sword somewhere. It could have been hidden here long ago to prepare for the Searcher."

Geof rose to his feet. "What the heck," he said as he rubbed his hands over the uneven stone surface.

Jon ran to Geof's side, furiously touching every inch of the wall in a manic parody of wax on, wax off. The wall was painstakingly examined, but nothing was found. Geof looked down at his feet. "Well, so much for that theory."

Uriah was not easily dissuaded. "We did not reach all the way up."

Jon frowned. "Up? Up where? Up there is the same as down here. I have eyes. This is just a big rock wall, and there ain't no sword in it. I know what a sword looks like. I saw one in a Victoria's Secret ad."

"Me too," Geof said. "They're long and flat and sharp, and they have big handles with jewels and stuff in them."

Uriah slowly looked at Geof, who looked at Jon, and all three looked up at the bejeweled crown. There were jewels there all right, but from their angle, it was not possible to tell whether the eye-catching stones were part of a sword, a sculpture, or simply the vision of a drunken artist.

"Okay. So how do we get up there?" Geof asked, verbalizing what everybody else was thinking.

The crown was at least sixteen feet off the ground. Geof was six feet four, Jon was five feet ten, and Uriah was a cocker spaniel. End to end, they only added up to twelve feet.

"Isn't anything easy in this joint?" Geof grumbled.

"It might be," Jon assisted. "If I could get on top of that crown thing, I could check it out. Better yet, we could throw Uriah up there."

"I have no desire to be the object of your amusement," Uriah dismissed.

"It's not such a bad idea. Do you have any ideas, Geof?"

"I got nothin'."

They re-engaged their inspection of the steep walls. The objective now was to find a way to get to the top of the sculpted crown. Their mission was cut short by the sound of footsteps coming from above, an uncomfortable indicator that the games were about to begin. The elite of Mu-jin casually strode in laughing and chatting as though they were about to watch a command performance of *Swan Lake*.

"I think we just ran out of sword-hunting time," Geof moaned.

By now, Trixi-lyn and Irishka-ru reached the outer wall of the tower. Irishka-ru led Trixi-lyn a quarter of the way around the wall and stopped at a small window with iron bars four feet from the ground. The elder princess looked carefully around to see if they were being watched, but they were alone. Irishka-ru reached up, grabbed the bars, and jiggled them vigorously. To Trixi's surprise, the bars, frame and all, popped free from the stones surrounding them. The weight of the iron bars caused Irishka-ru to fall to her back with a shriek.

Trixi-lyn grabbed the frame and slid it off of her sister. "How come I did not know about this?" she asked breathlessly.

"You were gone. Halb-ean showed it to me. It is how he slipped in and out of the castle without being seen. He did not trust my father and said this knowledge might someday be important as a way for me to escape."

"And instead, we are using it to break in. How ironic."

"What is iron... ironic?" Irishka-ru quizzed.

"Just a word from the other side. One day you will have to tell me about Halb-ean."

"Let's go," Irishka-ru prodded.

The princesses climbed through the window and found themselves in a small room filled with weapons, armaments, and unpleasant devices designed by Vandu-un to re-establish loyalty to the king.

"This place gives me the creeps," Trixi-lyn mumbled.

Irishka-ru took her sister's hand and guided her to the smallest of three doors. They entered an unlit hallway of such serpentine nature that it was impossible to see who, or what, was lurking beyond any turn. This made things decidedly uncomfortable, especially when Irishka-ru admitted to her sister that she was not exactly sure where she was going.

"How are we supposed to find my friends?"

The princess's answer was preempted by the distant sound of the hailing of the king. In keeping with his position and out of control ego, King Bu-usah insisted on being announced anytime he entered a room, regardless of the reason. As such, his every move was discreetly shadowed by not only Vandu-un, but by his official greeter, Riqu-in. Riqu-in was a tall, skinny fool with uncharacteristic reddish hair. He drooled over Bu-usah, laughed unabashedly at his jokes, and trumpeted his arrival at the most mundane events. Riqu-in had the reputation of being an obnoxious bore and not too bright. But for whatever reason, Bu-usah kept him around and enjoyed his enthusiasm, an iron-clad guarantee that no rational Mu-jinian would dare publicly reveal their disgust for him.

The hated strain of Riqu-in's high pitched, nasal voice screeching, "King Bu-usah" made Trixi-lyn cringe. It meant they had to work fast.

"We have little time," she said. "We must go."

"I am with you, sister. The arena must be close." Irishka-ru hesitated. "Uhhh," she said slowly. "Do you know what we are going to do when we get there?"

"Not really," Trixi-lyn shrugged. "But we have to go. We will think of something."

"Right."

The girls crept cautiously toward the annoying sound of Riqu-in. The upward-sloping hallway was deserted and very dark. It had a damp smell, though there was no visible moisture. As they advanced, they could hear the buzz of Bu-usah's guests milling around and laughing with anticipation of another great Joneva show. Time was running out.

CHAPTER 36

Trial by Joneva

King Bu-usah accepted his introduction with appropriate grace as each guest acknowledged his arrival in mock admiration. Joneva performances were one of Bu-usah's favorite activities, but this was a special treat. If these two "farmers" and their loudmouth dog were the phonies Trixi-lyn said they were, they would be good play toys for Joneva. But if they were truly the Searchers, Bu-usah would crush the only viable resistance to his evil plan.

Bu-usah swept majestically to his platform and peeked into the pit containing the talent for today's performance. He leaned over and looked at the rat-like trio scurrying around below. "Your wasted energy amuses me," the king spat down at them. "But I like your tenacity. So many just give up when they know they are about to meet Joneva."

"Thanks a lot, Your Lowness," Jon snarled back.

Bu-usah frowned at Jon. "I am particularly going to enjoy seeing your feet protruding from Joneva's mouth."

"I don't suppose you want to tell us why you're doing this," Geof yelled. "I mean, we just met."

"Do not take me for a fool. I very well know who you are, or who you think you are. Either way, we both know I cannot allow you to live." Bu-usah nodded in the direction of the giant door, and a grinding sound from an unseen mechanism signaled that it was opening. Geof, Jon, and Uriah huddled as far from the door as possible, which was not far.

"Okay, look," Jon said. "We have to look at this as an opportunity."

"Well, thank you for proving that fear drives people bonkers," Geof shot back, his eyes transfixed on the slowly opening door.

"Yeah, but dude, when the door opens, you have a straight shot to the Sceptre."

"We don't even know—"

"Look. This thing is supposed to have two heads, right?"

"I hope not."

"So, if Uriah and I each keep a head busy for a bit, you can run in, grab the Sceptre, and booyah! No more snake, no more Bu-usah, and no more war."

"You surprise me, Jon. It is a good plan," Uriah agreed as he trotted to the opposite side of the pit.

"Okay, but be careful," Geof warned.

"Be careful?"

"Never mind."

The door was about three-quarters of the way open when a figure emerged from the darkness. Joneva slithered into the arena and looked appreciatively upon his lunch offerings.

"Ohhh, crap!" Jon exhaled at the extent of Joneva's magnificence. His multicolored head was nearly four feet tall. The rest of his forty-foot body quickly came out, including the second head. The first head was triangular, and the second round. The two heads moved independently of each other as they surveyed the board of fare. At times, it seemed the two heads were in competition with each other, small comfort to the boys and Uriah, but a possible advantage.

The triangular head fixated on the boys while the round head was more animated.

"Look at their heads," Jon said. "They're different."

"Yeah, one is triangular, like a poisonous viper. Stay as far away from that one as you can," Geof cautioned.

"Good advice. Yo, Uriah. I get the round head."

"I didn't say the round one wasn't deadly. But it may not be poisonous."

"I want it anyway. That triangular head keeps staring at me like it knows something I don't."

"It does. If you look into the eyes of any snake, you will see that it knows all," Geof muttered.

"Say what?"

"Nothing. It's Rudyard Kipling."

"Thank you so much for that," Jon spit. "I'm sure that knowing that literary tidbit will make me taste better."

"Sorry. Just trying to stay in denial. Are you ready?"

Jon and Uriah nodded. They positioned themselves as far apart as possible while leaving an open path for Geof to the Sceptre. They jumped around and successfully attracted the heads. The triangle head focused on little Uriah, seemingly oblivious to the round head mimicking Jon's swaying movements. At times, the two heads snapped at one another as if each head wanted both boys.

Uriah darted back and forth with a speed that kept the triangle head off guard. Jon had it harder. The round head moved slower and was not faked out by Jon's evasive maneuvers. Slow as Joneva was, catching this boy would be just a matter of time.

Geof was able to slip behind the round head and into the unguarded doorway. The lair of Joneva had a putrid smell and was laden with human skeletal remains. But as promised, the Sceptre was there, lying alone on a ledge on the wall. Geof expected something more Hollywood, like laser beams or glowing translucent rocks protecting it. But there were none. He snatched the Sceptre from its resting place and held it tightly in both hands. He closed his eyes and tried to summon the power of Walking Horse but felt nothing.

King Bu-usah was relishing the terror in the pit when a messenger ran up to Vandu-un and whispered nervously in his ear. Vandu-un recoiled and raced the few steps to where the king stood. Vandu-un never looked fearful when addressing the king until now.

"Your Highness. The princess has escaped."

"*What?*" he bellowed. "That is not possible."

"I am told Princess Trixi-lyn assisted her in this treachery."

As hard-boiled as the king was, he was stung by the news that the apple of his eye had now turned against him. "Trixi-

lyn betrayed me? How can this be? Where are they?" he asked through gritted teeth.

The courier nervously shuffled forward. "We believe they have left the castle," he wheezed.

"Enjoy yourself, Joneva," Bu-usah yelled to the snake below. "Come." He motioned to his entourage with a grand sweep of his arm, and all followed obediently.

The king's departure left the viewing room deserted. The princesses ducked into a dark entryway to a thick wooden door with a large crossbar securing it. Trixi-lyn looked at Iriska-ru. "The cage of Joneva?"

"I think so. Let us remove this beam so we can enter the lair and help your friends."

They removed the beam and flattened themselves against the door in time to see the king and his minions, including Jok-imo, storm by in the main corridor. As soon as Bu-usah and his entourage disappeared, the girls quickened their pace in the opposite direction. The hallway circled upward and became progressively brighter. They knew they were close because they could hear the sound of desperation in the pit.

They peeked into the viewing area and found it deserted. Adrenalin pumping, Trixi-lyn ran to the barrier surrounding the pit and looked anxiously over it, expecting the worst. But the Searchers were still alive. Unfortunately, so was Joneva.

Geof emerged from the lair, Sceptre in hand, and inched his way around the writhing body of Joneva. Uriah was successfully avoiding the triangle head, but Jon was in trouble. He was growing weary, and Joneva was getting closer with each strike.

Joneva drew back his head for another shot at Jon but was distracted by Geof. He held the Sceptre out before him, hoping that whatever magic it had would come out now. But nothing happened to stop the snake's strike. Geof deftly dodged the huge round head as the yellow eye of Joneva grazed his chest. He smacked the snake on the head with the Sceptre, and it whirled around for another shot at him.

"Maybe there's a magic word," Jon shouted.

"Yeah... yeah." Geof pointed the Sceptre at Joneva again and shouted, "Die!" But again, nothing happened.

"Try something else," Jon implored.

Geof could barely think straight. "Uh... mongoose... abracadabra... drop dead." But nothing worked.

"This Sceptre sucks! I want my money back!" he yelled at Uriah. "Why doesn't this thing work?"

Uriah momentarily fixated the triangle head by swaying back and forth like a snake charmer. "I do not know. Maybe you are not the one."

"Not the one? Not the one? Now is not a good time to tell me that."

Round head found Geof's back a more favorable target than the slippery Jon. He reared back and struck at Geof. Jon covered four steps in a blur and hit Geof with linebacker force. Geof dropped the Sceptre and sprawled face-first on the ground with Jon on top of him as the deadly head of Joneva flew harmlessly by.

Jon pushed himself off Geof, his mind in a fog. Joneva knew he had him. The great snake opened his mouth and zeroed in on the disoriented teenager.

Trixi-lyn screamed, "Look out behind y—" but before she could finish, she was knocked aside by a man hurtling over the wall. The man landed on the triangle head and bounced to the floor between Joneva and Geof. The stranger jumped to his feet and wedged Jon's staff in round head's mouth so he could not close it.

"Jok-imo!" Geof yelled.

Round head waved wildly as he tried to dislodge the pole.

Round head's gyrations brought triangle head out of his fog, and in a split second, he struck, clamping on Jok-imo's chest. Jok-imo screamed in pain and pounded his fists helplessly on the snake's head. Irishka-ru shrieked as triangle head flipped Jok-imo like a rag doll against the wall. His paralyzed body slumped motionless to the ground. "Jok-imo!" Iriska-ru cried in agony.

A spark of light caught the corner of Geof's eye. It was a jewel in the handle of Jok-imo's sword, which had fallen from its scabbard to the floor. Triangle head again turned his attention to Uriah and Jon. Geof grabbed Jok-imo's sword. When the sword touched his hand, Geof could feel the ancients stirring within him, and he knew that the Sceptre had no purpose here. In the den of Joneva there was no cheating. It was man versus snake.

Geof raced past triangle head and drove the sword into the throat of round head. Blood spurted from the wound, and round head thrashed wildly about while Geof held firm to the sword.

Triangle head zeroed in on Geof. Geof pulled the sword from round head's neck and used it to keep triangle head's deadly fangs away. Round head, exhausted and weakened by the wound in his throat, crashed to the floor, breathing heavily.

Triangle head struck at Geof. He avoided the venomous fangs but banged his temple as he was hammered against the wall by the snake's enormous head. Geof dropped the sword, and Joneva moved in for the kill. Uriah jumped in front of Geof and opened his mouth with the biggest roar he could muster. The snake recoiled at the sight of a mouth as wide as his own, but his bewilderment was brief. Uriah raced toward the semi-conscious body of Jok-imo with triangle head slithering at his heels. Uriah circled to the middle of the floor, stopped, and faced the snake. In the background, Geof tried feverishly to summon the powers of Walking Horse, but the well was dry.

Trixi-lyn shouted, "There is a door in the other side of Joneva's cage. We unlocked it."

Uriah's ear flicked in the direction of Trixi-lyn's voice. He stood fearlessly facing certain death as the serpent closed in, dragging the groaning round head behind him, its mouth still propped open. Jok-imo's sword was trapped under the snake. Uriah knew he was out of options and the best he could do now was buy time for Geof and Jon. "When he strikes me, you must take the Sceptre and go," he said without emotion.

"No!" Geof cried.

"Go!" Uriah ordered.

Jon saluted Uriah, grabbed Geof and the Sceptre, and dragged him into the lair. Uriah watched them disappear and faced the snake and his death with the dignity of a true prince.

Joneva slowly opened his mouth and drew back his head. Uriah closed his eyes. "I love you, Felinah and Theri," he said quietly.

A bolt of lightning shot through Geof, and he felt the power of Walking Horse stir within him. His blue eyes flashed, and he bolted from the lair. "Not today," he yelled, holding his right hand out before him. An orange mist burst from his fingertips and engulfed the triangle head.

The mist drove the snake mad and drew his attention away from Uriah and onto his own round head. Also crazed by the orange vapor, the round head twitched violently and roared furiously back to life. Round head spat out the staff like it was a toothpick, lunged at triangle head, and sank its teeth into his throat. Triangle head twisted and bit down hard on round head's back. Uriah and Geof nimbly dodged the huge serpent as it attacked itself. The snake's body imploded and fell limp to the floor, breathed erratically for a few moments, and moved no more.

Geof and Jon gawked at the lifeless serpent, grabbed each other, and jumped around in a circle. "Ahhhh!" they shouted over and over.

"Welcome back, Walking Horse," Jon trumpeted.

Uriah walked solemnly past them to the mortally wounded Jok-imo. This distrusted man, savior of them all, lay with his head against the wall gasping.

Trixi-lyn and Irishka-ru rushed down the corridor to the back entrance of Joneva's home. Irishka-ru pushed the door open and raced through the lair and into the pit where Jok-imo lay. She dropped to the floor in front of Jok-imo and cradled his head in her arms.

"Jok-imo, my love," she sobbed. "Please don't leave me."

"What," Trixi-lyn said, stunned. "I thought Halb-ean..."

"Halb-ean is Jok-imo's father," Irishka-ru whimpered.

"I have heard this, but...."

"Vandu-un found Jok-imo and me together and was going to tell our father. But Halb-ean was also there and convinced Vandu-un that it was he who was my love. Even with the age difference, as captain of the guard, Halb-ean was an acceptable suitor. Jok-imo was nothing."

"But if Jok-imo was Halb-ean's son, he should have been suitable too."

"We lied about who Jok-imo was," Irishka-ru said between sobs. "Halb-ean knew it was only a matter of time before his activities were discovered, and he wanted to protect his son. So, to the king, Halb-ean was my consort, and Jok-imo was nonexistent." She stroked Jok-imo's face, and he squeezed her hand. He weakly looked at her and then at Uriah. Uriah came forward respectfully and listened to Jok-imo's barely audible voice.

Jok-imo labored, "Tell—tell them. Tell Constantine and Queen Alma that I was loyal. Tell them."

"You have my promise. Your bravery and loyalty will be forever remembered by all in Sergel-tuteron." Uriah stepped back, brought himself to his full height, and put his right paw on Jok-imo's right hand. "I, Uriah de Lancer, First Defender of the Secret City and Prince of Lantuc, declare you a citizen of the Secret City, now and forever."

Jok-imo looked at Uriah and gasped. "Prince Uriah de Lancer?"

Uriah leaned forward and placed his mouth against Jok-imo's ear. He moved his right paw to Jok-imo's forehead and began to whisper. Jok-imo's eyes came to life and fixated on the wall across from him. As Uriah spoke, a wide smile obscured the gravity of Jok-imo's condition. Uriah spoke for nearly five minutes. With each word, Jok-imo's face grew more peaceful. He looked up at Uriah and said, "It is more beautiful than I ever could have imagined. Thank you."

"You shall share an honored place with Sergel Tuteron and all the revered heroes in the Hall of Remembrance," Uriah said.

Jok-imo looked up at the tearful Irishka-ru. "Carry my heart with you into battle and get justice for our people," he choked.

"I will. I will," she whimpered bravely. Irishka-ru clutched Jok-imo's head in her hands.

Jok-imo closed his eyes, "Victory is ours, my love." He smiled and fell into eternal sleep.

Irishka-ru held him tightly in her arms and called his name over and over. She sobbed uncontrollably as everyone stood solemnly by.

Geof walked around the dead body of Joneva and gathered up Jon's staff. Handing it to him, he said, "Don't lose this."

Trixi-lyn bent over her sister. "We must go."

Irishka-ru wanted to hold Jok-imo forever, but she knew she could not. She gently released his head and rose to her feet. She rested her head on Trixi-lyn's shoulder and cried softly.

Jon looked baffled at Trixi-lyn. "I—I thought you were—"

"I was, maybe. But I realized how evil my father had become, and there is a reason for the Song. I saw the suffering of my people as a child and pretended it was not real. And now I see that with all your faults, how pure you and Geof and Debbie are. The world I want for my people is like Sheridan, not like Mu-jin."

As wrenching as it was to leave Jok-imo lying in the pit, there was no choice. Bu-usah soon would have the entire castle teaming with reward hunters. Geof, Jon, Uriah, Irishka-ru, and Trixi-lyn carried their heavy hearts through the den and into the hallway. Irishka-ru led the group to her special window. She poked her nose outside, exited, and motioned for all to follow her.

Uriah gathered everyone together. "My friends, we have accomplished our mission. We have the Sceptre."

"Big deal," Geof frowned. "It don't work."

"Possibly. But Bu-usah no longer has it."

Trixi-lyn interrupted. "There is something you should know." She told the game-changing story of the Unborns. It meant nothing to Geof and Jon, but Uriah looked crushed.

Geof crouched down to line his eyes up with Uriah's. "Is it that bad?"

"Disaster," Uriah said. "We have two paths before us. One is to stop the Mu-jin navy. The other is to stop the Unborns. We would be lucky to do one. I do not see how we can do both."

Geof stood up and looked at his friends. He flipped the Sceptre into the air, and confidently caught it. "I think it's possible to do both. We, too, have power. We already did the impossible and rescued this worthless Sceptre. We killed the giant snake. We are now free to choose our destiny. Let's do as Walking Horse would do. Sit with me, pool our wisdom, find our strength, and decide as one."

The Searchers sat in a circle. Geof raised his head and spoke. "I don't know if the Sceptre I hold in my hand is magic or fake. I don't know if we are the Searchers or if it even means anything if we are. Heck, I don't even know if the Secret City is worth saving. But I do know this. We have met the good citizens of Sergel-tuteron, and they are in grave danger. And as far-fetched as it sounds, maybe, just maybe, we can help. So, the way I see it, we can drop the Sceptre off at the Secret City and bail, or we can stay here and find out who we really are."

Jon faced Geof squarely. "Carpe diem pal. I say go for it."

Trixi looked at Jon. "Because of you, I am no longer who I was. I will go where you go."

Irishka-ru hugged Trixi. "I go with my sister. My very wise sister."

"What about you, Mr. Searcher?" Jon asked.

Geof reached into a pocket in his tunic and pulled out a yellowing piece of paper. He slowly unfolded it. "Dad gave me this long ago, and I'm never without it. He told me when I was lost to use it as my compass. I brought it with me."

"Oh yeah," Jon cried. "That Teddy Roosevelt thing. I love that thing."

Geof stood up and read aloud. "Far better is it to dare mighty things, to win glorious triumphs, even though checkered by failure, than to rank with those poor spirits who neither enjoy much nor suffer much, because they live in the gray twilight that knows not victory nor defeat."

Jon pumped his fist in the air. "Now that's what I'm talkin' about!"

Irishka-ru shook her head. "I do not understand what that means."

Geof gritted his teeth. "It means Jonster the Monster and the Bear are gonna kick ass."

Uriah buried his head in his paws and cried, "Thank you, brave Searchers!"

High fives, hugs, and back slaps enveloped the energized Searchers. Geof peeled off and walked alone to the edge of the garden. Time and distance merged as he peered into the vast unknown. Taking a deep breath, he slowly raised the Sceptre and pointed it in the direction of the Secret City. The Bear's hand was steady, and his eyes were steel.

"Hang on Debbie. I'm coming."

The End

But chill out. Jonster the Monster and the Bear
invite you to continue their adventure
in *The Secret City*.